NOTEBOOKS OF THE YOUNG WIFE

by

TARA BLACK

Cover image by www.cunning-linguists.com

This novel is fiction - in real life practice safe sex.

Chapter 1
Pickings

Joanna Heathcote was her name before she married Sir Montague Everett not long after the death of his first wife in 1727. Her eighteen years against his fifty was no doubt the occasion for gossip but she was, it seems, devoted, and soon with him in thrall to the latest sexual sport of eighteenth-century England. Neighbouring tongues would have had plenty to wag about had it been known that the young mistress was embarked on a meticulous catalogue of their activities in the rather arch contemporary style. She referred to the opus as *Commentaria Perversa*, and it hardly takes a Latin scholar to decipher the title. Not that we knew of the project as such from the start; in fact there were very few who suspected the existence of so thorough an effort, and from a *woman* at that. But getting our hands on more than a few choice morsels of the thing, that was something else. However, if I'm going to tell this story, I'd better go back and start at the beginning.

That would have to be when Judith delivered the package from the Archive, an event that is now - the gods save us - almost a whole year ago. It was a Saturday morning in May and the spring air must have got to me - rising sap and all that. While I didn't exactly plan it that way, I was rather deeply involved with our secretary when the buzzer went to announce her arrival. Well, to be more precise, *he* was the one in deep. Right up to his balls in my arse. I knew that because they were banging against me as he ground my hips into the desk. The intercom was only inches from my face; the question was what to say into it. I could have asked her to wait in the entrance lobby for the short time needed to finish the job, but I didn't. A demon had hold of me that day, for I stuck a finger on the control and burbled into the microphone that she was to come straight on through.

To spring such a scene on a close acquaintance would have been naughty, but Ms Wilson and I had never met. For some moments, as Dominic did a disappearing act and I hauled up my jeans, I thought I'd gone too far. The mutual introductions were decidedly awkward, but then I started wittering about not giving the wrong impression, I hoped, since I was of her own predominantly lesbian persuasion and things seemed to gel. In no time we were settled amicably in my den with a dram and a pot of freshly ground Java. To my mind, a spot of buggery and a dash of malt whisky is the perfect prescription for starting the weekend off on the right track.

The goods that it had been thought unwise to entrust to the postal system consisted of a batch of CDs, whose innocent exteriors hid evidence of the far-from-innocent activities of many of those laughably known as 'the great and the good'. A right pervy bunch, as clip after graphic clip left the viewer in no doubt. Just like me, and just like Judith, though with one crucial difference: *we* weren't sitting in judgement on what others did or attempting to censor sexual materials. Some of *them* certainly were, with an agenda that included curtailing the resources I had then so recently been put in charge of. But they had already met resistance and were going to encounter more of the same. For I had no compunction in playing dirty.

Quite appropriate as it happens, since that's what I was dealing with for a living: dirty books. Still do, in fact. *The* dirty books, one might say, since they are the ones that form part of our national fabric. Yes, the British Library has, over the years, built up a stockpile of erotic writing that is, as far as we are aware, unrivalled in its scope and depth. People know about what's called The Private Case, which used to be held at the British Museum and is open to (cough) *bona fide* researchers. But that consists mainly of two, albeit large, bequests; what I preside over is more, much more. There is a full section of 'Rare' Books - Thomas Bowdler's spirit lives yet - that is housed in the new complex. Or rather, *not* in it, but across a tree-lined street at the back in two terrace houses converted for the purpose. Says it all, really.

I've been told I shouldn't complain. Surely to have a young(ish) woman at the tiller in such a field is an achievement, isn't it? Well, I beg to differ. Just cast an eye over what's been coming out in this country and in the States in the past few years and you'll see the authors are all female. Ninety percent, anyway, and they're doing all the best stuff. I suppose it's something to have penetrated, so to speak, what used to be an entirely male preserve *here*, but then there were special circumstances. My predecessor was a man of, shall we say, the old school, engaged in all manner of shady deals and backhanders. One in particular, with the dodgy German-Czech outfit known as The Program, lost us two quite irreplaceable eighteenth-century editions. When this all came to light it must have seemed like time for a new broom, and there was I waiting in the wings with a DPhil plus a whole decade of squeaky-clean service in the ivory tower.

So that was it: Dr Jane Barrett-Greene was appointed Keeper of Rare Books and the collection acquired a new figurehead. But my job isn't public relations, which is just as well since I have neither the looks nor the aptitude for it. No, I have been blessed with a blonde bombshell of a PA to fend off the sweaty hacks from the redtops should scandal threaten to break. I am no match for Judith in that department - few are - which brings me back to her visit and the start of my story.

After we had chortled over a few of the clips and swallowed more whisky, talk turned to the new premises in Soho. While she'd been frolicking there with the best, as befits one barely into her twenties, it seemed there was a strong pull to one girl in particular. Playing therapist, I soon learned that the conflict was a recurring feature in Judith's life, though it had come this time to a crux. She was, in short, resolved on settling down but was having a deal of trouble resisting the temptations that appeared at every turn. Well, I'm afraid to say that I seized my chance and spun her a yarn about my stepmother's cane. I don't mean it was invention (indeed those events get a reprise in what is to come) only that I angled its telling to the needs of the occasion. In effect I drew a lesson from the taming of my wild youth that 'paying' for ones 'sins' could help draw a line under the past and allow one to move forward.

She looked unconvinced, so I produced the instrument and passed it over for inspection. Constructed from a core of synthetic resin bonded into a hard rubber sheath, it was both denser and more flexible than the standard article. As these qualities became apparent in her handling of it, I could see Judith's mind working. Capital! She was a woman after my own heart, drawn to the memorable experience such a weapon could provide.

'As you see fit,' she said, echoing the words I'd quoted to her, and bowed her head. I told her it would be twelve and asked her to place an upright chair in the centre of the room. She went over it, feet apart and back arched in the manner of the true devotee, and gripped the legs low down on the far side. The posture thrust the tightly sheathed buttocks into prominence and the high line of a thong made it plain there was no intrusive underwear. And what buttocks they were! For a young woman she had acquired a formidable reputation as a stalwart under the rod, and was blessed with the bodily resources to support it. The pulse was thudding in my temples as I flexed my black implement and studied the target area being presented. The fleshy mounds were well dimpled and of a full roundness that gave an overhang at the tops of the thighs despite the bent position. It was there I would land the final cuts, I decided, and raised the cane high above my head.

It was a beating that stays with me to this day; a classic seat-of-the-pants affair, though I doubt there was a schoolboy presented the equal of that arse to his housemaster. Each stroke left its mark imprinted on the cloth, and the light that fell across the scene from the window threw into relief the rising welts. Judith made not a sound, though I drew from her some sharp intakes of breath, and when I had done, the cool formality of the handshake could not quite conceal the effort that went into it. I would have liked nothing better than to peel off the trousers and apply remedial treatment of the most intimate kind, but to do so would have betrayed the whole point of the exercise. Besides, I could see that there was a sort of glow about her as if the cane had communicated directly with the moral sense we had spoken of, and with that in the air she took her leave.

We have remained in contact, though not of a disciplinary kind, and she is still living with her partner. I like to think I did my bit to further that outcome.

Well, Judith may have made an exit with head in the clouds, but I was left severely randy. There was nothing for it but to reactivate the secretarial organ for a much needed clitoral workout. What would I do without him? I remember wondering. Then it was only after I was stretched lazily out back in the den that I found the envelope nestling in the package that had brought our precious discs. It was addressed simply to 'Jane', so I took out and unfolded the crisp sheet of headed paper inscribed in Samantha's bold hand, and what she'd written brought me wide-awake at once.

Did you hear that Monty has pegged it?

Not before time, it might be said.

I'm told the estate is to be split up so there could be rich pickings if we move on the matter. Phone me.

In his prime Sir Montague Everett had been a chip off the old family block. While any kind of sexual excess was on the agenda - and his efforts became more bizarrely creative with advancing age - he took after the ancestor and namesake we've already met, who had been caught up in the general enthusiasm for flagellation that overtook the aristocracy. I'm speaking loosely, of course: to imply a craze for the rod is to overstate things a little. What we do know is that schoolmasters were keen on chastising their pupils and masters their servants, especially if young and pretty. At the time, too, there was a surge in erotic writing that features the birch in particular as a sex aid whose application causes ladies to faint from sheer voluptuousness and gentlemen to acquire a 'yard' so virile their ardour could scarcely be quenched.

Lip-smacking stuff, and we have some fine examples on our shelves. But there are serious gaps in the collection, and what makes it worse is that we know what many of them are. For example, a source from the mid-century enthuses about the several manuals that supersede the *Treatise on the Use of Flogging in Venereal Affairs* (1718), and condemns it as being of doubtful accuracy and limited compass. That is a volume we possess, in no less than three variant editions, but having been critically informed, one's perusal of them is an unsatisfactory affair, spoiled by hankering after the superior successors that are missing. The country house that has accumulated a library over the centuries is just the place where such items might be found, so the news was exciting.

As a sometime dominatrix with rooms in the capital, Samantha's extensive contacts have led us to come to an 'arrangement'. How it works is that we give up a few cherries in return for being alerted to possible sources of material. The Nemesis Archive she runs - as the severely titled *Miss* James with her deputy Judith - is devoted to the chronicling of aberrant desire among women, and if there is even a whiff of male engagement in the thing it is usually declined. Now I have to say that an engorged penis onstage, strictly under female control of course, rather heightens the proceedings to my way of thinking. But there you go; each to her own. The outcome is that the bulk of any books or papers we get to inspect by this deal can be snaffled up for The Library. With a capital L. And those we agree to relinquish will be available for consultation at the Archive itself by scholars dedicated enough to journey the sixty-odd miles north.

For the time being I was obliged to curb my impatience: it was a Saturday and the redoubtable lady would not be available until the Archive opened for business on the Monday morning. Fortunately there was something else to occupy my mind that day. An appointment had been made for one of the senior scholars of an exclusive school just a short taxi ride from our own establishment. It was the habit of the Principal to keep an eye on persistently 'difficult' girls that might benefit from what she termed 'Dr Greene's treatment'. A woman of my own persuasion in these matters, she had an uncanny ability to home in on one of a similar, if latent, disposition. Twice she'd called on my services in the space of some eight months, and her judgement in each case was spot on. So I was looking forward to the event with a degree of relish when

Dominic's head came round the door to announce that our visitors had arrived.

I followed him in to the office and greeted the rather elderly woman in black. Her manner, as before, gave the impression there was a bad smell under her nose she was trying to ignore.

'Miss Marston, I'm pleased to see you again. And this is...?'

'Miles of the fifth. Her taking in hand is long overdue, Dr Greene.' The surnamed pupil was regarding her shoes with a scowl. That suited me fine; a pleasant smile and a cheery hello were hardly appropriate to the occasion.

'Very well. Let's get on with it.' I extended my arm in the direction of the door I'd come through and waited until the reluctant eyes met mine. 'After you.' She took a couple of paces and the ageing mistress made to follow. I stopped her with a gesture, knowing she was a believer in corporal punishment *tout court*, without the special interest her senior and I brought to the subject.

'I make it a rule that the first time should be private, Miss Marston. Be so good as to wait here and I promise you the hand will be a firm one.' She was not pleased but I could see she was not going to challenge my authority. Thus it was that I ushered the wayward fifth-former into my den and drew the door closed behind us.

Chapter 2
First Time

I motioned her into the centre of the room and sat in my desk chair, swivelling round so we faced each other. She stood shifting from one foot to the other, looking thoroughly out of sorts.

'Ms Miles, let's not beat about the bush. You have come to me to be punished, have you not?'

'Well, er, yes.' The reply came after a long pause but it came without prompting. That was a start.

'And am I right to say that you elected so to do?'

'Elected? If you mean I chose to, then yeah, I did. But it wasn't much of a fucking choice.' The nose crinkled with rebellious emphasis and I warmed to the show of spirit. But I couldn't let her see that so soon and kept a deadpan face.

'You mean that pressure was applied to get you to comply?'

'Pressure? Shit. I'd call it blackmail. How would you like to spend the whole of next term confined to barracks?' I made a mental note to speak to Sylvia about her methods. Even allowing for a degree of exaggeration on the girl's part, it was too much like coercion for my taste. However, having come thus far I was of a mind to continue the novice's education. It was too much to hope for gratitude but her fate might come to seem less deserving of four-letter words.

'I take your point: you are here under duress. But you are, all the same, here, and I have a job to do. You will please prepare yourself.' While the attitude was straight out of a *Just William* story the gear was anything but. The single-breasted jacket was short, revealing a skirt that flared elegantly below contoured hips. Both were of a tailored mid-grey cloth that matched the muted stripes of the tie knotted loosely an inch below the collar of the off-white shirt. Off-white too, were the finely spun knee socks and the whole was heightened by the shine of patent-leather pumps. It was a most attractive sight. My request, however, had produced only a furrowed brow, so I decided it was time to be explicit.

'In order for your bottom to be spanked you will need to remove your jacket and skirt. I shall begin over the knickers, but they are to come down after a while to complete the operation.' I stopped speaking and watched the crimson-faced girl strip to her shirtsleeves and tug at her zip. When she was ready I took the clothes from her and placed them on a chair. I had one more thing to say.

'You may have noticed that I have not lectured you on the conduct that has brought you here; nor shall I. It is none of my business. Nor yet do I intend to humiliate by taking you across my knee. The position provides close contact, which I think important, and is simply the most efficient for my purpose. That is to cause you the pain of acquiring a very sore behind - one more tender than it may be possible for you at this point to imagine. Right. Enough of words; let's get down to business.'

Perhaps I'd overdone the little speech: my audience had become open-mouthed and was seemingly rooted to the spot. So I took hold of an arm and led her gently to the chaise longue that stood against the far wall. It is the ideal piece of furniture for an over-the-knee spanking of one of adult size. A chair has the recipient literally over-lapping, hands awkwardly on the floor for balance, whereas if one sits at its open end, the main body of the couch supports the torso while the legs slope down leaving the buttocks in prime position to be soundly slapped. In such manner I guided the first-timer into position and watched her settle in apparent comfort. I had already been struck by the expressive face framed by dark hair cut close to the shape of the head; now I was able to take a good look at the hindquarters that swelled enticingly in a swathe of silk. Perhaps such an item was the regulation underwear of the institution she attended, but that seemed unlikely. I was going to assume instead that I was honoured with a show of the Sunday best.

I smoothed out a crease at the leg elastic and let my hand rest on the bare flesh below. Under the fine material the cleft between the mounds showed dark and there was a wisp of hair where the gusset disappeared between the legs. A sharp stab of lust brought me back to myself: the girl was to be spanked, no more, no less. I cleared my throat.

'I am going to begin. It goes without saying, I hope, that I expect no unseemly struggling.' No reply was called for, nor came one, so I raised my hand and brought it down smartly on the right cheek, then repeated the action on the left. I fell easily into a rhythm of quite hearty smacks and was rewarded by a deepening blush that was visible clearly through the sheer covering. Ms Miles herself was behaving in exemplary fashion, silent apart from a kind of throaty mutter and a small jerking movement at a particularly well-judged slap. Before very long the colour I was raising had extended well beyond the boundary of the knickers and I decided it was time to take them down.

'Right, up on your feet. Let's get you ready for part two.' She stood biting her lip, with downcast eyes not meeting mine. But there was no resistance as I took hold of the waistband and lowered it over the hips. The crotch clung briefly between the thighs and I longed to test below the pubic triangle with a finger. But it was not to be - not *then* - and I remember sighing as I eased the girl back into place and ran my hand over the fiery cheeks. As if inspired by their heat I spanked with gusto, savouring every bounce and ripple of the bared parts. The new vigour had an immediate effect: though she wasn't fighting me, the body twisted and writhed at each stinging crack of palm on flesh. My hand was holding up remarkably well, but the lower curves of the crimson globes were a smudge of purple bruising. Then all at once came tears and great gulping sobs.

'No, please! Oh please, that's enough!' I held her tight while the spasm passed, then spoke quietly.

'Twelve more, as hard as I can. Then we are done. Agreed?' There was a sniff and a croaked 'Yes', and I proceeded to count out, in slow time, the dozen full-force blows I'd promised. Each set off a wailing that had to be fully audible in the office, and Miss Marston, at least, would no longer think her trip wasted.

Once the girl had calmed I helped her back into an upright position. Her face was flushed and there was still a catch in the breathing, but she looked little the worse for her experience. I watched as she stood with almost a meditative air, hands gingerly exploring her bottom.

'Ouch and double-ouch. I am *sore*.' After some more rubbing she continued. 'It's hard to believe just a hand did this. And I bet you use other things too.' She was looking at me with something of the old spirit; not defiant exactly but very perky for one who'd just had her first ever spanking. In response I beckoned her over to the corner cupboard and opened its two doors wide. On one side hung a row of punishment straps while the other held a set of many-tailed whips. There were two shelves of paddles, including a vintage English tapette, and beside them a fistful of canes sprouted out of an upright stand. Her eyes flitted from item to item with a look of awe and I selected one that would augment that impression.

'This is a tawse, a genuine three-tail Lochgelly. Eight-millimetre gauge leather, heavy yet supple. Feel it.' She took the instrument from me in one hand and slapped the business end of it lightly against the other. Her mouth made an 'O' and I guessed she was wondering how it would be to experience its forceful application. 'Memorable,' I said with a smile, and the answering flush confirmed my supposition. I leaned over and gave her bare bottom a little pat. 'Just a few strokes would leave these pretty cheeks red raw and throbbing for the whole day. But I'm afraid we must bring this occasion to an end: your chaperon will be getting restive. You should get dressed and I'll take back the strap. Not in its league, of course, but I hope the encounter with my hand will stay with you for a while.'

'Oh yes.' She pulled up her panties and zipped up the skirt then paused, jacket in hand. 'Dr Greene, what I said before wasn't true. I know a girl in the sixth who was here once. I mean, she wouldn't say anything except about the hand and I got kind of, er, really curious. So I wasn't actually forced into anything.' Jacket on, she straightened her tie and smoothed down the collar of the shirt. 'And by the way, it's Becca. Becca Miles.'

'Then it had better be Jane.' Apart from a slight redness around the eyes, the girl had a colour that exuded well-being, and even her hair seemed to have acquired an extra gloss. 'Do try to look just a touch woebegone, Becca dear, or I'll be accused of failing in my duty.'

She suppressed a giggle behind her hand and was gone. I returned the solid piece of leather to its place and closed the cabinet on the array of implements. Whatever else I did, the delectable Becca had to be nudged into a return visit. One in which the firm 'hand' could use some carefully chosen back up.

As soon as I heard the outer door bang shut on our departing visitors I called Dominic in. He'd already served me well that day but I was confident he could be relied upon to rise once more to the occasion. Masturbation was an option, of course, but chastising the schoolgirl's virgin curves had brought me to the kind of high-voltage state that would be best discharged by the work of an active partner. When he entered with a querying look I was ready with a leather paddle behind my back, which I produced with a flourish.

'I had an idea that the breakfast six of the best might need a little refreshing. If, that is, the thought appeals...' The dark-jowled, slightly stolid face lit up with a crooked grin.

'She must have been hot.'

'*She* took what I dished out like a real sweetie. But that was it - no hanky-panky - so I'm the one who's hot.'

'Okay, boss, I get the picture. Wish I could have played peeping tom.' He opened his belt and I undid the metal buttons on his jeans one by one. Underneath was a black satin jockstrap, already bulging, that I lowered along with them so I could take the growing erection into my hand.

'Good start, my boy. Now let's do what we need to pump it man-sized.' He bent over in a practiced gesture, legs apart, so that the garments stayed bunched around the thighs. The rounded backside bore the fading tracks of the morning's cane and jutted provocatively as if asking for more. He was by no means a fully-fledged masochist, merely a young man who was turned on by the idea of being beaten, particularly it seemed, by a woman who was his superior and more than ten years his senior. I gathered girlfriends of his age came and went with whom he behaved in a largely conventional fashion. I took the paddle and rubbed its surface over his bare bottom.

'Six plus six is what I have in mind, all right? Be warned I'm going for the full swing on each one.' I cracked the leather oval hard across the centre of the left cheek, then the right. Running my hand over the area I waited for the colour to come up, then delivered a second pair of blows. After a third I announced the end of the first half dozen and caressed the hot red flesh. He did colour beautifully and I could see the full erection straining between his legs. The second six proceeded in like fashion, except on the final stroke he yelped and sprang up, grabbing his behind. Dominic was always a model of decorum in the receiving of discipline, so that could mean only one thing. I smiled to myself: it was his way of asking for more.

'Tut, tut.' I pushed him back down with the instrument and pressed it against the glowing rounds. 'What do we do, boy, when the agreed number of strokes has been given?'

'We wait to be told before we move.'

'That is so. It will be six for your impertinence. You may express your gratitude in advance.'

'Thank you, ma'am.'

'That's better. We'll make a young gentleman of you yet. Brace yourself.' I lay on as hard and fast as I could, but though he gasped and squirmed the hands remained locked round the ankles. When I'd done they stayed put until I reached down and took them in mine. I steered him to the couch and he lay back with an 'Ow' when the tender buttocks made contact with its surface. I grinned at him and took the pole that sprouted from his groin between my fingers. While it was my firm belief that a man's body was never the object of my truest passion, I was not keen to forswear a stiff member primed to oozing point and entirely at my disposal.

On that occasion, the encounter with just such a thing came close to perfection and remains vividly in the mind. My threadbare 501s were all that stood in the way - I can't abide any impediment to the feel of that seam tight in the crotch - and they were discarded in a trice. Then I straddled the boy and eased down until the engorged head slid by my throbbing clitoris into the mouth of the vulva, where I held it, gently rocking. And held it, and held it, quivering with lust while long seconds ticked past. The face below me was contorted with desire so intense it was as much pain as pleasure, and I could resist no longer. I thrust down just as he pushed up and, awash with juices, cock and cunt squelched into orgasmic union. I remember a great yell - from me, from him, more likely both - and a delirium of pumping bodies, and then a slow slide into the torpor of satiation.

How long we lay in blissful languor I do not recall, but I do know it was very much the end of *that* day. For me, I should say. Dominic took himself off muttering in the way he often did after sex; I could never quite work out whether it was a general post-coital malaise from which men are said to suffer or a more specific sense of being used. Which of course he was. I'm afraid that once I discovered his predilection I was quite shameless in exploiting it for my own purposes. Women I was accustomed to bed in a more reciprocal fashion; I took pleasure in perversely treating men as they are commonly held to treat us. That disposition, however, was to be challenged by the improbable affair that came at me out of nowhere. Indeed, neither was there back then a hint of the gallivanting in store to secure the return of the missing notebooks.

No, all I knew was that there was very probably a large mass of disreputable materials up for grabs. The Everett name was a byword for aristocratic depravity but my acquaintance with the history of the house was sketchy. To be honest, I wasn't very sure even where it was. However, I decided that any research into these matters would keep until morning. I was too spent even to contemplate banter over a jar or two round the corner at the *Hellfire Tavern*. Instead there was the remains of a bottle of Bruaichladdich in the flat that would send me pleasantly into oblivion, and to that end I let myself out of the back door and headed up the stairs.

Chapter 3
Uxor Studiosa

The morning had started well. Ardingley End was easy to find online in the Country House Index, which delivered the basic facts. Begun in 1610, it contained a Jacobean core that was later flanked by wings with rooms by Robert Adam. The Everetts came into the picture by acquiring the property in 1695, and stayed with it from generation to generation until Monty popped his clogs and brought the line to an end. But then my luck ran out. I searched the usual sources like Ashbee, Porter, Hitchcock and so on - any commentary I could lay my hands on that was indexed - only to find they contained no mention of the family name. It was common, of course, for disreputable items to appear under a false name or no name at all, but the pen names of particular eighteenth-century enthusiasts like Perry or Ireland had often been cracked. Not so with Everett, it seemed, if indeed there were any original materials to be had.

I ground up a quantity of beans and set the coffee machine hissing and bubbling while I racked my brains. We knew about the interests of the present - or rather, late - Sir Montague, and through him of the fact of likeminded ancestors. Had any of them published flagellatory erotica copies would be preserved in his own collection, and it was unlikely that they'd have been left to lie in scholarly oblivion. Not at least by one of Monty's aptitude for self-promotion. I glanced again at the clutch of books I'd hauled upstairs from the basement. At the bottom was the imposingly titled *Organum Venereum*: a recently acquired nineteenth-century reprint of the 1787 original. I had put it aside for reason of its lack of index, but now it occurred to me that it may be worth a quick scan, since it contained material from an earlier period than the rest. Earlier, and therefore thinner on the ground.

Coffee poured at hand, I settled to the task. The main body of the book was a dissertation on the medical or pseudo medical works that purported to explain why a good whipping of the buttocks inflamed lechery, while in the process dwelling lasciviously on all the bodily details. At another time I would have been diverted, even titillated by evidence of preoccupations like my own two or three centuries in the past. That day, however, they were a source of irritation and I skimmed hastily through on the lookout for names. I saw there was an appendix entitled *Incident & Anecdote*, and without any real expectation turned to it. And struck gold.

The third entry ran to four pages under the heading *An Educational Use of the Servant*, and at the end of it I found,

A---- E-, in the County of --sex.

The Month of June in the Year of 1728.

Uxor studiosa scripsit.

It had to be. Academic caution always goes out of the window when I think I'm on to something and I just *knew* the piece was from Ardingley End, Essex. But the last three words made me gape. I was familiar with *scripsit*, meaning literally 'wrote', and for use after the author's name at the end of a letter or document. *Uxor studiosa*, though, was a turn up for the book. Wife, of course, and not merely studying, but keenly so. 'By the zealous wife' might do as a translation. With a slightly unsteady hand I turned back the pages to read what she had written.

I am scarce one Month wed and my Husband's Course of Lessons is underway in earnest. This Day we are gathered - that is my Abigail and I - in the Morning Room where a Space has been cleared for an Article of Furniture that I am most desirous of viewing in use. At last the Footmen enter - it is they shall play a vital Rôle in the Drama we are to witness - and bowing under its weight bring the Item to the Centre of the Floor. At first Sight it could be taken for a kind of Seat, possessed as it is of a slatted wooden Top curved as might fit the Shape of an Arse. Yet a Glance at the festooning Straps and the Timbers enclosing the four Legs that extend a Yard fore and aft suggests otherwise. Indeed, the Apparatus is concerned with posterior Matters, though not in the Mode of Sitting. One may rather be sure that when its Function has been discharged, that very Position will be one best avoided. For the thing is a Whipping-Bench, no less, made out of the finest Oak to a Plan drawn up by Sir Montague's own Hand. It is unique to the House and I hope to see it become the Envy of the Circuit.

The Housemaid arrives who is to be the principal Subject of our Staging and casts a nervous Eye over the Frame. We ready her for the Event by removing the outer Garments, with the Observation that while there may be some trying Minutes, they will become as nothing in the final Consummation. From the Calves and Shoulders that have come into view, Martha is a well-built Girl and I tell her that having survived, as she has, the Strictest of Upbringings there will be nothing in today's Exercise to cause her undue Alarm. She is reassured, it seems, and stretches over to embrace the Frame. I send Nabby to the left and together we cuff the bare Arms to the forward Struts. At the other end we take the hem of the linen Smock at each side and between us fold it up until it is able to be held under the broad Belt that I buckle tight across the lower Back.

What a Moon has risen on the Scene in response to our action! I catch my Servant's eye and make with my Hands the form of the two resplendent Hemispheres that lie uncovered, but we stifle our giggling. I do not wish my Husband to surprise us in a state of foolish Levity, so we bend again to our Task. Now the Refinement of the design becomes apparent in the placing of the Straps that circle each Thigh close to the Knee. The Distance between their fixing Posts is such that when they are drawn tight the Legs pull apart into an inverted V. The Consequences of this are, it seems, apparent to our Volunteer who gives out an 'Oh', while her Muscles strain to undo what we have just done. It is to no avail. Despite the ripeness of the Buttock its lower portion is split wide to expose the pink Folds of the Quim.

'Don't fret, Martha,' I say, 'it is a pretty sight. And the Master tells me that once a young Woman has been warm'd she forgets to be shy.' The words are opportune, for no sooner are they uttered than the double Doors are flung wide and Sir Montague himself is among us. He greets me with formal gravity and hands to the Footmen a Parcel wrapped in greased Paper. My Curiosity is great but he chides me gently with a wagging Finger.

'Patience, my dear. Once you have seen the Action and Effect of these Items you may inspect them at your Leisure.' Bending over the Hindquarters we have rendered at his disposal he is moved to express satisfaction at their Size and undoubted Resilience, all to the Confusion of their owner. He chucks Martha's Chin and promises that the splendid Nether Cheeks will soon blush as brightly as the ones on her Face. 'And then,' he announces to the company, 'it will become clear that the Whip may prick into Venery not only those who inflict the Lashes or suffer them, but those too who are mere Spectators of the Event.' At that point he directs at me a Look of such Lechery that it is my turn to colour, being left in no doubt of his Intention once Martha is dispatched.

Now, though, it is time for the little Play to begin, and he sets himself down amongst the Cushions of an Arm-Chair as befits a Peer of the Realm. We humbler Mortals, the Wife and her Maid, stand forward for a closer View and a little to one side in order not to obscure his. The Footmen have taken up their Positions to left and right of the bench'd Figure, each holding in Readiness his Taws. Fine things, we think, seeming to consist of a long Slab of Leather cut into Tongues, and our judgment is confirmed when the first three Strokes are deliver'd. Crack! Crack! Crack! they sound, reverberating from the Walls of the room and almost at once the Imprint appears vivid across the whole Breadth of the Orb. The second Man replies in like Fashion, and the two-pronged Attack is then reprised. One Dozen delivered, and at each the Recipient squeals and wriggles, diverting us with the most lewd Gaping of what we cannot, in Conscience, continue to term her private Parts.

They repeat the whole, then on Instruction from the Chair finish in rapid alternation. We close in around the Tether'd Form, and while Nabby wipes away the Tears with a Handkerchief I put a Hand to the radiant heat of the Whipt Globes, marvelling at how the once snowy spread has been turned a flaming Scarlet. And below, there is what could be Sweat from the force of her Writhings, but I venture to believe it Juice of a different kind. For the Footmen's part, their tight-breech'd Condition makes it plain they are thus affected and on the Nod the first moves to unbutton. The Length he draws out stands Proud by its own Means and he eases into place between the open Legs, bending a little at the Knees and pressing forward. Leaning over, I part the Hot Cheeks to observe without impediment the Shaft's entry into the fleshy Purse, while beside me

Nabby cranes her Neck to follow the Course of the Action.

It is no drawn-out Affair of much thrusting, for a Conclusion is upon us almost at once. Martha gives voice, crying Oh! Oh! Oh! and the man pulls out, pressing to the Bum a Head that under his manipulation spouts Copious Milk into the Crack. Now comes the turn of the Second, whose Member swells impatiently in the owner's hand. Without more ado he brings it forward, and knowing its destination, I open again the Channel between the Mounds where there winks at us a Hole as yet unbroacht. Careless of his Fellow's Spending that bedews the Entrance, with a single Push he spreads wide the Ring and then works his way by Degrees until the whole Truncheon is gone within. From the Maid there issues a moaning so low it seems to be forced out of the very Depths to which she is Penetrated, and I am transfixed.

A Tug at my Sleeve brings me back. It seems the State of the Master induced by what he has seen requires urgent Attention without the cover of Privacy. My Abigail has bared the relevant Area and a Purple-Headed Beast rises to greet me. It is of a Girth to shame the younger ones that have excited my Lust, and I move quickly. Clutching at my skirts I kneel up on the Seat. Nabby lifts the garments high so that I may lower myself with some Precision on to the Manhood that awaits. It is done, and what shudders begin to run through me! Quim stuff'd with Cock I rock slowly, making the Clitoris rubb'd, and to cap it all my Naughty Servant has a finger up my Bottom-Hole. Of what more could a Young Wife have need?

(I am trapp'd by the form of a Rhetorical Question, for which I beg pardon. The reader who has dallied awhile may be pleased to return at a later date for the Answer to it).

Return? Return *where?* Contained between the brackets was as close as one was going to get to a '...to be continued', and there was no indication in the collection that it was anything more than a one-off. I searched for clues in the preface and for footnotes or endnotes that might clarify the matter, but with no success.

All the more reason to pin my hopes on the late Monty's collection. If there was more, I thought, that's where it would be found. Surely the writing of the prized young mistress would be a thing to be treasured, or at least kept safe. *Uxor iuvenis.* I was beginning to think of her in the Latin manner she assumed, though in classical times there was a more likely designation that would have put her firmly in her place. *Domini puella*: the master's wife, or indeed, slave girl; it said a lot that the language of the day didn't bother to differentiate. But what a gem! Something of the feistiness and humour made me think suddenly of the Irish girl I met the week before in the place in Soho. She was a gem, too. I picked up my mobile and scrolled through the directory. There it was: Niamh. We got on well enough for me to be given her number, which allowed me to distinguish myself by knowing how to spell the name. If she was answering and amenable to the idea of a pub lunch, I might be in the running for something more than a second opinion on a piece of text.

Chapter 4
Quimshots

'Well, I think the girlie's for real. What a great character. And the q-word is ace.' The way she looked up from under her shaggy fringe gave me a jolt I remember to this day. I'd returned from the bar with the two plates of goulash aimed at filling our empty stomachs and suddenly I had an ache in the groin that would need to be fixed as well. Later, with a bit of luck, is what I thought. I didn't realise then how lucky I was going to be that Sunday afternoon. I sat down and we toasted each other with the glasses of claret before tucking in. Niamh had as good an appetite as I, and there wasn't a lot in the way of conversation until we'd finished the food and started on a second bottle. After a quick canter round some of the classics of early pornography - in which she proved herself to be surprisingly knowledgeable - she glanced at me over her wine and said, 'I do cunt pics. Fancy a go?'

'I'm sorry?' I just stared, no doubt looking completely stupid. I heard the words quite plainly, of course, though they'd been spoken quietly enough not to turn heads at neighbouring tables. But it was a case of the mind refusing to accept the input to the ears.

'I take photographs of female genitals. Preferably wet ones. If you've nothing planned for the next hour or so, Jane, I reckon you'd make a good subject.'

I didn't need asking a third time, so we downed the rest of the bottle, paid up and headed off to her base round the corner. She had taken up a term of residence at a joint called the Art of Correction, dedicated to the induction of novices into the ways of discipline. It was situated down a side alley we ducked into through a brick arch, and was not going to attract the attention of anyone not in the know. The sign above the door was the sole indication of its purpose and that was enigmatic enough. One had to look hard at the picture of a girl who seemed to have been interrupted in the proofreading of a manuscript to notice that the interloper's hand held a punishment strap.

Niamh used a key to let us in, and I followed her along a corridor and up a narrow flight to the first floor. The place seemed deserted. Under a short fleece she was wearing a skimpy T-shirt and cotton Bermudas that emphasised the curves of her solid figure. I reached out and took hold of the waistband, bringing her to a halt on the turn of the stair. There was a glimpse of a dark cleft, then her body was against mine and I squeezed a full buttock.

'You like that, yeah?'

'I like, very much,' I said into her ear, nuzzling the neck.

'I've not been spanked for days. We want you nice and juicy and if that would do the trick...'

I kept a hold of her while she steered us into a room and locked the door. She went over the table on her elbows and I peeled down the shorts to find an arse that swelled out completely bare, without even the minimal cover of a thong. Here was another knickerless girl after my own heart. Spanking was what she was going to get, but first I gave in to the temptation to inspect the goods at the closest quarters. Far from raising an objection, when I hunkered down behind her the Irish girl obligingly arched her back to present me with an even better view. Covered in a fine down, the skin was pearly-white and indeed without hint of bruising, and I explored its soft resilience with my two hands. Then I straightened up and crooked an arm round the compliant waist to deliver the first smack.

'Uh-uh.' It was a throaty noise that encouraged me in my task. But this was to be no punishment session and I stroked and caressed as much as I whacked with a stinging palm. I was making love to a young woman in a way we both understood. When the area had turned a beautiful salmon-pink I stood back. She rose from the table holding her bum, blew me a kiss and fired up a floodlight on the computer desk in the corner. Camera in hand she waved me up onto a table that resembled nothing so much as the examination table in a doctor's surgery. It was equipped with the stirrups appropriate for a gynaecological examination, and I understood that her photography was going to be of the most intimate kind. I was already juiced to dripping point inside my jeans and stripped them off to climb up so that my calves could be lifted and positioned.

'Fucking beauty.' Niamh bobbed about between my spread legs, eye glued to the viewfinder as she stored image after image of my seeping cunt lips for the delectation of future generations. It was a heady experience that I have to say made me ooze still more. I'd heard of the injunction to 'smile!', but this candid camera had me doing something decidedly more earthy. Then she laid aside the device and looked up at me from squarely between my parted legs.

'Um, Dr Jane Double-Barrelled: the important person who keeps the national smut safe. I asked if my lens could get in there, but I didn't check if you were up for a tongue. Well, I know you are in theory, but I mean like mine. Here and now.' The charming creature had taken a fit of shyness and I just fell totally in lust.

'You should be warned that while I showered this morning, since that time the young wife has had a go, then your gorgeous arse made me wet my pants and this fevered snapping of cunt pics has got me leaking all over your table. So it's likely to be strong stuff down there, sweet girl.' By the time the sentence was finished she was wearing the biggest grin I'd seen all year and pushed her face right into the nitty-gritty.

I'd been taken into the charge of an enthusiast - a self-proclaimed 'muff-diver extraordinaire' - who in seconds flat had me at that pitch of sensation where pleasure crosses into pain. And held me there while time stopped. In the end I begged and sobbed my way to the release that was, at last, granted. As I lay back gasping from the intensity of it all I thanked the gods out loud for the continuing silence of the building beyond our small room which brought a chuckle in response.

'Well, the bar isn't open and after the sesh last night the others are either off or dead. But you shouldn't have worried. I'm in here kinda regular with the camera and all, so nobody passing by thinks twice about the noises.' I had the grace to blush at my assumption of special status when I was merely one among many to receive the treatment. But Niamh seemed not to notice and bundled me cheerily into the small bathroom conveniently en suite. After she climbed on a stool to pass me down a towel from the top of the cupboard, I seized the opportunity to sit on it, take her across my knee and complement the spanking with a bit of deft clitoral manipulation. A pale shadow of the efforts of the *maestra* herself, I feared, but it seemed to do the trick and she showered happily enough once I pushed her into the tiny cubicle on her own.

When I emerged later, the Irish girl was swathed in her robe and bent over the keyboard staring at her monitor. 'I'll print you out some in A5 to take away, and if you fancy one or two I can do them big. Be good framed on the office wall, right?'

'Right.' The impish grin made me want to start all over again with a hand to the bottom, but as I gazed it was replaced by a look of slight perplexity. 'See, Jane, I don't want to speak out of turn, I mean you being the expert and all that.' She stopped and stared at me again.

'No turns needed, girl. Just spit it out.'

'Well, that girl who was writing in seventeen-whatever, you're thinking it would be a big find if a lot of her stuff was in this country house. That she's like a little-known figure.'

'As far as I know, yes.'

'Then you'd better cast your eyes over this.' I moved in closer and, peering at the screen, read:

...Uxor studiosa. When I was researching the book I only ever found two pieces by her under that name. It seems there might be more in a collection over in England but they wouldn't let me near it. V frustrating! But I know a lady in SocHist with contacts in the scene so I'm gonna keep on the case.

Now, as regards the query about how things got published back then...

I looked up puzzled while Niamh began to explain.

'It's just a post, right, but what we've got here is what the engine found on an earlier trawl and that's got corrupted. The link to the current page is dead so you can't get to register and sign in. The site must be a goner. It was the only hit for her name, so it's true she's not exactly famous.'

'But can we find out how long ago it was, er, posted?' Not being a chat-room sort of person, even in their more academic manifestations, I was content to show my ignorance.

'Tricky. You'd think it would be the easiest thing in the world but the buggers don't usually give you a date. Though hold on a minute...' She scrolled down the entries then jabbed a finger at the words that appeared. 'Look, here's a bit about a forthcoming conference, the next month it says, and there's the name of it too. You could find out when that was, yeah?'

'I should think so.' The girl was brilliant.

'Okay. I'll print out this little lot and you can take it away. Along with the pics.' She flashed me one of the dirtiest winks it had been my pleasure to receive and my groin responded with a throb. But away was where I had to go: with a spot of luck I might be able to get more than a date. If the writer of the posted text had been doing research for a book then she ought to be on our records. I took the sheets from Niamh and just as I was stowing them in my document bag there was a tap on the door.

'Nevie, are you in? Open please, it's me.' The key was turned and a pony-tailed blonde stood in the doorway. 'Oh sorry, I intrude.'

'Come in Helga. Meet Jane. She was just about to go.'

'Hi, Helga.' I studied the ice-blue eyes as Niamh pulled her into the room by an arm. The Nordic-type beauty was dressed in a charcoal bodysuit that was fetchingly snug, and seemed to have locked on to her fellow worker to the exclusion of all else. I bowed out with a thank you to my host, catching sight as I did of the zip of the garment coming down. It was time to leave the youngsters to it. But the glimpse of breast and crotch I caught suggested one layer was the rule at the AOC, and as I closed the door on them I resolved to call back soon.

When I got out of the cab security was on the prowl. It was a twenty-something guy I'd not seen before, and as he checked my ID I thought of asking him in to look at my dirty books. If he wasn't a reader, there were plenty of pictures to tickle a young man's fancy. But I had things to do, so I suppressed the urge and headed up the stairs at the back of the building. Courtesy of the Library I was installed in a flat carved out of three top floor rooms; it was tiny but had all the essentials like a kitchen, a shower and a king-sized bed. The lounging about that passed for work - as well as that with no such pretence - was mostly done in the den off the main office, and I went straight down to it.

The symposium referred to in Niamh's printout rejoiced in the title of *Sexual Herstory: New Explorations*, and was an easy one to crack with an online search. It had been held in Chicago at the very beginning of March, so that put the interchange on the web page at two months or more back from the mid-May we had reached. So far so good. The next step was to identify the author of the post. It had already occurred to me that research for the (unnamed) book would almost certainly have called upon some of our own resources at the BL and those, of course, were on record. But where to start? Applications for access to the collections came in at quite a rate, and if work on the project could have begun five years ago or more that would make a long list. And in any case, what would I be looking for? No, it would make better sense to jump in at the other end: if the lady had been to us at all, the *Organum Venereum* would have been one of the titles requested. So what I needed was the log of its consultation.

I keyed in the two words with the date of 1787, clicked on 'accessed' followed by 'sort by date', and there it was: ten entries that stretched back over the five-year period I'd chosen. The most recent could be set aside, being mine, for the volume still lay with the others on the corner of the desk. The next most recent was on the 12th of the 2nd and credited to '573D', that my master-list revealed to be one Jonathan Squires DD, The Old Rectory, Wythingford. I wondered briefly what he might have made of our *domini puella*, but I couldn't see a Doctor of Divinity in the Shires having much truck with 'herstory' so I passed on. Two more from December were English academics, also male, and anyway I had it in my head that I was looking for an American.

With number five that is exactly what I found. The October before Belle Torman PhD, Assistant Professor of History and Women's Studies, spent three days with the learned tome and it was hardly credible that its one female author could have gone unnoticed. The clincher for me was the fact that her appointment was with the University of Chicago, explaining her familiarity with the conference arrangements. But even assuming I had found the poster, it was her interest in the Ardingley stash that singled her out for attention and a degree of alarm. Had she managed to give it the once-over or was she still trying? And what was I going to do about it?

All these questions called for an inspirational dram so I opened the implements cupboard and took out the bottle of Laphraoig that was nestling amongst coils of braided leather. The scald of smoky peat at the back of the throat jerked me awake. I didn't need all the answers; what I needed to do was to get to the house myself. Sooner, not later. I looked at the wall clock: it was coming on to eight. I couldn't get the director herself until the morning, but a deputy freshly returned might well be checking things out at work before the new week. While she'd be sitting more comfortably by now, I was prepared to bet that our little encounter would still be in Judith's mind. It was just possible she would be favourably disposed enough to pick up the phone. As it was, I faced down the answering machine five times before I heard a live voice.

'Nemesis Archive.' She sounded a little peeved.

'Judith, you are there. Don't be cross with me, please.'

'Ah, that's Jane, isn't it? After our last meeting, I'll go for the polite and respectful option. Just in case.' I permitted myself a chuckle, then launched into what I had to say.

'I'll be brief. You know about the Everett hoard, I take it. Well, it seems someone was sniffing around back before the old man snuffed it. An American academic.'

'I see. So you're wondering if they got in. I don't know a lot about it, to be honest, but I thought the place was tighter than a schoolboy's arse...' an apologetic cough came down the line '...as the saying goes. In, er, some quarters. I'm rather immersed in stuff on first times just now.'

'That's encouraging. I mean about the security. You see, I reckon there might be a real gem or two to be had.'

'So you want to move fast, yeah? Well, there's nothing I can do for you but the boss will be in at eight sharp. And she'll be as keen as you are to get things moving.'

'Thanks, Judith. Sorry to pester. Call in and see me anytime you're up, won't you.'

'Sure. Perhaps I'll wear an extra layer or two the next time.' There was a little laugh. 'Sorry, I'm back in the housemaster's study again.'

We said our goodbyes and I poured myself another tot. It would be easy to let the mind fill with images of the behind I caned only the day before, but I pushed them firmly to the back. There were a couple of things I needed to sort if we were to be ready for an assessment of the house's contents. However, as I prepared to set up the laptops that would travel with us, I promised myself the reward of an unopened bundle of photographs from the early twentieth century depicting the discipline of young males. Between Judith and me it was becoming the theme of the moment.

Chapter 5
House Rules

I rang Samantha as soon after eight as I dared, then got through to the house before nine. By eleven in the morning we were actually on the road and were aiming by twelve-thirty to be in the vicinity of Ardingley End. In the meantime I was folded into the passenger seat of the shiny new Porsche, swathed in a boom of drum 'n' bass. Tamsin, of course, was at the wheel; strawberry-blonde locks pulled back from a face decked out in wraparound shades. The rest was a jacket in pearl-grey over a mauve micro-skirt and glossy tights. The shoes would have been something special too, but I couldn't see from where I was sitting. All of which was rather beyond the scope of a salary from the BL, though where the money actually came from it always seemed to me a little indelicate to ask. As was the habit in these infrequent excursions from the world of denim I had opted for a low profile black: leather jacket, roll neck and chinos. Not that I needed to work on being unobtrusive in Tamsin's company.

That's the PA for you. She's not actually personal to *me* as the letters might suggest. In fact, Administrative Assistant is her actual title, but AA might carry a whiff of TT with it that would be entirely out of character. Anyway, Ms T Bingley has kept our show on the road since I came on the scene: about six months at the time of the jaunt I'm describing. I know her better now than I did then, though we have been able to work well together from the start. Tamsin's not by nature as pervy as I delight in being, but I have yet to see her fazed, and she deals as well with the stuffed shirts of the hierarchy as she does with the women-hating bully boys of the tabloids. Both types take her for Essex-girl stupid and they don't stand a chance. Best of all from my point of view, is that we don't have to pretend there is a lot in common: when there's a job on we do it; when we're just travelling to one conversation is happily precluded by the endless supply of what she calls her 'bangin' choons'.

But we did talk that day over lunch at *The Greene Man*, whose name seemed too apposite to pass up, even though my particular quest was for a woman. The village pub was less than a mile from the house we were bound for, but it was hard work to winkle out even a snippet or two of gossip while we waited at the bar for the food to arrive. I don't know what the tight-lipped landlord had us down as, but when I revealed that we were interested in acquiring the collection of books, he opened up a touch and leaned over the counter.

'I would say you'd better be careful going out there. It's only what I hear, mind, but there's two maids partial to them alcopops on a night off, and the lads round here tell me you wouldn't believe some of the stories they come out with after they been plied with a few.' There was the bang of a door in the distance and he glanced sharply in that direction. 'I'll just say this. It's not pranks they're up to at the End, but something that sounds very similar... if you get my meaning.' With an embarrassed smirk he drew back as his wife clattered in with two steaming plates of hotpot and a crusty loaf. I avoided Tamsin's eye until the dishes had been served, and then behind the cover of a partition we succumbed to a fit of the giggles.

'Oh, jeez. It's so bad to him he couldn't get nearer than a bleedin' rhyme.'

'Yeah. If only he knew...' That set us off again like a couple of schoolgirls until the smell of the stew took command. Only after we'd both taken bread and swallowed with it some meltingly tender chunks of mutton did she look at me again.

'Okay, guv, so when we arrive there, what's the agenda? Any idea how long a job we're looking at?'

'Well, we both packed a toothbrush as instructed. But beyond one overnight it's impossible to say. Even if we knew how many books I was given no clue as to how they are catalogued. If they are catalogued at all.' The PA made a face then popped another piece of meat in her mouth. I did the same. The lunch was too good for pessimism to take hold at that point.

'So we just hole up in the library and get stuck in, and take it from there, right?' I cleaned up my plate with the last of the bread and pushed it aside.

'Yeah. Though there was one thing about a house rule that I didn't understand, largely because Samantha was being coy. Laughing up her sleeve would be a better description, now I think of it. Said we'd find out soon enough for ourselves, as indeed we shall. Better move, eh, Tams?'

The driveway wasn't one of those tree-lined ones that delivers the visitor gaping before a gigantic façade; instead it snuck round the side of an ornamental garden to reach a relatively modest front entrance. There was pretension in the later eighteenth-century wings, though drawn shutters gave them an air of abandonment. The older central section was of three storeys, crowned at one end by a square tower, with a profusion of ivy around richly curtained windows. I gave the iron lever a sharp tug and we waited in a burst of warm May sunshine for the door to open.

'You must be the ladies from the Library: Dr Greene and Miss Bingley, if I remember right. I'm Mrs Jencks. Perhaps you would be so good as to come with me.' She could have been anything from a weathered forty-five to a youthful seventy, and the clipped tones suggested a lady unaccustomed to having her instructions questioned. We followed meekly in her footsteps until we reached double doors that stood open.

'The Great Hall,' she said, with an emphasis that signalled capital letters. 'As you can see, we have prepared for your arrival.' It was a splendid room. Not huge, but long and low with a massive fireplace framed in carved wood from floor to ceiling. However, the scene contained no obvious explanation for the housekeeper's words.

'Er, how exactly do you mean, Mrs Jencks?'

'Ah, perhaps you were not fully informed. But Miss James assured me there would be no difficulty. There is a tradition by which guests are introduced to the house and we are of the opinion that the Master's demise makes its observance all the more important.' There was a hint of amusement, even relish in the gaze that moved from mine back to the further end of the room. Then I saw what she was looking at and everything fell into place. It stood waist high with a stepped side, to the uninformed eye resembling nothing so much as a mounting-block that might be found in a stable yard. But I knew better. This was not a device for mounting anything else: it was to be mounted by one destined for the birch. And on that day the one was to be me.

'I see.' I remember the effort it took to appear unruffled when instinct was telling me to leg it. 'I take it you intend to proceed forthwith, Mrs Jencks.'

'Indeed, with your leave. As to the details, Dr Greene, it is not our practice to count strokes, but to continue until a rod is quite used up. Given your expertise in the area, it was decided that your welcome will require the employment of two.' It was no time to explain that while I knew a lot about the literature and was an enthusiastic spanker, my experience as a recipient was limited. I had, in fact, never in my life been birched. Think of it as a piece of first-hand research, I told myself sternly.

'Very well, so what's next?' As I spoke a maid appeared at the end of the corridor and the housekeeper called her over. 'Molly will see to you. By the way, Dr Greene, I hope you understand that all the staff are summoned to witness these events. Now, Miss Bingley, shall we attend to the matter of the accommodation?' Flashing me a 'what can you do?' kind of look, Tamsin went with the older woman in the direction of the car while the maid led me across the Hall into a small antechamber.

'You're going to sort all them books, are you, Dr, er Dr...'

'Jane. Call me Jane,' I said, handing over my leather jacket before bending to unlace my shoes. Unpractised though I was in the ways of the block, I knew it required a bare bum. 'That's right. We're going to tackle the library once I get past this inauguration, if that's the right word. I hope it's worth it.'

'It'll be your first time then?' I sat down to pull off my trousers and she took them from me with a smile. She was a pretty little girl with a snub nose and I was getting a buzz from stripping in front of her.

'I'm afraid so. Any tips?' The question went with the offer of a pair of knickers and she laughed.

'Well Jane, I'd say straight off forget about these after. Cos when you heal up they'll be sticking.' First pair on for weeks and I was to lose them: Fate plainly intended me to go without fulltime. But I didn't like the sound of the bit about healing. 'Don't be worried. If you get it as often as we do you don't think nothing of it. What you got to remember is it feels a lot worse than it actually is. I mean, it smarts like the skin's being flayed right off your arse but the truth of it is just a few wee cuts and grazes.' I got to my feet a touch reassured. By then I was dressed in only a short top and a pair of socks, and Molly's eyes went straight to my groin. It had slipped my mind that I'd indulged a recent lover's whim to shape the bush into a heart that she'd then dyed red. I could feel the colour rising - what would the girl think of such behaviour in one of my advanced years? - but she giggled and hoisted up her long pinafore dress to reveal a day-glo pink tuft above a prominent clit-ring.

'Snap!' she cried. 'Well, sort of.'

I shook my head. 'You've trumped me, Molly. No contest.'

Her laughter was interrupted by a noise outside and she dropped her clothes back into place. 'Quick, Jane, we'd better get out there or I'll be following you over that thing while it's still warm.'

The Hall was still empty but the block had been joined by a tall tub from which protruded the handles of two bundles of sticks. I was aware of the technique of soaking the instruments and Molly confirmed that they might stand for up to a week in a mixture of brine and vinegar. At the sound of approaching voices I knelt in place, pleasantly surprised to find the step cushioned. No doubt the principal source of pain was considered to be sufficient without making the victim's lot any more uncomfortable. A wooden bar was fastened across the calves just below the knee, which turned out to be the only mechanical restraint.

'Laura'll be here too and we'll each hold an arm to keep you right forward. If you want to dig your nails in, feel free. I'll just get you back later.' But the time for humour was at an end and I lay over the domed top as the audience began to troop in. The last thing I wanted to do was to look openly at those who would be viewing me *in extremis*, but out of the corner of my eye I got the impression of some twenty souls assembled for the occasion. What I did see, all too plainly, was the woman who came to take her place by the tub. There was no floury apron - that must have been left hanging behind the kitchen door - but the food-marked white tunic said it all, and she was endowed with arms that would have graced a female wrestler. Mrs Jencks called for silence, the maids took the strain and the cook pulled out the first dripping rod with a massive hand. I thought desperately of *uxor*: her education had undoubtedly included just such experiences as the one I was about to undergo. I was in good company, and if I was ever to read more...

'Begin the welcome.'

Since then I have been birched in the manner of much early erotica where the circulation is fired and a deep lasciviousness induced. That afternoon, however, the rods were lean, mean instruments far removed from the veritable brooms that appear so often in illustrations. Imagine the switch cut from a sapling that is a straight yard, budded toward the tip. On its own it is capable of a smart cut to bare skin. Now think of five such bound tight for the first quarter of their length, and thereafter free to fan out into five individual switches that strike the target at the same time, again and again. I can report that the shock to the system of such treatment is extreme and through it my conception of smarting pain has been irrevocably extended. The experience was one I have vowed will never be repeated.

I'm going to gloss over how it feels to have the vinegar and salt of a fresh birch beaten into already raw flesh; suffice it to say that the Great Hall has quite an echo if put to the test. Eventually, of course, the thing was done, the second instrument, shredded like the first, discarded and the spectators gone. Molly was a perfect gem. She left me alone to catch my breath, then returned with a bowl of cool water and sponged down the abused hindquarters to remove all traces of irritants. Then she helped me up and over to the cubbyhole where she poured a good slug of brandy into a tumbler. Not in the same league as malt whisky in my view, but then it was exactly what I needed. After a couple of good slow swallows while the maid carried out another bum inspection, I was ready to think about getting dressed.

'You ain't too bad, Jane,' she said, touching me gently with the tips of her fingers. 'A bit gooey in places, but with them loose trousers you'll be all right.'

I offered up silent thanks I'd not come poured into a new pair of jeans. 'Well, sweetie, you could always come along and check me out again tonight. I mean later, when everybody's safe in their beds.' She laughed and steadied me while I got one leg and then the other into the chinos.

'That'll be right. You'll be putting me in trouble with the groom. He don't hold with me having another woman, unless he's there to fuck the two of us, that is.'

'I know the type.' Alcohol running in the veins, I was about to give her my go-for-it-dyke pitch when Tamsin opened the door. She looked me up and down with a definite air of disappointment.

'You look pretty good to me, guv. As usual I've gone and missed all the action.' Then behind her came the housekeeper and a cook still flushed from her exertions.

'Not quite, Miss Bingley. Now that we've caught up with you, there is still the matter of your own introduction to the End. However, I believe a private dose of the kitchen strap will serve for a subordinate.' There was an open-mouthed silence caused as much, I guessed, by the designation as the threat, but after a couple of seconds the PA rolled her eyes theatrically.

'Okay, okay, okay. I surrender.' She turned to go and I could see her eyes widen at the girth of the sweaty lady's arms. 'Let's get it over with, eh?' That's my girl, I said to myself, never one to whinge when there's nothing to be accomplished by it. I watched them head out into the passage, past the maid who was busy with a broom and shovel at the scene of my excoriation. Messy business, the birch. Now compared with the clean open palm and the precise cane...

A tug at my sleeve jerked me out of the reverie. The impish face and scruffy knee breeches gave the odd impression of a street urchin out of time, then the frame shifted and I saw an older teenage lad with a mop of light-brown hair. He put a finger to his lips and peered out into the corridor. Then with a whispered 'come on' he disappeared and I followed, intrigued. We passed a double door through which I could see a stack of pots and pans, then he ducked into a kind of pantry with stone jars of flour and meal. From there a door with two lights in its top half opened on to the main space of the kitchen and we looked each through one at the scene beyond.

Centre-view was Tamsin, or rather her rear end, framed by the raised band of skirt above and the rolled-down tights below. Mrs Jencks held her forearms from the far side of a counter while the formidable cook took down what looked like an old-fashioned razor-strop from a hook on the wall. It was rather cheering to know I would not be alone in nursing a sore bottom that evening. Also I had to give credit to one who was scarcely what you'd call a devotee of s/m, for she took three cracking strokes across the centre of the cheeks without a murmur. How many was she going to get? And how long could she play the cool stoic?

I was just settling in for the duration when I became aware that there was something else happening right beside me. While the gaze of my fellow voyeur was fixed on the reddening buttocks, I could see the fly open and the thumb and forefinger busy working the shaft of a very presentable erection. Our PA's behind made for an enticing view, but I'd seen it before, if rarely. On the other hand, the sheer effrontery of the act of masturbation at my elbow was giving me hot stabs of lust and I couldn't take my eyes off it.

'Three more, my dear, and brace yourself. Cook, your best if you please!' The announcement from the kitchen brought matters to a head. At the first crack of leather on flesh the beast tensed and spat and by the third and last the fingers were squeezing from it a final drop. He looked up with a grin splitting his face and stowed the shrinking organ back in his pants. Then with half an eye still on me he rubbed the spilt semen into the floor with the sole of a shoe.

'Hey, boy,' I hissed, pulling him back from the door, 'you've got some nerve! I ought to put you across my knee and give you a good spanking.'

He twisted out of my reach with a chuckle then turned round on his way out. 'Yes please, Miss. Later.' I leaned weakly against the wall, with little heed of who might come and find me there. Suddenly it was all too much excitement for one day, for the expression on the boy's face had been utterly serious.

Chapter 6
Perverts Two

I pulled myself together with the realisation I had no idea how to find my way around. But I managed to make it back to the Hall where all traces of the 'welcome' had been removed, and was glad to find its rigours already fading from my mind. So much so that when I saw the maid Laura passing by - she who had kept such a tight grip of my right arm - I was able to hail her in quite a matter-of-fact way to ask for her help. She pointed out where the books were to be found behind a door off the lobby, then showed me to the pair of rooms we had been allocated on the first floor. The mullioned window in mine commanded a view of the ornamental garden, and the furnishings were a large bed with a carved headboard and a heavy wardrobe also equipped with shelves.

I felt at home immediately under the low ceiling, and was soon soaping under a warm shower in the compact bathroom.

When I emerged I checked the guest quarters opposite, but there was no sign of the PA, so I went down to take a first look at the library. It was a well-appointed room, with upright chairs around a polished table and deep armchairs by the fireplace. I wandered around finding whole sets of Dickens and Thackeray, to say nothing of a complete shelf of three-deckers, a large number of political biographies and a whole section devoted to the locality: its history, geography, flora and fauna. There was even a substantial astronomy collection housed between the two windows that included atlases and detailed charts. Someone had been, and relatively recently, a stargazer. Some of these things might have been the means of whiling away a wet afternoon in the country, but none of them was even remotely connected with the cause of our being at Ardingley End in the first place.

Just then the door opened and Tamsin appeared looking a little flushed. 'Sorry, I got held up.'

'No problem. Are we sitting comfortably yet?'

'A lot better now.' The expression was almost coy and there were definite spots of colour in the cheeks. I began to suspect the strapping in the kitchen had not been the end of it. 'But how about you? Was it bad?'

'Sheer bloody hell. But it's right what they say: a birched bum soon mends. Or words to that effect. So I'm fine. All I need now is someone to tell me where they've hidden the dirty books.'

'They're in here,' she said, going over to a small door in the corner, and led me through into another book-lined room that was about half the size of the one we had left. I pulled down a volume at random that proved to be Millet's *L'Escole de Filles* of 1668. We possessed a slightly tatty copy, but the one I was holding was in pristine condition. On the next shelf was *The Serving-Girl: Her Morals and Discipline*, a rare anonymous text dated 1725 that I knew of only by reputation. It was a promising start.

'There's about five hundred of them, at a rough estimate,' offered Tamsin, opening up her laptop, 'and then there's that little lot.' She pointed at a counter against the far wall that was piled untidily with box files, some spilling their contents.

'Oh dear. And have you chanced upon anything resembling a catalogue?'

'Nope. Matilda - I mean Mrs Jencks - says there isn't one as such.' I let the slip go by without comment thinking I could probe later if I wanted. 'However, there is a list of additions up to eighteen hundred or thereabouts. And the books seem to be arranged on the shelves more or less in chronological order.'

'Right. So you know the deal: we find enough to hook Samantha and she'll put in an offer for the lot from the coffers that Oceanus, Inc keeps overflowing.'

'And then goes on to donate the ninety-nine percent she doesn't want to us?'

'Just so. Now we've got a couple of hours before dinner and I want to root through some of these papers. How would you feel about starting a scan of the titles for pornographic gems?'

'Sure thing, guv.' I was expecting acquiescence but Tamsin seemed positively enthusiastic. 'That's strictly f-f stuff I'm looking for, yeah?'

'Well, with goings-on between women providing the main thrust of it - and not too much literal thrusting unless it's dildoes. And you can check anything you turn up against their catalogue. I was told it's bang up to date.'

By the time twenty to seven came round I'd had enough of dusty papers, most of which were meaningless through elisions made for the purposes of concealment, or if decipherable, uninteresting. I could bear only so many repetitions of statements of the type: T-- gave G-- 2 doz with the b-- after which they c--ed. The fact that this particular birching and copulation (?) took place at M-- H-- on the 12th June 1731 helped not one jot. Tamsin, on the other hand, was looking well pleased with a pile of six or eight volumes at her elbow. When she saw me glance over, she nodded up at the clock.

'We're getting dinner on the hour and there'll be an aperitif laid on first.'

'Enough said, my girl. Lead on. I take it you know the way.'

It was as well she did for the modest dining room, though in fact the neighbour of the study we left, was reached only by approaching it from the other side. Both had windows overlooking a rising stretch of parkland topped with a crown of trees that, just at that moment, were caught in the rays of the setting sun. I did the honours with the bottle of Brut sitting in an ice bucket alongside a bowl of mixed nuts. We stood in silence before the view for a bit, and when the glasses were empty I refilled them.

'So is this courtesy of Mrs Jencks - or should I say Matilda?' Tamsin blushed and I repented of the remark. 'Sorry, I'm being nosy. Perhaps I should make a confession instead. When the cook was practicing her swing on you, I'm afraid I was watching.' I don't know quite what made me say it - some kind of rush of bubbles to the brain perhaps - and it was an anxious moment before I saw the smile breaking.

'Shit, I had a funny feeling about it. That's in addition to the far from funny feelings in my bum.'

'Let me explain.' I jumped in quickly in case her mood changed. 'It wasn't my idea. A lad came on the scene, took me round the back into a pantry and there you were through the door. Next thing I knew he had his cock out, pumping for all he was worth and to save my life I couldn't have taken my eyes off it till the business was done. So there you are: I wasn't exactly ogling your peachy bits, but he certainly was.'

The PA gave a chuckle and munched on some nuts. 'Nice to know, really, but I don't reckon I'm cut out for s/m stardom. Not when there's muscles like that at the back of the strap.'

The talk was interrupted by the appearance of Laura, to set down hot plates and a stock of red wine. She opened up a hatch to the kitchen and carried over a dish of lasagne and a large bowl of green salad. We agreed that we certainly could help ourselves and ring the bell when we were done. So with that she left us to it and we tucked in. It was soon apparent that cook was good for more than swinging the arm.

After a while, with inroads made into the second bottle, Tamsin said, 'I'd better come clean too. You'll twig anyway if I don't.' I made well-only-if-you-want-to kind of noises, but she seemed set on telling the tale. 'After I'd been whacked, Matilda - I may as well call her that, okay? - said how well I'd taken it, and it must have been an awful shock, and if I'd go up to her room she'd give me something to make it feel better. And she did. Fucking jeez she did.'

The girl took a swig and swished the dregs round in the glass, eyes fixed on what she was doing. 'Well, this time I got the tights right off and the skirt too and she put me over these two pillows on the bed. Then out came this bottle of aromatic oil, I don't know what kind, and she starts on a massage. But not like any massage I ever had before. It's not just the arse, it's kind of from the waist down to the thighs, and in ten seconds flat I'm ready to come. But I don't, well not like a big climax that goes whoosh and fizzles out. This just goes on and on, and fucking on till I don't know whether I'm laughing or crying. Jeez!'

There was just a splash of the red left and I put it out in the pause. 'Something else, eh, kiddo?' I said gently. 'So you're going back for more.'

For the first time she looked me straight in the eye. 'Bloody sure I am. Look, Jane, I get a sore bum and get into sex with a woman twice my age. I mean it's not been sex sex yet, but it will be and odds on there's going to be more strapping. What kind of perv am I?'

'Well, Tams, just consider this. Older and supposedly wiser than you, I spend the afternoon captivated by the self-abuse of a boy who's of an age to be my son. I'm living in hope that he'll appear in my room later and the gods know what *that* might lead to. You and I plainly make a good pair of deviants. Let's drink to it, I say.' With that I reached for another bottle from the sideboard and stabbed it with the corkscrew. The PA's worried face creased and before the cork was out she was doubled up with laughter. That's my girl, I thought for the second time that day, and filled both glasses to the brim.

Later, after coffee, Tamsin insisted on resuming the search for hot lesbian titles of earlier ages, but I ducked out of any more library work until the morning. I lay back on the vast bed in my room meaning to rest weary eyes, only to find myself waking with a start to an insistent tapping on the door. Head muzzy from the wine, I gulped a mouthful from the glass of water on the table and turned the key in the lock. He sidled in, the perkiness tempered by a certain hesitancy. I was suddenly struck by qualms.

'Just how old are you, boy?' I blurted, assailed by the prospect of banner headlines proclaiming BRITISH LIBRARY PORN WOMAN CLOSET PAEDOPHILE.

He shrank back, looking alarmed, then rallied. 'Seventeen, all but. Honest, Miss. I can prove it if you like. It's just I act like a kid a lot of the time.' From where I stood at the grand old age of thirty-six, seventeen was pretty kid-like, but I let the thought pass. The lad had made the running to that point and was keen enough to have showed up. So I fixed him with a stern eye and wagged my finger.

'That was an outrageous stunt you pulled today. Playing peeping Tom is bad enough, but you have to go and drag me into it. Well, I told Ms Bingley the whole sorry tale and she has generously allowed me to deal with you myself.' I was warming to the rôle and for his part the boy was grinning happily until he remembered to be the penitent.

'I'm sorry, Miss. It won't happen again, I promise.'

'That may be so. However, a young man must be taught that misdeeds have consequences. Am I not right?'

'Yes, Miss.' He was looking down and shifting from foot to foot. The little scene was shaping up well.

'Painful consequences.'

'Yes, Miss.'

'So bad behaviour will be punished in order that a boy may learn his lesson. Perhaps you can tell me the form this punishment takes. What exactly is it that happens to a naughty boy?'

'He gets spanked, Miss.'

'Very good. It seems we are of a like mind on the matter.' I moved over to the bed and sat on it, patting my knee. He came to me and without any fuss dropped over my lap with his upper half on the covers and his feet on the floor. The cotton cut-offs he was wearing were not tight, but they were thin and I was able to smooth and tuck them so that the bottom cheeks were clearly outlined. I was pleased to see that there appeared to be no underclothing. 'Ready?'

I began with slow, measured slaps, enjoying the resilient feel of the target, and increased their force until I was drawing a small grunt with each one. After a while I stood him on his feet and reached for the fastening at his waist, looking up at his face. He was flushed with a bead of sweat on the upper lip. I was feeling decidedly warm myself. 'I am going to bare your bottom,' I announced, trying to keep the emotion out of my voice. When I opened its zip the garment fell from his hips and the erect organ I'd felt pressing into me hung between us. I took hold of it and it stiffened further. 'All in good time,' I said quietly, and guided him back down. 'First there's a spanking to complete.'

The smooth buttocks were prettily pink but it took little to redden the fair skin, and I had a mind to show the lad what could be done with the unaided palm. And so I did. From the sting of my hand I knew he must be on fire, and when I'd done he jumped up and clutched his crimsoned backside, gasping. I waited till the rubbing subsided then pulled him closer to put my unused palm to the hot flesh. Another touch to the penis brought it back full-standing, and as I stroked it a drop formed at the urethra. I had a towel at the ready and worked the shaft between thumb and forefinger, all the while caressing the cheeks I'd spanked with all my might. Two more drops ran clear then a milky jet spurted, once, twice, three times before the deflating member subsided into a dribble.

I rolled the doused towel into a ball and held him sitting beside me while we both caught our breath. Then he made for the bathroom without a word, from where came sounds of flushing and washing and then silence. I got up and stretched, flexing my aching hand, and drank the remains of the water. Vigorous exercise, even if only of the right arm, had done wonders in clearing the head.

29

Then he came out and what I saw gave me quite a shock. Nothing in the physical appearance had changed: there was still the worn sweatshirt and the odd three-quarter length breeches. But all of a sudden he looked every bit the age he'd claimed, if not even more. I stared, tongue-tied, and he said, 'I used to help the old man with the books and papers when he couldn't get about so well. Is there anything special you're looking for?'

I went blank with surprise for a minute, before the *Commentaria* came to mind. 'Er, yes. The young wife of the first Everett here, Joanna I think, she wrote things. Called herself *uxor studiosa*.'

'I know that name. Can't remember exactly where, but I'll see what I can find. Time's getting on, I'd better shoot.' And that was it. He was gone leaving me struggling to come to terms with the transformation from spanked boy to potential colleague. In which mode would I meet him next? On the form thus far Ardingley End was the place to keep a visiting librarian on her toes.

Chapter 7
Cock & Taws

After that the only problem I had was that I couldn't sleep. By the time one in the morning had come I gave up the struggle and pulled on a bathrobe. If I was awake, I might as well go back down and have a go at the record of the collection's earliest items. So I stuck my feet into the leather mules by the bed and slipped out into the darkened corridor. I could just make out the head of the stairwell, and was waiting for my eyes to adjust to the near dark when a sudden shaft of moonlight through the tall window picked out a figure pressed into the alcove on the landing. The shock sent my heart thudding before I had a chance to register that it was only Molly.

'Sorry, sorry,' she whispered, putting out a hand, 'didn't mean to startle you. I was on my way, but then I heard the door open and bottled out. Suddenly thought you might have just been joking.'

'Sweetie, my come-ons are never jokes.' It was difficult conversing in an undertone so I pulled her back into my room. She was wearing only a shift, and as I turned the key I spotted something through the fine cotton and lifted it before she could stop me. 'Hey, now what are these? As I recall, the idea was you were going to check out *my* bum. Among other things.' I ran a finger along one of three plum-coloured lines.

'It was *him*, of course. And he would've done more but I weren't having it. So when he started calling me every name under the sun I just buggered off. Stuff him!'

She looked thoroughly mutinous, but there was a trembling lip and I eased her down beside me on the bed. 'I've got some herbal oil here in my bag, the perfect thing to soothe some fresh stripes. So why don't you just come over this way, that's it. Just get good and comfy.'

I settled Molly over my knee and pulled the shift right up out of the way. For the second time in only a few hours I had a body across my lap, bottom bared. Difference was, this one wasn't for spanking and was lusher, broader-hipped than the earlier example. I set to work and before long she was moving in response to my hand, with little noises in her throat.

'Come right up on the bed,' I murmured, and rearranged the compliant girl into a sixty-nine position where her genitals were mere inches from my face. She made to push her face into my crotch but I told her later. I wanted no distraction from my close encounter with a fresh cunt, all whorls and dimples of slick, engorged flesh. I delayed as long as I could but it seemed all too soon that I was wrestling with jerking hips as the climax broke. Then she took charge, turning herself round to face me, head busy between raised, spread thighs. She seemed to sense I was too far gone for much teasing and homed straight in to the clitoris in a way that sent me spinning off into space.

Afterwards we lay twined, and as I was hovering on the edge of sleep I thought of Chicago and the internet poster. Mrs Jencks had assured us we were the first viewers of the collection, but at the time there was something about her manner that didn't ring true. Something that had stayed with me to surface in one of those strange twilight states. I turned over and muttered into Molly's ear, 'Visitors, gorgeous. Had any visitors lately?'

'Mm-mm.' She snuggled into me and I tried again.

'Anyone come to the house in the past month?'

'Visitors. Not since the Master got ill.' The voice was thick with sleep and I was about to give up when she mumbled, 'I'm wrong. A lady in the library. From some college. Didn't see her myself. Mm-hm...'

The news should have put me into a state of alert, but instead I too slipped quietly away to that land east of Eden. Perhaps I'd been used up by the long, intense day and deep down knew it would keep till the next one.

As it was I woke in a rush to see the time had passed nine o'clock, I was alone in the bed and there were a few sheets of paper that had been left beside me on the table. I scooped them up and scanned their contents: there was no heading but the last line contained the familiar words *uxor studiosa scripsit* under the date of July 1728. If my memory was to be relied upon, that was a mere month later than what I'd seen already, and oblivious to the fact I was making a late start even later, I began to read. This time there was no heading, and the pages had been printed, presumably in recent times, by a modern device.

The Day I record here is one of Work, for we are enter'd into strenuous Rehearsals, the End of which is a Display propos'd for the Great Anniversary of the 15th Day of August. The Scheme of my eminent Husband is that, as the Culmination of a set of Scenes, I shall be Bench'd, Whipp'd and Plugg'd, and in said condition, receive the Lordly Member into my Mouth. Some are saying the Event will be on a Par with the taking of the Sacrament, but I keep myself apart from such Matters of Controversy.

This Afternoon is set aside to accomplish two things. Since no Organ, let alone that of the Master, has yet entered through my Lips, I am in sore need of Tuition in the Art. My Abigail, while being no Expert - or so she insists modestly - has agreed to teach me what she knows. In addition to that Deficiency, I lack first-hand Experience of the Taws with which I am to be Lash'd, but wish to approach this Matter by Degrees. Thus it is that I shall lay them across Nabby's Backside a few times at the start - with her full consent, I must make clear - so that we may take note of the Condition and Progress of the Marks while I undergo my Primary Instruction.

The first of the Footmen to do Duty for us is let in to my Chamber bearing the Instrument of Correction for our Scrutiny. I am equipped with a Rule and determine its Length to be a little more than two feet, and its Breadth a total of one and three-quarter inches. It is made of Leather a full quarter-inch in Thickness, and for half its Length is cut into the three Tongues that give the Name to it. One Face has been polished to a high Degree, which we reason is the one designed to strike the Skin. We have finished our Study so my dear Maid raises her Shift and kneels at a Stool, bending to present her white Posterior for my Action.

'Hard now, Mistress,' she begs, 'or we sha'not learn what we should,' and I take her at her Word, standing forward so that when I swing the Taws whips around the Globes to Bite the far side. Two Lashes as we have agreed produce two Squeals, then I move to deliver a Brace backhanded to the Left to make two more. Nabby leaps up and rubs with her pretty Mouth open, but when she stops there is but a little Red to show for it. I am disappointed, but it is no Matter, for we have the main Business to attend to.

The Young Man is now divested of his Livery and stands waiting in an open Shirt and Breeches. Before even he is unbutton'd it is plain he has enjoy'd the View; thus it is no surprise when Nabby draws out a Polony as firm and long as it were come fresh from the Continent. However, once the Mouth is put to work it is not to munch but rather to suck as though she were holding one of the new-made Lollypops between her Lips. In a while it is my Turn, and Nabby shows me to take the Organ in on to my Tongue and then close around it. I do so and at once Retch as the Head touches the Roof of the Mouth. 'Easy as she goes, Mistress,' says my ever-helpful Abigail, counselling me to take a little of the Shaft at a time. Thus I get on better and am soon, by Variation, licking at the Head as I am instructed. There is suddenly a Drop at the End that is not, I think, of my Spittle and Nabby takes it back, declaring the Finish to be near.

The Aid is enlisted of the Footman to take the Member in his own Hand, for we are desirous of its Discharge into a shallow Dish. He pumps rapidly perhaps a dozen times, then the Juice squirts. The Deed is done and the Equipment has shrunk to the size of a Slug, which Nabby wipes and returns to its Place in the Clothing. Once the Lad is dismissed, she takes a little of the Pool with the tip of her Tongue and asserts that it is a Fine Sample. I follow her Example and although I am not best pleased with the salt Taste - which fact I keep to myself - I join her in licking the Plate clean as though we are two Cats at the one Bowl of

Milk.

It is when my Maid rises to put it aside that I see a Sight to make me clap my hands with Glee. For the Area that showed before so little mark'd is now aglow! We move to a Mirror so she too may see what has excited her Mistress: each Buttock bears the Print of the Taws emboss'd in pink on the marble-white Surround. The Flesh is hard, so that one may trace the rais'd Outlines with a Finger, and I cannot resist to kneel and press my Face to the Heat. Though the very Picture of a Slapp'd Bottom it is sore only to a Degree, avows Nabby, which bodes well for my Experience in the Month to come.

We are all a-flutter when the second Man arrives, so straightway he is treated to a full Examination of the rosy Object, after which the Cock springs eagerly from his Trews. I take a firm Grip of the Stem close to the Ballocks and concentrate my Efforts on the Head. Soon he declares the Moment is upon him leaving me to sit agape - and no little aghast - while the Spending coats my Lips. Crying to me 'don't move!' Nabby shoos him, still buttoning, out of the Door, then she is at me with her Tongue. Sans Impediment, the Male Seed is dispersed among the Saliva of our Mouths and when she raises my Smock to gain access to the Nether Lips I am easy prey to her Love-Making. In Truth, dear Reader, there is little in it to shock, for my Abigail is become of late no Stranger at Night to the Bed we disport ourselves upon.

I gulped down some essential, if stewed, coffee that had been left in the small dining room as fast as I could, but it was still almost ten when I hurried through the library. In the study Tamsin was sitting at the screen of her laptop surrounded by books.

'Busy night, guv?' she asked without looking up.

'It had its moments. As it seems did yours.' I stared pointedly at the cushion that separated the mini-skirted behind from the wooden top of the stool, and was rewarded by a blush. 'A memento?' I suggested.

'Sort of, except it's not going to last.'

'You'll just have to book in for weekends, Tams.'

'Too right.' She grinned, at ease again, and waved at the pile of leather-bound volumes on the counter. 'They all meet the criteria of girl on girl and absence from the Nemesis collection. Will I deliver them on the way back?'

'If you don't mind the detour. Just make up a list for, er, Matilda, will you? And there is one thing. She told me that we were the only ones in here since the death, but I heard that's not exactly true.'

'And you want me to do a little probing.' Tamsin made a face. 'I'm just going to ask, right? No tricky stuff. Now I'll just print out these titles and then I'll get to it.'

When the PA had gone I settled down with the early record of literary acquisitions, whose first entry was for January 15th 1700. The family had been already five years in residence, so it was perhaps the new century that prompted the keeping of a log. That was all it appeared to be on a cursory glance: essentially a bibliography by date of purchase that ran through to a final entry of

1787. Since the shelves were similarly arranged it was easy to check that the first three titles were indeed present, as were another three selected at random from the first decade. Then it occurred to me to look at the records for the year of 1728, when, from the scanty evidence I possessed, my *uxor juvenis* was busy putting pen to paper.

The start of it noted the arrival of a copy of the pseudo-medical treatise *Gonosologium Novuum* in an edition from 1725, and further down I spotted the rare *Rod of Venery*, hot from the press in that very year. Then at the foot of the page there was a line of writing dated September 19th and enclosed in square brackets. The ink had faded more than the entries above and I shone the desk lamp directly on it to make out the following lines.

J copied for me a fortnight since Scene No. 4 from the purpos'd *Commentaria Perversa*, which is set fair to be a Work of the most debauch'd Kind! The same was deliver'd to MR of Covent Garden, who this Day returned it with a Note that he is 'greatly interested' in her Endeavours.

The penultimate word clinched it: J had to stand for Joanna, the young wife. Not only was she writing, there was a larger creation on the agenda than the brief pieces I had seen and it looked as though a London publisher had been contacted. Indeed the MR was readily expanded into the contemporary Martin Roberts, who had printed two of the early items in the collection. It was the first time I had come across the putative title, and I decided that while *perversus* could be a simple adjective, it would be preferable to read it as a past participle, carrying the implication that the Notebooks were not merely 'perverse' but had been 'perverte*d*'. Aside from these points of translation, one thing was immediately clear: whatever stage the project had actually reached, and in whatever form it survived, we had to unearth it.

At that point Tamsin returned to say that the housekeeper had changed her story. The visitor Molly recalled was confirmed as having come on a particular errand. She was offering a high price for one of two identical copies of an item from 1810, and Matilda had obtained the blessing of the by then terminally weak earl.

'I'm not very happy about this, but the book checks out. I can't help feeling the story could well change again.'

'Who was the lady, do you know?'

'Yeah, a Dr Torman and she'd come from Queen Mary's College. Anyway, that's it guv, I'd better shoot.' She got up and moved over to the door.

'Okay. I'll be one, two more days max. Can you hold the fort till then?'

'Sure thing. See ya.'

I could look into the academic connection when I was back in town. For the present I was more concerned to locate what there was of the *Commentaria* and there was an obvious first source to tap for help.

I went through the Great Hall and out to the back, where I'd been inveigled after the trying encounter with the block. The pantry was much as I'd seen it before, except that this time the glass panes in the door afforded a different view. Cook was in residence, as then, but sans punishment strop, and wrestling, or rather trying to wrestle, the boy into position across her ample lap. I breezed in with a cry of: 'Oh, here's the young man I'm looking for, and in trouble again!'

'Nothing but trouble, this one, ever since the Master took him in.' She gave up the struggle to subdue the unwilling boy and shook her head at me. 'See that,' she said, pointing at the smashed pieces of what had been a large earthenware pot. 'He comes up behind me with a shout and it slips right out of my fingers. Pure devilment, it was.'

'Well, I think you're quite right, Mrs, er...'

'Beaton, and I've been told you're Dr Greene.'

'Indeed I am.' It was a novel experience to exchange formalities with a woman whose brawny arms had been only the day before lashing my bare arse for all she was worth. But I'm not usually one to harbour a grudge. 'And I'm with you on this, Mrs Beaton, that it is definitely a spanking offence. How, I ask myself, can the lad not agree?' For the first time I looked him in the face; he had seen what was coming and the lips were pursed in wry resignation.

'Well, Dr Greene, what boy does not try to escape a hiding? Now if you were to see fit to lending me your support—'

'Then we shall have him under control in a jiffy.' By that time Cook had hold of one arm, I took the other and he was down. Then I moved round and took his head in a scissor-grip between my legs while she dragged the trousers down clear of dimpled cheeks. I thought I'd seen all there was to see of over-the-knee events, but what followed was a scorcher. The broad hand was powered by muscles to do it justice, and the arm rose and fell at a pace that had the boy screeching from the outset. As in the popular disciplinary recipe, it was short, very sharp, and the shock of it could be gauged from the decidedly flaccid penis glimpsed when the recipient grabbed for his trousers on release.

However, by the time I took my leave, hustled him up the stairs and applied a cold sponge to the inflamed parts, he was flaunting a specimen I was soon able to work up into fine spurting condition.

With the act completed and clothing restored, I put my own needy crotch determinedly out of mind and bade the boy sit. I had questions to ask, and after a little petulant squirming to play up the soreness of his bottom, he seemed happy enough to leave aside the spanked urchin persona and tell me what he knew.

Chapter 8
Tales

The story I got wasn't much, but it did contain one crucial lead. While I was aware that Monty had spent his time in the manner of a rakehell from an earlier age, it was news to me that he had been diagnosed with an incurable illness in the autumn of the previous year. Soon after, he decided to live out the remainder due him by putting in order some of the papers to which he'd paid little heed before. He could no longer live the life himself, so he would take what vicarious pleasure was to be had from the recorded exploits of his predecessors. For some two or thee months, before the final stages confined him to his bed, the old man employed a secretary to turn certain items into text documents that could be stored and later printed. The boy's job was to help scour the stack of box files for anything of greater interest than routine letters and accounts.

It was by his assessment a boring one until the day that the invalid chanced upon a piece by *uxor studiosa*, whom a scribbled note in the margin allowed him to identify as his earliest namesake's young wife. Or so I understood. The tale was told in rapid-fire spurts that put me in mind of his prowess with an organ other than the mouth. *Later*, I told myself, and tried to clarify what the boy was saying.

'So that was what you left for me to read.' He nodded assent. 'And were there more, or was that just a one-off?'

'One-off, yeah. Written out nice. But then he found the books. All full of writing like a spider.'

'Books? You mean notebooks, like a diary?' Again he agreed. 'And did the secretary transcribe any of it?'

'Some. You can see for yourself. There's a thing in the desk.' That was it. I marched him downstairs through the library and hovered while he opened first one drawer then another. Eventually, going back to the first, he pulled out a CD in a plastic case. He fidgeted and I drummed my fingers as we waited for the laptop to boot up and then to load the contents of the disc. At last, there it was onscreen: *The Ardingley End Project*. Scrolling down the table of contents brought us to the entry Everett, Joanna (1727-9) which unpacked into a list of three items. The first I'd read in one of the BL's own titles and the next was still lying by my bed; only the third, of a mere two pages in length, was new.

'Well, no matter,' I said brightly. 'Once we've got our hands on the original notebooks there'll be loads of stuff to pore over.' I looked at him and he looked back at me in silence as a horrid suspicion began to form in my mind. 'You don't know where they are, do you, boy?' He shook his head dumbly and fidgeted some more.

'They were always out. On the desk, right there.' He jabbed a finger at the space beside my computer. 'Then she was gone. Two months ago. I couldn't find them. Anywhere.'

'But what about the Master? He must have known where they were kept.' He shook his head again.

'*Did* know. In his bed, past caring. That's why she stopped.' My frustration must have been evident and the poor lad seemed to take it to heart. So much so that when maid Laura appeared to say there was lunch, he declined and insisted vigorously that he would search both rooms from floor to ceiling.

On invitation I opted to join the small group at the kitchen table where I was soon seated in front of a big round of cheddar, homemade pickles, spring onions and freshly baked bread. Introductions were made to the striking Ama, a mechanic and driver who looked after the collection of classic cars, and little kitchen maid Jill, who came in with a huge jug of what proved to be porter sent from a small local brewery. Cook, of course, presided at head of table and once her tankard had been filled the ale was passed round.

'Simple fare, Dr Greene, but all of the best. Help yourself.' I needed no encouragement and was soon spreading creamy butter onto a slice of the crusty loaf. 'May I ask, did you get what you wanted from the boy?'

'Well, Mrs Beaton, it was a start and I left him searching for the notebooks we need to find. There is one thing you could tell me, if you will. I've been calling him "boy" since I got to, er, to meet him.'

'And "boy" it is, I'm afraid. Unless anyone knows what I don't.' She scanned round the table but there were no offers. 'Mrs Jencks must have a name for him but I've never cared to ask.'

'I reckon that's what he prefers,' said Ama, spearing an onion with her fork, 'though I tried at first. Especially when we arrived on the same afternoon, two newcomers together. And I expect you can guess what that meant, Dr Greene.' Before she swigged from her glass I thought I detected a wink.

'Would I be right in thinking of the Great Hall and a certain wooden block? In fact a rather *broad* block if memory serves.'

The black girl giggled. 'Got it in one. Two targets side by side, eh, Mrs B?'

Cook cleared her throat, for once not quite in control of the situation. 'Well, the Master insisted on it, so—'

'Fair enough. But did you really have to keep cutting me long after you'd finished with the boy?'

'My dear, I didn't mean to treat you worse, and you know that.' The large lady clicked her tongue. 'I never before took the rod to a coloured—'

'Black.'

'All right, a *black* girl. And the marks are a lot harder to make out. Now if you wanted me to get more practice - no? - well then, let's change the subject. You're just trying to embarrass me in front of our guest.'

When the meal was done and we left the kitchen, Ama lingered by the back door. 'Tell me to keep my nose out, but you're a bit struck on the boy, yeah?' I mumbled something, feeling the colour rise to my face as she went on. 'You'll think I got some nerve saying this, but I'd bet he hasn't actually been doing it.'

Gobsmacked is not a word I'm attached to, but there are times when no substitute is adequate. In the silence I stood fixed by eyes set deep in the oval face rimmed by hair braided tight to the scalp until I made myself speak. 'No, but it's early days, surely. I didn't want to rush the lad.'

'Oh God, of course not. You must think me completely crass.' The furrowed brow diminished the young woman's beauty not one jot. 'Thing is, after we were birched together like I said, we got left alone to console ourselves. And he was rock hard till I made a move to fit the peg into the hole, if you get me. I never saw any stiffie wilt so fast.' I couldn't help smiling at the image that came to mind. 'See, Dr Greene, I reckon he's a gay boy pure and simple. He gets off on

Mom spanking him but he doesn't want to fuck her.'

'Jane, please. And you could well be right, Ama.' The learned doctor really didn't go with such a down-to-earth conversation, and besides, I was trying to digest the implications of the remark. Assuming the driver wasn't one to skulk about in the night listening at doors, the boy's taste for a hot bottom was no secret, at least at Ardingley End.

'I'm an awful snoop. To be honest, I fancied the pants off him myself, but after that bad start there was no chance. If you're in with one I'm plain jealous.'

'I'll keep you informed if you like. But now I'll have to rescue from his library search the one whose ears should be glowing red by this point.'

She flashed me a smile that demolished any defences I had left, and touched my arm. 'Look, Jane, call in on me in the workshop. Anytime, I'm usually alone there. I mean, don't get the wrong idea - I play both ways. Especially if there's a cane about the place.'

'So do I, Ama, so do I. And you may expect a visit.' I watched her go, head a-whirl with the adrenaline rush of a sudden proposition no less suddenly accepted. The blue cotton of her boiler suit clung to the curve of the hips and the buttocks bounced enticingly as she walked across the yard. And the c-word had been placed very deliberately on the table. Only after the goddess had disappeared completely from view did I become earthbound enough to turn and head slowly away in the opposite direction.

Back in the study I found the subject of our conversation sitting with his tousled head in hands. A pose, possibly, for the benefit of my entrance, but suddenly I felt for the strange creature we'd been discussing. He was down in the dumps after a search that had borne no fruit and I pulled him gently to his feet.

'Let's see the state of you.' I eased down his trousers and turned his backside to the desk lamp. There were a couple of faint dark smudges but otherwise no ill effects of cook's heavy hand. 'You'll do, my lad,' I said, noting the semi-erection my inspection had produced, 'and don't fret. We'll think of something. Of course it would have helped if you'd seen where the things were kept, but we can deal with that lapse at the end of the day. And if you could find something like a leather paddle - to save my hand - that would put you right back in my good books.' At these words the cock had become its fine upstanding self and I gave his bottom a slap.

'Put that thing away, boy, and go and get some lunch,' I ordered. 'You may report to me later.'

'Yes, Miss.' With the cheeky grin back in place he made for the door while I sat in the desk chair and tried to get the brain working. I'd not foreseen the diversions that would be on offer within the confines of a secluded country house, albeit one with an extensive collection of old pornography. In less than twenty-four hours I had been publicly birched, drawn into the spanking 'n' wanking games of a teenage lad, and after frolicking with a maid half the night been given an s/m come-on by the beautiful mechanic. No doubt an uncertain future had something to do with the frenetic living for the moment, but that didn't make it any less distracting. Not that I was actually complaining...

Suddenly there was a raucous *brrr-brrr-brrr!* that brought me to myself with a start. The noise was coming from the black telephone receiver I'd marked down as a museum piece, and I grabbed it before it went off again. When I said hello a voice said, 'Incoming call, I'll put you through,' and there was Samantha on the line.

'Jane, is that you? I wanted to tell you at once that the books are splendid. Absolutely top notch. To find such explicit dealings between women from such an early period is a real tonic. So the deal is on, my dear, if you are still so minded. I gather from your assistant - such a comely girl! - there may be some half-dozen more titles for us, and then the rest is yours.'

'That's very good, I'm glad you're pleased. And whatever Tamsin said goes.' I wondered briefly if Samantha had acted in any way on the PA's 'comeliness' before she went on to give me news that took my full attention. Apparently the debts Sir Montague left behind were much greater than initially supposed and the sale of the house itself would be required to settle them. With some good fortune a very distant but very wealthy cousin had been found in the US: a Southern patriarch keen to inspect a possible family seat, and in all likelihood sooner rather than later. Since a library of antique (if pornographic) books would no doubt be seen as a desirable asset, it was rather important that the contents of the study be spirited away before that date.

'Mr Wilkes, who is handling the estate, an admirable man who shares an interest in such materials finding a good home, is contriving to make the items appear to have been sold while Monty was still with us. They will be identified simply as the, ah, Rare Books Collection, but naturally, the details of what exactly it consisted of will prove to have been lost.'

I chuckled at the nod to my own department at the BL, and was still smiling when I replaced the receiver on its stand a few moments later. For a practicing domina of a severe disposition, the Archive's Director had a remarkable way with the pillars of middle English society. And thanks to her information, my principal duty was all but accomplished: I needed simply to phone Tamsin in the morning and arrange for the books and papers to be picked up. If I knew my organisation, the fact that a substantial free acquisition could be at risk *in situ* would have the job done by the weekend. However, I'd taken on a personal mission in my short time at the house: to obtain for myself the records made by the self-styled *uxor studiosa*. And that aim was no further forward.

Then there was a tap on the door and Molly's head appeared. 'Er, Jane,' she said diffidently, 'I don't mean to disturb you—'

'Please do. It's exactly what I need. What's up, sweetie?' The pretty face was wearing a rather downcast expression.

'I just got a big lecture from old Jencks. "Telling tales out of school" she calls it - that's *me* telling *you* about that college woman visiting.' Obviously the housekeeper had not been impressed with Tamsin's questions on the subject. But how did she know the informant was Molly? The maid looked sheepish.

'I don't reckon she did know, but I gave it away. Never was much good at porkies.'

'Being an accomplished liar can be useful, but the best people often can't hack it. You're in good company.' When I didn't manage to raise a smile, I guessed that telling off wasn't the end of the matter. 'So I get the impression there's more?'

'Too right. I've been sent to the woods, the part where all the birch trees grow. And I don't have to explain that to you, do I?'

I was outraged. 'That's just not right, Molly. She's the one up to the funny business, not you. I ought to go and—'

'And she's the one who either puts in a word with the new master or she doesn't. So just leave it, Jane, or you'll make things worse. But if you wanted to come and keep me company that would be nice, and you can learn how the things are put together too.'

It wasn't going to help to say anything about who the new employer might be, so I kept mum and followed Molly to get kitted out with a pair of wellington boots.

The afternoon sun was warm as we walked up the slope at the back of the house, but among the trees there was a dank carpet of dead leaves underfoot. Not much was yet in leaf and the slender birch wands Molly began to cut were full-budded. I thought, I'm afraid with a degree of *schadenfreude*, that she would in due course be stinging just as much as I'd been the day before. After watching the curved blades of the large secateurs at work, I chipped in that I'd heard the inclusion of an ash plant of a similar thickness gave the whole thing an extra bite.

'Very likely true, Jane, but I can do without suggestions like that when it's my bum that's to be on the block.' She was looking at me in a kind of playful pique that sent shivers through me. I moved in close and squeezed the article in question.

'And a very tasty bum it is too. Will it be a private affair, or can I sit in?' Molly stuck out her tongue.

'You're just one of them - what's the word? - sadists. Like that Marquis fellow. You want to see a poor girl get a good hiding.'

'Oh yes, please. Especially when she's as sweet as you. If you let me watch I'll give these cheeks the best in aftercare.' By that time I had the top button of the jeans open and a hand down the back roaming over the chubby globes.

'Well, it'll just be herself. Cook wouldn't go along with something like this. But there will have to be someone to hold me down.'

'Better and better. Consider the position filled.' I was worried I might be showing a bit too much relish, but Molly didn't seem to mind. In fact, she kissed me hard and when I eased her pants right down the vulva was slippery to my touch. While she knew as much as anyone how painful it was going to be, the girl was aroused by talk of the birching to come.

Spotting a handy tree stump, I shucked my own jeans down and pulled her across my knee so we were bare skin to bare skin. With the legs spread I was able to stroke the wet folds from the clit down with one hand, while the other kneaded the buttock cleft. Soon she was moaning and in short order the orgasm was on her. While it subsided I sucked on the fingers that ran with her juices and then she pulled me up and got down on her knees, and a very few seconds of her sucking and nibbling had me jerking about as though I'd been given a mains wire to hold while the other end was stuck up my arse. Whatever one may say about rural life, my brief exposure to it was doing no harm at all to the quality of my orgasms.

Chapter 9
Plugg'd

In the late afternoon as we trooped back with the bundles of cuttings I asked what my companion knew of the boy's history. Mindful of how Ama had at once seen the sexual heat beneath my disinterested pose I was ready to drop the subject, but if it bothered Molly she didn't show it.

'Not much, to be honest. I expect you found out he isn't keen on his name, well, it's like he wanted to leave a lot else behind as well. The Master took him in not last year but the year before.'

'Took him in?'

'Yeah. He was in some trouble with the law and the magistrate agreed to let him off if he was given a home here. Well, I suppose it was probation, like, 'cos he had to report in every few weeks. But not any more.'

'Any idea what he'd done?'

'Lord knows. I heard he was living rough for a bit. Whatever it was, he soon settled in here - if you can call being a shiftless layabout settling in.' I was a touch taken aback by Molly's dismissive assessment of the lad, but there was no chance to respond. We had reached the gardener's shed and it was time for further coaching in the ways of the birch.

'We've got a decent collection here, all about the same thickness. So when they're like this you take five of them, no more no less - that's how we do it anyway - and line them up straight as you can. Then you get a hold of the ball of twine and bind up anything from a quarter to a third.' I watched her at work, thumb on a loop of the cord that served to pull through the end at the finish. Absorbed in passing on a practiced skill, the maid had forgotten for the moment whose bottom it was that would be wasting her creation painfully into tatters.

With a little help I managed a passable effort myself, and then Molly did up a third. 'Just in case one comes apart,' she explained, 'you've got a spare. Not that it will if you do it right.' In a corner stood a tub I remembered from the Hall, and Molly thrust the business ends of the rods into the liquid, swirling them round.

'So how long do you leave them to, er, pickle?'

'Could be a week or more, but these'll be coming out day after tomorrow. That's plenty time.' She shook her head resignedly but there was the hint of a smile. 'I don't know what I was thinking of; we should have botched them up a bit. As it is, these are too bloody good by half.'

'Don't worry, sweetie, I'll be holding your hand.'

'Holding me down, you mean. That's not quite the same thing.' But despite the words she was grinning and I took the chance to get a hand back down her jeans and kiss her. There was a good hour before dinner and I was suddenly of a mind to bolt the door and take advantage of our privacy.

The meal was a disappointment after the convivial lunch earlier in the day. The lustrous Ama seemed preoccupied, saying little and none of it to me, and cook was grumpy and taciturn. Perhaps the addition of the groom and two other unidentified males was responsible, or perhaps there had been an incident of which I knew nothing. Whatever the cause, I was glad to make my excuses as soon as I could and escape to the seclusion of the study.

Once there, however, I found it difficult to settle to anything. First I began to check some of the early acquisitions against the entries in the log kept by the original Montague. The *Gonosologium Novuum* of 1709 that he mentioned was there, as was the *Satyrica Sotadica* in an edition of 1720, both handsomely bound in what looked like calfskin. The rare *Flagellationis Scientia* of 1695 was another treasure of the pseudo-medical variety with its straight-faced recitation of the physiological benefits of regular whipping. I knew it only by reputation, and its fine engravings depicting callipygian maids and matrons frolicking under birch and lash kept me occupied for some minutes. So did another handful of titles - all present and more than correct - but after a while the pointlessness of what I was doing came home to me.

The books weren't the problem. They were going to make a valuable addition to the BL collection and if there were a few missing that was only to be expected. It was the notebooks of *uxor studiosa* that I wanted to get my hands on. There seemed little purpose in conducting a search of my own: I was certain the boy would have been only too pleased to produce them if he could. As far as I could see, all the disc had done was to channel suspicion in another direction. Before we had an academic from town who had come in search of a book, and, it was claimed, only a book. Now there was a secretary too who could possibly be implicated in the absence of the *Commentaria* if only through the fact we knew she'd handled them.

However, it occurred to me that the handwritten pages from nearly three hundred years ago might warrant a glass case in a local museum, but were of no real value except to a specialist in old erotica. While this pointed back in the academic direction, I thought it was still more likely that they had been put away somewhere we were just not thinking to look. I opened the contents list of the transcriptions again and tried to see if any more use had been made of our young wife's writings, but all I could find were the extracts I'd already noted. The third one was at least new to me, so I decided that in the absence of the means to print it for later perusal, I might as well read the piece where I was. Once I had it on screen, I was pleased to see that the writer jumped in with both feet as usual.

To a Young Female Person the male Organ, once tam'd and at her bidding, is properly a Thing of much fascination. My previous Epistle concerned the Act of Suckling at the Member till it gives up its Milk; the present one removes its Focus to the opposite End of Matters. I am, as the keen Reader shall have already discern'd, speaking fundamentally, that is, of that Aperture through which emerges the Residue of what is taken in by the Mouth of our earlier concern.

My Guide, as by Habit, is my Abigail, who will have no Truck with long Words in this, nor any other, Domain. The Thing is, she insists, a Bum-Hole and it is the Stopping-up of it with a Cock that is the Subject of today's Lesson. We must begin, I am told, by rendering it free of Impediment to the Entry of its appointed Bung. To that end she has prepared a Bulb of Rubber, filled with warm soap'd Water that is joined to a glass Pipe around the Thickness of a Finger, and we have taken up a discreet Position by the Privy at the back in order to proceed with the Evacuation.

I lift my Smock to allow Access to the Opening and Nabby inserts the foreign Object with a firm Push. It is a strange Sensation that becomes yet more so as the Liquid is forc'd into my Innards. Once the Bulb is emptied, she bids me hold tight closed while my Lower Belly is treated to a Massage. Of a sudden the Pressure overcomes me and I reach the Seat in scant time to direct my Explosion into the Stench of the Pit below. When I emerge, much reliev'd, there awaits a second Dose and then a third, after which my Tutor declares the Bowel to be in Prime Condition for its Entrance to be plugg'd.

These Diversions concluded, we climb the Stair back to my Chamber where we entertain the first of the Footmen to do us Service this Afternoon. He is a well-proportioned Fellow, and from the stretch'd Nature of his Breeches needs no Reminder of his earlier Visit. Nabby lays a Hand on the Cloth to counsel Patience while the Ground is prepared for what is Bulging beneath. By this Wisdom she refers not only to the Application of Oil that will ease its Passage, but to the warming of the surrounding Cheeks. Thus it is that I am arrayed over the Horse, Legs wide, for my Abigail to anoint the purified Anus and then strike me a dozen Times with the Taws.

The effect of this Latter is less a Sting than a furious Itch, and after the Treatment I writhe till the Organ pins me down with a great Thrust. I am ready to swear that its Dimensions so far exceed those of my modest Hole that I shall be split in two, but Nabby soothes me with a Commentary on its Progress to the Hilt, at which point I am compelled to admit being unharmed, if full. Then my Alarm is quell'd altogether when, under expert Direction, he begins to move, slowly at first, to Pull out and Push in. It is an Action that rubs my Parts against the Ribb'd Edge under me at the same time that it quivers my Insides, and all at once I am in a high Excitement. The thighs press my sore Posteriors as the Shaft swells in Discharge, then I too am Seiz'd and cast a rich Shower on to the Leather that supports my Belly.

There is scarce Time to draw Breath, for my Teacher has become Hot with all she has witness'd and is no longer content with the Part of Watcher. So the second Man is call'd in as the first departs and she hoists her Cloathes, spreading herself forthwith to show what shall be the Object of his Endeavours. While it is now my turn to swing the Taws, I hang back, concern'd that my good Abigail has not been Sluic'd in the Manner I had understood was requir'd. However, she assures me it is but an hour since she was deliver'd of two plump Turds and the Void remains yet, ready to be Fill'd. Given this Intelligence I hesitate no more and begin to make the Bottom present'd me bounce and shake under the conjoin'd Trio of Whips. Such is my enthusiasm that poor Nabby is obliged to cry Mercy to remind me that a Dozen was my Limit, but it is clear that our little Show has been appreciated. For when I release the Buttons of his Confinement the Actor springs out with a Dewy Eye, in little need of the Drops I am spilling on his Target.

With no delay his Head pushes wide the Ring while I hold to Nabby's Shoulders and peer closely at the act of Penetration. I am seeing the Result of Practice, I surmise, for it is a Vigorous Play in which my Maid forces herself on the Member as much as she is Impaled by the Man's Movements. Whatever the respective Contributions, it is a Sport of small Duration as with contorted Features he withdraws his Weapon for it to rear up and shoot its Contents. When that is done, what a Sight is before me of my dear Servant's red-streak'd Mounds dripping Gouts of White. I cannot resist to lick him clean of the Dregs, after which he stands full ready for Engagement with the untried Opening that his insatiable Partner pushes at him entirely without Shame.

Thus it is I am acquainted with the Elements that will go to make up the Display, and announce once we are alone the Need to rehearse them with Assiduity in the few Weeks that remain before that Event. It would seem that my Abigail concurs, though busy as her Lips are with the nether Counterparts they have lighted upon between my Legs, it is not easy to be sure. (I must own, too, that I am a little distracted from making the Effort). What I am resolv'd to make quite certain of, however, is my own Preparedness in the Month ahead of us to serve the Master's Will.

Uxor Studiosa scripsit, July 1728.

Back in my room I set the taps to fill the freestanding bath with its clawed feet. From raunchy Mistress with her Maid to the *domini puella* of the closing homily, she had made me keener than ever to see more, but for the time being that would have to wait. While it was barely nine, I decided to cut the day off with a long soak, then curl up with a glass of malt and the copy I'd brought up with me of the wit and wisdom of the famed Lady Termagant Flaybum. Half a century later than *uxor*, she was at that juncture about the closest I was going to get.

When I emerged eventually from the steam, towelling my hair, the boy was waiting inside the door. How long he'd been there I didn't know, but I made no comment and took from him the leather paddle he was holding. I sat on the bed, patted my lap and without a word he lay across it. That part of our relationship at least required no special negotiation. I pulled the cotton covering tight over his seat and brought the instrument down several times with some vigour. It made a fine noise and once his erection began to press into me I stood him up and dropped his trousers to the floor.

The penis pulsed in my hand and I stroked its meaty thickness, feeling my own loins contract. So much was becoming habitual, but that night I was of a mind to move things on a little. With a nonchalance I was far from feeling, I opened the bathrobe and my legs enough to enfold his hardness with my thighs when he came back down. Thus I held him with the tip of his glans a bare inch from my aching vulva while I resumed the spanking with a bare hand. Whatever he thought about the new departure he made no complaint. Quite the opposite, in fact: as I fell into a steady rotation of smacking and fondling the reddening bum, the boy's movements too acquired a rhythm that pressed the cock into the limbs that gripped it. I stroked his balls and drew my hand up the crack to the puckered hole. It responded at once, opening to my fingers, then he made a noise in the back of his throat and I felt the hot spurting between my legs.

And that was it. He lay quivering a moment, then he was up and into the bathroom grabbing at his pants. I sat frozen and when he returned it seemed to my fevered mind that he pointedly kept his eyes off the spattered flesh still uncovered. Perhaps so, indeed why should he not have been as embarrassed as I by my clumsy attempt to bring cock closer to cunt without the dreaded 'gay' wilt, of which I'd been warned. As it was, there seemed to be something else on the boy's mind.

'Secretary,' he muttered, from under the fringe that had fallen over his eyes, then tossed it out of the way. 'She might know, right? Not far down the road. We could go.'

It took me some seconds to wrench the sex-fixated brain into gear. He was talking about the Notebooks, of course. The woman who'd transcribed some of their contents might be expected to know where they were kept. It was certainly worth a try and I warmed to the we: an expedition might lead us to other places than our literal destination.

'How about after lunch tomorrow?'

'Yeah.' He made his unceremonious exit, releasing me to go and clean up in an almost cheery frame of mind. I planned to call on the lovely mechanic in the morning, and with a little help from the gods I could end up with the use of a car thrown in. The day was shaping up well.

Chapter 10
Sub-Frame

I passed a restless night battling with monstrous images of walls and furniture that sprouted orifices I could find no means to fill, though I was somehow desperate to do so. The dawn light was creeping round the curtains so I threw on sweatshirt, jeans and thick socks and tiptoed down the stairs, wellies in hand. Outside the back door I pulled on the boots and set off over the dewy grass in the direction we had followed to the birch wood. After five minutes the fresh air had banished the oppressive residue of dreaming and I sat on a gate at the top of the rise just as the sun pushed up its rim towards the salmon-pink clouds. The combination of *uxor's* anal exercises and the real-life hole I'd been probing were enough to explain the lurid scenes my mind had concocted, but I was tempted to see more in it. I'd been angling to get the boy into the fucking position; the theme of the night put me in the driving seat, as it were, though frustrated by anatomy. Well, there were ways around *that*, and a certain young lady in my thoughts might be just the person to have the equipment for the job.

As I surveyed the house from my vantage point my eye was drawn to a group of outbuildings. A sizeable thatched barn closed off one side of a yard in which stood a couple of cars under tarpaulins. At right angles to it was a more recent brick structure with machinery visible inside, and at the end an outside stair led to an upper floor. All of a sudden golden sunlight picked out a window at the moment curtains were drawn back and a dark-skinned face looked out. It was unusually early for a social call, let alone the serious business that had been mooted, but the event had the force of an omen. Ama was up and about and I'd been apprised of the fact. On an impulse I waved a hand high over my head and she threw open the frame and waved back. The conclusion was inescapable: I had to visit her there and then.

I made myself concentrate on negotiating the rutted track until I reached concrete on rounding the corner into the enclosure. The door to the accommodation above was open, so I climbed the steps before I could think better of it and left my mud-caked boots at the threshold. The smell of newly made coffee hit me as I put my head round, tapping on the wood.

'Come on in, Jane. I hope I don't need to tell you not to be shy.'

At the poised milk carton I said, 'Just a splash,' and took the steaming mug out of her hand. 'Thanks, Ama. And I don't think I'd be here at all if I were afraid of taking a plunge.'

'So I can hope you're not just stopping by, welcome though that would be, of course.' We were in a small kitchen area and Ama pointed me to one of two high stools by the polished counter. She disappeared behind the partition at the back of it, past which I could see a large divan that occupied the far end of the living space. When she came back my host took her seat, placing a long black rod carefully on the surface beside us. I recognised the nature of the beast at once, though to be quite certain I tested the feel of it with a finger.

Pulse quickening I said, 'Resin bonded into a hard rubber coating. A formidable instrument.' She was watching me as I spoke, but I couldn't make out the expression.

'You are familiar with such a thing, Jane.'

'Indeed. From both ends, so to speak.' There was a silence in which Ama seemed to be considering her words, and I waited it out. Give her time to put her own spin on what I was by then in no doubt I was going to be asked to do.

Through the window the sun was warm on my back and the bright spring morning was out of joint with the dark thing that had been brought into it.

'I mean, I actually hate the whole idea, everything about it. All the baggage it so often gets laden with. Men's fantasies of compliant schoolgirls for instance, or uppity wives getting beaten into obedience. For fuck's sake, have you seen those magazines?' She looked up from the coffee mug between her hands and turned an indignant gaze full on me. It was not the time to confess to my own partiality for schoolgirl bottoms, so I suppressed a twinge of guilt and nodded in agreement. 'But between women I try to tell myself that's a different thing. Not that I've really got a *choice*.'

Ama got up and leaned against the sink, frowning. 'If I try and ignore it I just get more and more wound up. Fucking obsessed, can't think about anything else. If it comes to it - and it has done - there's a lady in town who'll...' she broke off, shaking her head, '...but I won't go into that. You've got a reputation, Jane, and you've come along at the right time. If you're up for it, of course.'

'I'm up for it, Ama, the question is, are you?' I was a touch irritated and let it show. However, in response her face cleared and there was the suggestion of a smile. She led me out round the dividing wall and with the air of playing a trump card positioned me in front of an object shrouded in some dark material. Plucking off the cover, she stepped on a pedal, threw a lever and with the sounds of machined parts slotting decisively into place, four steel tubes swung out from a stout pedestal bolted to the floor. There was a kind of double saddle in the centre and the padded cuffs at the extremities were sprung open.

'Once I'm on, I'll have to be. Up for it, that is. I don't get off till you decide it's finished, right?'

'Right.' I echoed the word trying to get a grip on the situation. 'Is it, I mean, did you, er...?'

'My design, my execution.' It was now less of a smile and more of a smirk. 'Although to be honest, the conception owes something to the modern dentist's chair, and to various kinds of fuck seats. You know, aimed at facilitating position ninety-six-and-a-half from the Kama Sutra. Though the occupant of mine is going to have an experience rather more toward the dentist end of things.'

I grinned at her, delighted at the enthusiasm propelling my beautiful black acquaintance towards a sound thrashing. I was keen to make it one she would not easily forget and my loins were turning to liquid at the prospect. She showed me how each of the hefty tubular spokes could be moved through ninety degrees horizontally and close to a hundred and eighty in the vertical dimension; once locked into place the apparatus was a punishment frame as rigid as any that stood on four feet in the traditional mode. And much more flexible: the body could be secured jack-knifed, limbs together, at one extreme or spread-eagled flat at the other; or of course, in any chosen position between the two. Furthermore, the central pillar could be raised or lowered in the manner of a hydraulic jack and, in addition, the whole of what it supported could be titled fifteen degrees forward or back. I was mightily impressed: Ama's use of the thing might be only occasional but was important enough to have motivated a labour of love.

I was itching to put the piece of equipment to a practical test, and to that end retrieved the cane from the kitchen. As I swished it a few times it occurred to me that while it was, if anything, slightly heavier than my own, the weight was concentrated into a perceptibly narrower form. While I planned my application of the rod to be quite unrestrained, I did not want to break the skin.

'Ama, is there something you could wear? Thin, but tough is what we need.' She nodded with what looked very like relief and turned to fish something out of the chest of drawers at her back. It was a pair of Bermuda-style shorts in a fine red leather, closed by zips that ran from the waist to the front of each thigh.

'I had them made last year. After... after a time when...' She broke off, biting her lip, and I squeezed her shoulder.

'Put them on, sweetie. You should have said.'

'I didn't want to look like I was chickening out.' I tsk-tsked while she wriggled into the garment and then discarded the robe she'd been wearing. I had just time to register breasts with nipples like cherries before they and her belly were pressed into the upholstered rectangle at the machine's centre. I pumped up the height of the whole and angled it forward, then secured and positioned the arms ahead in line with the downward slope of the back. Once I'd fastened the legs well apart I stood back to survey the field of action. The design of the shorts was on a level with that of the apparatus as a whole: the target area of the buttocks, that formed the apex of the tethered figure, was covered in a smooth second skin from hip to hip. While it could be removed in a moment, the fastenings were tucked safely underneath. I took hold of the waistband to feel the material between my fingers: strong yet light, it would prevent the skin from splitting while allowing the most forceful impressions to be created.

On a shelf under the window were half a dozen dildoes and strap-ons, and at the end, between a blindfold and a complete headpiece, I spotted a ball-gag. 'I would reckon this sufficient for the occasion, if you agree,' I said, stooping to address the head poised a bare foot from the floor.

'Your call, Jane. About the number. I, er, have been known to take twenty...' It was suspiciously like a weakening of the will and I jumped in before she could finish.

'I shall give you as many - or as few - as I see fit. And you will take them.' Without waiting for a response I pushed the ball firmly between her jaws and tied the band tightly behind the head. 'In my book, safewords and suchlike belong in parlour games. And I'm not playing.'

Having delivered myself of this little homily I turned my gaze back to the luscious arse awaiting my attentions. Despite the acute angle of the body two full globes rose to meet me with the fat vulval purse clearly outlined between the spread legs. I laid the last two inches of slender black rubber against the fold and rolled it back and fore until I saw the dark stain of wetness show through. The victim was primed and ready: it was time to begin.

I'd already decided that the protective layer would allow for something rather special, and with that in mind I measured up the first stroke with care, across the dead centre of the cheeks, a little below their highest point. Until my eye was in accuracy would be of paramount concern; nevertheless I managed a satisfying *crack!* as the cane bit and flesh rippled. Then, after pausing a moment or two, I walked round and took up position on the other side. For years I had trained myself to be fully ambidextrous in the use of instruments of discipline, if for no other reason than the increase in staying power it afforded. At that time, however, I was able to reap the direct benefit of such an ability. Now with my left hand, I laid the weapon precisely to the contour of impact preserved in the material, raised it high in the air and struck.

Swish-crack!

This time the whole body locked stiff in protest and there was the sound of air being expelled from lungs. Adjusting my aim by an inch at a time, I went on to deliver two more 'doubles' in short order, then stood quietly by until the limbs had ceased to wrench at their bonds. Inspection showed the lower quadrant of the buttocks to be encircled from hip to hip by three perfect hoops of hard, raised flesh. I knew the rod's tip had scored the sides like a brand, but I could also be sure that the repeated hits in the centre must be the source of some very lively sensations. I too was on fire, but with the fierce flame of old gods and ancient ritual. There was no more calculation, no more straining for exactitude of aim, only a duality that subsumed all into the giving and receiving of pain. For a space I was lost to the mundane world as the cane slashed, the body jerked and strangulated cries forced their way past the ball lodged in the mouth. And then, when it was done, the action stopped.

I came to myself, chest heaving in rhythm to the muscular spasms that racked the figure below. Not aware of having counted, I yet knew that two dozen strokes had been delivered in twelve scorching lines. I tugged feverishly at the zips, yanked down the back flap and pulled the soft leather out from between the legs. And there they were! The welts stood out like ropes that converged into a solid band at the sulcus, against the brown skin a shocking purple that oozed here and there a dark red. I gripped the still shivering hips between my hands and ran my tongue over the lines of excoriated flesh, tasting in between the sweat that had collected at the top of the cleft.

From there the anus demanded to be explored, and its slightly acrid taste was with me as I dipped between labia that welled up with juice in the wake of an addict's bout of extremity. For addict she was, and I felt no guilt at the sadistic treatment of her that sent my head spinning into orbit. Not that I was occupied with the ethics of our encounter at that particular point. Mouth smeared with the copious flow, I teased at the soft folds of flesh, at the same time opening the fly of my jeans to access the wetness of my own within. My tongue then teeth worked her clit just as I found mine with two fingers; her body bucked and the rush of sweet pain consumed me utterly.

Feet back on the ground I buttoned up the soggy crotch and retrieved the remote control from the bed. The figure on the frame was motionless save for the odd shuddering breath, so I set the auto-release for ten minutes and let myself out into the yard where the fresh morning air seemed filled with honey.

An hour later, showered, breakfasted and residually euphoric, I made the short walk back. This time the door was shut - as I'd left it - and horrid doubt clawed at me. Had the whole thing been an appalling mistake? Were that the case I had to know; there was no ducking it. So I gritted my teeth, turned the knob and walked in.

The kitchen was empty, and so was what I could see of the area containing the divan whose quilt was unruffled. Unaccountably afraid to call out, to make even the smallest sound, I tiptoed forward, heart in mouth. Around the partition the machine came into view, its tubular arms positioned as in its earlier use, though without the occupant it had then borne. And there she was: back to the wall, motionless, fixed in silent contemplation of the instrument of her recent suffering. Wearing only a short white top she made no sign that my presence had been recognised, and I too stood staring, at a loss. Then I noticed for the first time the bare pubes caught in the light from the window. The mound gleamed in a way that made me certain the hair had been removed, not shaved, and the sight broke my spell. In a flash I was in front of her, on my knees, pressing lips to the silky fissure as I cupped careful hands to the welted cheeks behind. She made no attempt to move away and I looked up to see her mouth twisted in a wry grimace.

'Jane,' she said, 'I own two perfectly good rattan canes. Full senior grade both. Another time remind me to try and interest you in one of them.' As the words sank in - another time, the angel had said *another* time - I ventured a chuckle and a little squeeze to the corrugations that lay thick under my fingers. 'Ouch, fucking ouch! Easy, girl, you've done enough damage in that department for one day. But the front bottom - as I believe it is politely known - now that is all yours.'

Chapter 11
Cane and Cork

I worshipped at the shrine of Venus until its black curator was brought to the heights that were her due. Then I posed her over pillows on the bed and gave her buttocks the most gentle but persistent massage with a herbal cream devised by Samantha's Rigorist Order in Brittany for exactly the present requirements. So visibly stimulated was Ama by the procedure that while she lay still undulating to the rhythm of my hands, I replaced my jeans with a strap-on from the shelf. The phallus was appropriately brown in colour and realistically shaped with the additional feature of a back-spur that pressed into the apex of my vulva. It slid easily into the slick vaginal opening and I fucked my partner with slow, deep strokes to spare her bruising, until the climactic end when the pain would be but one more strand in the overmastering web of sensation.

Later I helped her into a loose-fitting overall and broached the issue of transport. I explained that if I had wheels, the boy could lead me to the woman who had held in her hands the notebooks we couldn't lay ours on. Ama understood their possible significance and nodded in agreement.

'How about the Healey? The stick can be a tad clunky, but you'll turn plenty of heads. And it's just the day for the wind in your hair.'

I was privileged. 'Terrific. I feel I ought to say something about how I won't prang it.' She laughed and I reached for the dildo that still lay on the divan between us. 'This might come in handy too, if I may?' The black mechanic laughed again.

'Can I guess it's going somewhere tight that might need a spot of lube? Don't answer that, I'm just being nosey. Instead come on down and I'll show you round the car.'

I was spared the task of hunting for the boy. All it took was for me to draw up with a throaty growl of exhaust at the front entrance and he was there, watching as I climbed out of the cream leather interior and patted the shining red paintwork. He was already kitted out in a black polo neck and cotton trousers rather similar to my own. We made a pair and I had a mental flash of a placard hung from his neck that read NOT MY SON, placed in order that the world and her husband should know what we weren't. What kind of pair we *were* was a more tricky question, though I was developing some notions of how to push things along. As things were, I settled for a comradely arm round the shoulders to guide him towards the kitchen.

There we made an early lunch of thick vegetable soup and fresh bread with Mrs Beaton's home-cured ham. She left us to it, and as we ate I mulled over our expedition to the sometime secretary who went under the name of Edith Faversham. She had not been forewarned of our visit, so we could take her by surprise should she be party to any monkey business with the elusive Notebooks. I thought that unlikely, but we had nothing to lose by calling unannounced since her movements were restricted by a lack of transport. Our quarry lived by herself and was not a driver, so unless on a job that provided transport she would be found working at home. That was what the boy reckoned, unusually garrulous, and I was happy to take his word for it. The cottage, he insisted, was a mere twenty minutes away and the trip could easily be repeated.

After the burst of speech the actual journey took place in silence, and I was able to indulge myself hurtling along the surprisingly empty country lanes in the spring sunshine. All too soon we were slowing to pass through a nondescript estate of new housing, and pulled up at a gingerbread cottage that stood on the edge of the village green. Before we had time to get out of the car the door opened and a woman in a tweed skirt and brogues emerged. Fifty-ish, with broad shoulders and a heavy bust, she glowered in our direction, no doubt affronted as much by our choice of parking place as our loud arrival. Then her eyes fixed on the boy and her expression cleared somewhat.

'Oh, it's *you*,' she said, plainly no more equipped with a name than I was. I got out of the car and held out my hand.

'Jane Barrett-Greene. Miss Faversham, I take it.'

'Indeed so. How may I help you?'

'I've come from Ardingley End about the transcribing work you were doing a few weeks ago. You see, we can't seem to come across the books you were using and wondered if—'

'I looked *everywhere*. Did you make off with them, or what?' It was rather typical of the boy to find his voice, and a petulant one at that, when the situation called for a little diplomacy. Before I could undo the damage, the lady drew herself up to make an angry retort.

'I can assure you both that when I left for the last time, the volumes were returned safely to their proper place.' She looked fiercely at the boy and then at me.

'But that's just it, Miss Faversham, what is their place? Where can we find them?' I tried to sound ingratiating but she regarded me with pursed lips.

'I could tell you that, of course. However, I must say how much I resent the suggestion that I was not a proper custodian of such valuable materials.'

'I'm sure it wasn't meant the way it sounded. He's annoyed with himself for not being able to come up with the goods. Isn't that right, lad?'

'Um, yes, I'm sorry.' It was muttered at the ground while he scuffed a foot in the dust and I was not surprised when the words cut little ice.

'I'm afraid that an apology is not going to be enough. Perhaps, though, if you were to come inside...' We followed her into a low-ceilinged room shared by a sizeable computer workstation and a floral three-piece suite. From a stand by the door she picked up a wooden clothes brush and was regarding me with an expression I couldn't quite make out. Then the penny dropped: she was unsure of my proprietary status and didn't like to ask.

'Be my guest,' I put in breezily. 'I hold the opinion that regular bottom warming would be of benefit to young men in general. And especially those who have forgotten their manners.' It should have occurred to me that one who had been employed in Monty's library was likely to be favourably disposed to corporal punishment. As it was, my enthusiastic response had turned the frown into a quiet smile, while the boy eyed the item in her hand with resignation. The lady of the house wasted no time in pulling out an upright chair and after seating herself motioned him into place.

It was a broad lap that gave him good support and I had the impression he was going to need it. The trouser seat was a close fit, without pockets, and once he was bent over presented a smooth, wrinkle-free surface. Miss Faversham began at once with an admirable firmness of action, and in the confined space the long flat back of the instrument made a splendid splatting noise on impact. Soon each stroke was accompanied by a yelp, and after perhaps a couple of dozen she released him to spring up and rub.

'Let's have a look at you, my lad,' she said, reaching for the fastening at his waist. It was plain to me that she meant to inspect his behind, in order to judge if it should receive more of the same. But when the trousers came down that was not what caught our attention. Instead we stared, all three, at the engorged penis that stood to attention in front of us. Eventually the chastiser broke the silence.

'I don't believe,' she said carefully, 'that such a thing could, by any stretch of the imagination, be taken to indicate a suitable state of contrition.' I failed to suppress a chuckle, and under the scrutiny the boy's face turned bright red. Then I saw my chance to push the envelope of our disciplinary practice. In the hallstand I'd noticed a crooked handle amongst the umbrellas, and went to pull it out. As I thought, it was a decent length of rattan and I held it out to our host with a raised eyebrow.

'Do you think, Miss Faversham, the cane might do better to achieve the desired aim?'

'Indeed I do. And please call me Edith. You are Jane, if I heard you right.' While we were becoming more amicable through the swapping of first names, the boy without one was looking less than overjoyed at the appearance of the new implement. However, I saw no indication of outright rebellion, so I decided to take a direct part in the proceedings. Pulling him towards me by the hand, I bent him forward and circled his waist with an arm. His bare bottom, glowing rather from the action of the brush, was thus in prime position for the continuation.

'Perfect, Jane, if I may say so. And since you have him fast, I shall be able to exert myself a little. I've never been one to draw out a licking, believing that six strokes, if they really are of the best, suffice more often than not.' I agreed heartily and while tightening my grasp contrived a covert examination of the male organ below. Cheekily hard yet, in the face of adversity, its chances of staying so were, I thought, slight. Edith Faversham had a look about her that said she meant business.

She took careful aim for the first, but the remaining five were laid on with a grunting force that precluded fine control. Notwithstanding, they were beauties! At the last the boy twisted out of my grip, shouting and clutching desperately at his injured seat. When the contortions had abated somewhat I encouraged him to stow the deflated cock away and zip up while it was still a shadow of its recent self. Having returned the cane to the stand, the chastiser was bright-eyed.

'I have to own I enjoyed that, boy, and precisely to the extent that you didn't, I'm afraid to say. But I do hope there are no hard feelings.'

'S'pose not.' He was still rubbing but I could tell the worst was well past.

'Bertie doesn't get much exercise these days, you see.' She turned to address both of us. 'There was a girl in the village who did for me once a week and she usually made some blunder that would afford him an outing. By design I became convinced, though we never spoke of it. Unfortunately she moved away, and her replacement warned me that if I so much as glanced in his direction she would be "out the door". Her words. So there we are.' Miss Faversham sighed, then pulled herself up.

'That's enough about me. Now take a seat, do. That chair there has a good soft cushion, lad. And when I've made a pot of tea, I'll tell you what you came here to find out.'

On the return journey I lasted the three minutes it took to reach a field with an open gate where I could pull off behind the cover of a hedge. He was as hot as I, with an erection that strained in my hand. I stroked the shaft until the whole was slippery with his juice, all the while fondling the lumpy tramlines that crisscrossed the bum.

'Sorry to land you in it, boy, but you don't really mind, do you?'

'Not now I don't, Miss.' He managed a grin, but I got the hint that I should rein in the impulse towards greater severity. Pledging to behave myself in the future, I persuaded him to bend over and hold his ankles.

'Eyes closed, because I have a surprise for you. Don't worry, it won't hurt, but it might just stretch you a bit.' I opened the boot and took out the borrowed strap-on and a tube of gel. In a matter of moments I had jeans and trainers kicked off and buckles tightened around my waist and between my legs. The boy was obediently as he'd been placed, so I parted the welted buttocks as gently as I could and pushed a blob of lubricant into the anus. Then I smeared my phallus with a coating of the same and touched its moulded tip to the puckered hole. At once it dilated and I, or I should say my prosthetic addition, was in: the cork to the neck of the bottle.

It was a coarse, needy fuck on both sides: I pulled him hard into my thrusts and he clawed back at my body. In seconds flat the pressure on my clit sent spasms rocketing up my spine and I felt his hot flow over my fingers. A water trough stood by and I took my time to wash in it his penis and its artificial counterpart. By the time I'd done he was again as firm as ever and I was sorely tempted to bugger him - and by dint of Ama's device, me - slowly to another climax. But we had a job to do, so I contented myself with a last squeeze of punished buttocks and touched my lips to his foreskin.

'Later, boy, later.'

Back at The End, I stopped the car beside the entrance and we went quickly through the library to the study. Around the doorway through which we'd entered was a decorative wooden frieze whose abstract weave of lines was interrupted at intervals by the representation of an acorn. The third from the top on the left-hand side, Edith had said, and one was to press it just as one would a doorbell. I counted down and there it was, carved in a little more relief than its neighbours, and it did exactly what we'd been told it would. With a click a gap appeared in the frame of the doorway itself that allowed a panel to be slid back. Behind it was a cubbyhole set into the thickness of the wall and there, as promised, lay the first Parisian edition of *Les 120 Journées de Sodome*. But there was the signal absence of the Notebooks that were the object of our quest. Instead, tucked into the first page of the de Sade was an envelope addressed to Jane Barrett-Greene, D.Phil.

The lad brushed his fringe away from a forehead creased into a frown, while I frowned back. Then I made myself go over to the workspace, retrieve the silver letter-knife and with a show of calm resolution slice cleanly up through the top of the flap. Inside was a single sheet with a single sentence in a large, bold font.

Dr Greene, it read, now you've got this far it is time for us to come clean. Under the scrawl of a signature was the name of Belle Torman, c/o Queen Mary UL.

'The American. Came for the book.' He jabbed a finger at the print.

'Yes, and more, it becomes clear.' I was thinking hard. If she was, as the message put it, coming clean, it didn't sound like a simple case of theft. Plainly I had to make contact as soon as possible. It was already after four but I might achieve something by quick action. I looked over at the receiver on the desk, but it was an extension without any means of dialling out.

'Kitchen,' said the boy, divining my intention. 'Cook orders stuff on it.' I left him perched on a stool, apparently no longer troubled by the effects of the sharp six. Mrs Beaton waved me on to the wall phone by the door where I dialled the number I knew for London University, and negotiated my way through the arcane telephone system. Eventually there was a reply.

'History Department.' The voice was brisk but not unfriendly.

'Hello. I believe you have a Dr Torman with you. Is she in, please?'

'Ah, we do, but she isn't. And I'm afraid won't be until the end of next week.'

'I see. Is there a contact number? I do rather need to get in touch.'

'Sorry, but Dr Torman is out of the country.' I could have banged the phone rudely down in its holder in frustration, but then I had a thought.

'This is Dr Greene from the British Library. I don't suppose there was anything left for me?' I held on as instructed, through a brief silence save for the rustling of papers.

'Actually there is; a sealed envelope that you must collect in person. She was very clear about that point.' I detected the tone of an English secretary resenting a dictatorial American academic.

'Oh dear. You see, I'm not in town myself this week. However, I could have my assistant pick it up for me.' There was no immediate response so I plunged on. 'Tamsin Bingley is her name and she would be carrying the Library's full accreditation.'

'I'm not sure I can—'

'Tamsin is utterly reliable,' I said firmly. 'I shall receive the item as surely as if you had placed it in my hand yourself. And Dr Torman will never know the difference.' There was a noise that could have been a small chuckle.

'Very well, Dr Greene, please tell Ms Bingley that I shan't be in myself till noon tomorrow, but any time after that will be fine.'

It was as well I hadn't asked her to wait for Tamsin to do a quick dash before five, because I couldn't reach her at our own place or on the mobile. So I left a voicemail to say I'd ring in the morning and tried to curb my impatience. After all, we now knew what had happened to the writings we were chasing, and that was surely the first - if small - step towards getting them back.

Chapter 12
Closer

At dinner there was a buzz about the likely acquisition of a new Master.

'Well, it's not all signed and sealed yet, but I'm hearing that it's as good as.' Mrs Beaton leaned on the table, forearms bulging out of the rolled-up sleeves of the once-white tunic. 'He's coming early next week to look the place over. And that means the staff too. Us.' There were sceptical looks amongst the lower ranks that I guessed were at the inclusive nature of the pronoun. As if confirming it, Sally piped up.

'Pardon me for saying so, Cook, but there's staff and staff. You and Mrs Jencks, now you aren't the ones to be worrying.'

'By my reckoning that's just where you're wrong, girl. Who's to say the man will take to what I can provide in the kitchen, and he could well bring in a body to run the house the way he's used to. A maid, though, is a maid. There aren't too many different ways I know of cleaning a room. Of course, there is one quality I'm told will be an asset. But that's only what you should be familiar with from the old Master, *if* you take my meaning.' I followed her glance round a circle of blank looks before Molly chipped in.

'I get it. He's another of these disciplinary types. Am I right or am I right?' She made a sour face. 'Though, with what's happening first thing tomorrow I could do without being reminded of the subject.' Mrs Beaton wagged her head sympathetically.

'This one doesn't have my approval, remember. And you give me the chance to remind everyone that we are *not* going to attend. I can't stop the Housekeeper from what she's set on, dear, but I can deprive her of the audience she'll be hoping for. Anyone with other ideas will answer to me.' There were nods of agreement all round, but I suspected that the two young men were less than pleased at being deprived of the sight of a particularly comely rear gyrating under the birch.

'So what else do we know about the American, apart from him being well to do?' It was Molly again, and Cook seemed to be weighing up her answer.

'All right, since you're involved I'll tell you what I was told. But it's not much more than gossip, coming as it does from that young clerk at the solicitor's office. She's far too excitable for her own good, if you ask me. So let's not have any wagging tongues.' After a pause for effect - she needed no lessons in how to play an audience - Mrs Beaton bent forward with a conspiratorial air. 'It seems he's what they call a Southern Gentleman, getting on in years and old-fashioned with it. There's a lot of them never really got over not having their slaves any more. I had an aunt - no longer with us now, I'm sorry to say - who was married over in that part of the world so I know what I'm talking about. So how he's going to take to our Ama is a question. Which reminds me, I haven't clapped eyes on the girl since the day before yesterday.' Alarmingly, she looked directly at me as if somehow informed of our session.

'I think she's keeping to herself for a day or two.' I didn't add that it might be until she could sit comfortably with the rest of us. 'Perhaps she wants to have the cars looking their best for the man's arrival.' I was clutching at straws but it seemed to do, for Cook resumed her exposition without comment.

'The story is he's unmarried now, but there are two daughters from the wife that was. What happened to her we don't know. Twins they are, these girls, and only just twenty years old, too. And rumour has it that they are rather more to him than daughters rightly should be, if you get what I'm driving at. We're not a run-of-the-mill household ourselves, it has to be said, but this is a new one.' I pricked up my ears. We were back in the world of *domini puellae*; one where the distinction we would draw between a master's daughters, servants and concubines counted for little. All were there for the taking. The coming of such a patriarch to Ardingley End promised to be interesting.

There were more bits and pieces of information, including a taste for vintage cars that could provide a means for Ama to break down barriers. But I was in a restless mood and slipped away as soon as was decently possible from the rather familial gathering. The mechanic in my thoughts, I wandered over towards the workshop to be met by the view of a pair of legs sticking out from under the Bentley. Stiff and sore as she certainly would be, she was not the sort to let that stand in the way of work. Nor, in that case, should I. The idea made me all at once reluctant to engage her in talk, so I turned before my presence was detected and swung out of the yard in the direction of the tree-topped rise.

I leaned on a gate at the edge of the wood to take breath. In the fading of the day high clouds to the west were tinged pink, while behind me starlings jostled for space in the branches. With its hedgerows and small fields, the area was a small corner of gently rolling countryside spared the depredations of large-scale farming. As a light in the house below came on, and then another, the tranquil setting seemed oddly appropriate for the hotbed of perverse pleasure to which I'd become party. There was, however, one item of unfinished business that would not give way to the peace of the evening, and it turned my thoughts back to the note in the secret compartment.

Had it been planted in the expectation that I'd be led to it? The answer had to be: possibly. But then again, possibly not. Planted, rather, in *case* I was. The notion gave me a small feeling of achievement, of having overcome a hurdle, thanks of course to the boy's help. It made me wonder what the next stage in the game might hold in store and whether there might be a test more specifically targeted. As I was to find out soon enough, there was indeed to be. And it was perhaps as well I didn't know it then, for that was not of a kind to prove amenable to a little detective work.

But this is to run ahead of events. When I made my way back in the gathering dusk, by the kitchen phone I found an instruction to call our PA on her mobile. When she answered her voice was competing with the babble of pub or club, so I kept it brief. There was no problem, Tamsin assured me, in doing what I asked: collecting the communication from the College, opening it and reading its contents to me; all of this to happen as soon after noon as she could manage because I'd be waiting by the phone. It was all that could be done until the following day, and I went upstairs pondering how to fill the remaining hour or two of the present one.

Then, in my room, I found the boy sitting on the bed with the extract from *uxor studiosa* he'd found for me, and looking rather down in the mouth. I sat beside him and squeezed a thigh.

'Don't worry; we're going to get the whole thing back. And I mean *we*. Once I get the message at lunchtime, right?' I don't know quite what made me say it, but it was odds on there was going to be travel involved. At least it was clear to me that the Notebooks were not going to come to us. In any case, the statement seemed to cheer him up and I got him to his feet in front of me and unbuttoned his trousers with a sharp pang of desire. They dropped to the floor and his cock stiffened as I took it in my hand and worked the shaft. When in full flower I eased him down across my lap and looked at the dark lines left by the afternoon's caning. 'I'm just going to bring these up a touch, lad. Feel free to yelp if you want.' He twisted his head round with a grin, and I weighed in with a series of smart slaps that were just short of what one could properly term hard.

He was 'ow-owing' quite lustily when the door opened and Molly's head appeared.

'Sorry. If I'm interrupting—'

'On the contrary. Come and join in. I'm sure the boy won't mind.' He lay compliant while I caressed his neck. I could feel a rock-hard erection poking into me. 'He was given a lovely six of the best earlier. Have a closer look. Mind you, I don't think he enjoyed it quite as much as we did.'

She laughed. 'Oh, he'd get used to it if done regularly.'

I parted the newly pink cheeks and the anus responded at once to my touch. 'See this, Molly. We have an arse begging to be fucked. And if you wanted to help out...' I waved at the strap-on that lay on the bedside cabinet, and she picked it up.

'Well, I could certainly use something to take my mind off what's pickling in the tub.'

I pointed out the movable spur at the root of the life-like phallus. 'This thing here will get you well sorted, girl, while you're on the job of sorting him. Just try it out.' It took only seconds for the device to be strapped in place and adjusted, and seconds more to position the boy hands on knees with bum out. I supervised the lubrication and initial insertion, then on an impulse I hunkered down in front of him and shifted his hands onto my shoulders. I looked up at him and touched my lips to the wet tip of the organ.

'I have to say this is not my absolutely fav'ritest thing to do with a cock, but I do get the urge from time to time. All right?'

'Yes, Miss. Thank you, Miss.'

What a gem. I devoted myself to the task, moving in tandem with Molly's thrusts from the back, and in a short space of time little fluttery cries told me the end was near. I wish I could say it was a creamy mouthful as tasty as the boy himself. The mouthful part of it was never in doubt, from a teenager at the peak of his powers, but however appealing the productive apparatus, what it dispensed was the usual salty, unappetising goo. But it would have been uncivil to spit, so I swallowed dutifully and moved on to the altogether sexier task of sucking the cock back into full-blooded form.

Thankfully Molly had hit her stride with the appendage since I was in dire, seeping need. So it was over the bed rail, legs apart, and the black thing was into the wetness at once from behind. She pulled the lad in close and I reached back to pump his erection until I felt his hand taking over. The ridged head of the phallus prodded insistently at my clit and I was suddenly at the point of no return. Rocketing skywards in a fizzing rush of sensation, I was dimly aware of the boy's grunts and a hot spattering from the sperm factory on my bum. It was good. Bit by bit we were getting closer to where I really wanted him.

I awoke in the middle of the night alone, though I was able to retrieve a moderately clear memory of intertwined bodies before sleep had blotted it all out. Molly I'd expected to disappear with the event of the morning weighing on her, but I thought - hoped, even - that the boy might be moved to stay. I knew he had accommodation in a one-time gardener's cottage, though there had been no call before to track him to his lair. Now, I thought, was as good a time as any, and unless he had a secret assignation elsewhere I was likely to find him in.

Robed and shod, and blessed with the light of a full moon, I padded down the staircase of the silent house and made my way through to the back. As I expected, the kitchen door was unlocked so I turned the handle carefully, eased it open and shut it quietly after me. A few paces took me onto a short path, dark under trees. Small gusts of wind were rustling the branches with their new foliage, and I was glad to emerge from the shadow into the clear space in front of a low-roofed building. It was bright enough to make out some hoes and a rake through dirty leaded glass, so I passed by the entrance next to it. Then came the curtained window of what could be a dwelling, and beyond it a door that stood invitingly ajar.

Visited by a touch of apprehension, I told myself there was no harm in simply taking a look, and pushed it wider. There was no sound as it swung back and I stood on the threshold waiting for my eyes to grow accustomed to the gloom. After a bit I became aware that to the left another door lay partly open, and I pushed at that one too before I could think better of the whole thing. It clunked against some obstacle, the noise painfully loud in the hush, and I held my breath, but there was no reaction. Now in front of me I saw against the far wall a bed, *the* bed I supposed, and it was empty. The covers were thrown back into an untidy heap that suggested a hasty leaving of it, and I advanced a few steps into the room... *and froze rigid*. It was one of those reactions where the alarm signal reaches the brain ahead of the information that triggered it, and for a fraction of a second there was only the panicked lurch of the heart. Then I knew that in the space behind the door, at my back, there was a figure standing.

'Thought I'd pay a call.' My voice rasped in a dry throat as I forced myself to remain still.

'Heard you coming.' He was right behind me, his breath on my neck. Then two hands reached round for the waist tie and the bathrobe was off my shoulders on the floor. He fondled my bottom and I thrust back at him, feeling his cock hard against my hip. We moved forward as one body and in the pale light I saw laying on a bedside table the leather paddle I'd used before. Only this time I handed it to him. I felt his eyes probing mine, though the face was in shadow against the lit window and I could read no expression in them. Then he took the instrument and I went forward onto my elbows. We were in his domain and I was going to submit.

He hit hard, with stinging smacks that made me catch my breath. He was thorough too, ranging up and down and from side to side until my whole arse was on fire. This was not punishment though, it was lovemaking, and I burned for him.

When done with the paddle he spread me wide, and scooping juice from my sopping cunt he fingered it into my anus with a firmness that made me gasp. I was ready for, no, *aching* for the act that, however consensual, carries with it a frisson of violation. The boy could be doing it with a boy: there was no need of one of my gender for the purpose of buggery. It could well be the case he would rather do it to one of his own, and perhaps it was desirable to him only to the degree that my female differentia could be passed over in the dim light and the heat of the moment.

But I didn't care. Not then. For when he pressed the head of his cock into the ring of muscle it yielded, and it was as though from the top of my scalp to the tips of my toes every cell of my body shivered in a dark ecstasy. He fucked with a force that drove my thighs into the wood, and all the while his hands squeezed the flesh he'd paddled hot and sore. When the orgasm broke it came from deep inside, deeper even than the extent of his rough penetration. Once he pulled out I lay panting while the pounding of blood in my ears fell slowly away. When I hauled myself up the boy was nowhere in view, and I felt disinclined to search. A wave of tiredness hit me and I ached front and back. Suddenly I wanted out. At the door I steadied myself and summoned the energy to negotiate the short distance to the big house. Clouds had gathered in a freshening wind and I had to concentrate to follow the line of the path to the safety of the kitchen door. I was in and up the stairs in less time than it takes to tell it, and in seconds flat, in my own bed asleep.

Chapter 13
Après Birch

Morning came too soon in the determined beeping of my pocket alarm, and when I heaved myself up to shut it off the pain made me cry out. What the mirror showed was a gaudy band of discoloration across the front that quite eclipsed the decorous hints of bruising left by the paddle at the back. I sat down on the bed, queasily unnerved by the bodily evidence of the night's little expedition. To put it bluntly - and it seemed time for bluntness - what the fuck was I doing? It was one thing to offer up one's arse to the rituals of the cane, but rather another to invite a buggering that mashed thighs into rough wood. The former was an exercise in endurance with its own rewards: painful, at best keenly so, yet methodical and controlled. The latter, on the contrary, was given over to the unrestrained violence of passion, and the thought of it made me shiver. I had revelled in such treatment from a lad half my age when I ought to know better. That is, the grown woman who took pride in the exploitation of the male organ for her own purposes, *she* ought to know better. Or could it be that that persona was beginning to slip?

I shook a head that ached from too little sleep and tried to put the unsettling thought aside. Groping about amongst three days' worth of discarded garments for something to put on I came up with some loose cotton trousers and a clean shirt, in a suitably sober black. Molly's appointment with the pickled rods was in half an hour, and an alert savouring of the event was going to require a cup or two of good strong coffee. In the kitchen I found a Mrs Beaton willing to oblige me in view of the occasion, and though it was late for breakfast and early for elevenses, she had the machine hissing in short order.

'None of my business of course, Dr Greene, but would I be right in thinking you have an eye for the girl's charms? The one, I mean, who is booked to bare all on the block this morning.' I looked sideways at her, but she seemed engrossed in the progress of the brew dripping into the jug. Flesh of belly and thigh pressed to the raised surface while the birched behind burned and stung: it was a deeply lascivious image. Was Cook expecting me to bare my soul in a declaration of passion for the young maid? I hesitated, and she carried on.

'I don't mean to be impertinent, only she's had an unfortunate do with that groom, and with the changes that are bound to come with the new Master... oh dear. What I'm trying to say is that to have an older, that is, a more *mature* woman, looking out for her might be so much more suitable. And I know that she, um, likes women, if you take my meaning—'

'Mrs Beaton, I'm afraid you are a little late as a matchmaker.' I rescued the estimable lady with a chuckle and watched as realisation dawned. 'But I'm going to risk your disapproval by confessing that she is not the only object of my affections. Even here in this house. You will think ill of me.'

'If you mean the boy, Dr Greene, I did get the impression he had set his cap at you. But where's the harm, I always say, in one of each kind? Rounds things out rather well, to my way of thinking.' And if we add in a black mechanic to the equation...? Out of pure mischief I might just have voiced the thought had not the door swung open. Molly came in and flopped down on a stool, putting an end to our little seminar on the ground rules of sexual relationships.

'I don't reckon that'll do a lot for me,' she said, tilting her head at the coffee maker, 'but laced with a drop of your special brandy, Cook, it might be just the ticket.' Without a word Mrs Beaton reached up to a cupboard over the sink, took down a green glass bottle with a faded label and pulled out the cork. I half-filled a mug from the machine and held it out to receive a generous measure.

'There you go, my dear. Now sip away at that and enjoy your seat while you can.' The girl looked up at the clock and made a face; in only ten minutes' time she would be arrayed facedown in the Great Hall at the Housekeeper's pleasure. On the way there in the dim corridor I was moved to express my feelings.

'Think how wickedly sexy that bum is going to look,' I said into Molly's ear.

'You're a beast, Jane.' But she wiggled against my hand under the short smock and I took the chance to delve deeper.

'Don't exaggerate, sweetie. A few grazes will give me the excuse to get in close with the lotion. Not, I have to confess, that I need much of one.' When we kissed I got my tongue in but the adorable creature pulled away with a giggle.

'Come on now, or we'll be late and the old cow will be reaching for the extra one before she's done.'

However, there was no need to worry. When we entered the Hall was empty except for the block that stood in front of a fireplace, closed off by an ornate screen the colour of pewter. Sunlight streamed across the polished floor from the east windows, and gave the whole a feel of airy space under the dark wood of the ceiling. The progress of the whipping would be well lit and the arrival of Mrs Jencks set me tingling in anticipation.

I'd already decided against tackling the woman about her part in the removal of the Notebooks; Tamsin could do that better at the weekend. As for Molly's being unjustly punished for putting me on the scent, it was her will to submit in the uncertain climate attending the arrival of a new head of house. To complain could only make matters worse and, besides, as I made no pretence of disguising - to her or to myself - I was going to revel in the spectacle of the pretty young maid being soundly birched.

So I added nothing to the curt exchange of greetings, and while the black-clad figure examined the three instruments soaking in their tub, busied myself with fastening the girl's knees to the cushioned step and tucking the clothing well up into her back. Apart from the raised top padded out to a shallow dome, the device was the shape of a cube constructed out of thick oak planks, whose corner joints had been executed with the precision of a fine cabinetmaker. Plainly built to last, it prompted me to think of the succession of naked arses that would have graced its surface over the years. If it dated from as recently as the nineteenth century they had still to be numbered in the hundreds, and unless the thing had fallen out of favour for prolonged periods, one would need to add another zero yet to reach a probable figure. And imagine their variety: from the huge and spreading to the positively scrawny, from the almost eager upthrust moon to the sullen slab of blotched meat. Every stage in between and all combinations of properties of flesh swam before my mind's eye in a delirious parade.

Though no doubt it was the case that possession of a winsome pair of cheeks made the owner more liable to find herself close-quartered to the heavy wood, in past ages as in the present. Indeed, as on that very day. I came out of my brown study to detect a decided glint in the Housekeeper's eye as she advanced on Molly's ripe buttocks with her slim bundle of wet switches firmly in hand. At that moment the boy appeared out of nowhere at my side and without a word we took each an arm and pulled the unresisting figure forward. I gave silent thanks for his timing that had pre-empted the need for any other action. Perhaps he was feeling awkward too, after our intense encounter in the night, perhaps not. Either way, I was able to focus on the matter at hand.

Which was as well, for from the very first cuts the initially compliant maid began to fight us. At each hissing stroke the fine red lines spread and darkened in a manner that made me glad it was not my bottom being so treated. Certainly, Mrs Jencks was working with a fiendish energy, and it seemed an answering devil in Molly had decided that she was not going quietly. So, feet against the base of the block we heaved to keep the protesting figure in place, for all the world as if we belonged to a tug-of-war team, and a hard-pressed one at that. Hard-pressed, but not losing: it was the other side ordained to take a drubbing and I was determined to see it through. So when the second dripping birch lashed into raw, contorting buttocks, we dug in our heels and hung on until the yells died into gasps and the chastiser at last tossed aside the ruined instrument.

I undid the leg fastenings with relief, and the would-be refusenik was hauled to her feet and marched to the antechamber. She was panting and so were we; the boy's face was flushed with the exertion of the previous few minutes and I felt the shirt sticking to my back with sweat. I put on the crossest face I could muster and wagged a reproving finger.

'I have never been made to work so hard, ever, in the cause of a whipped bottom. When you are over this, girl, I'm going to find a horse and tie you to it so tight the pips will squeak. Then you'll find out what a good hiding really is.'

'Jane, please, it stings *so*...' The victim sniffed and a tear rolled down. Then she made a *moue* that kicked me straight in the groin and I just couldn't keep up the act. Muttering soothing noises I spread Molly over the table and signalled the boy to bring the bowl of water left ready. Carefully I sponged away the irritant residue of brine and vinegar then hunkered down for an examination. I had to own that they were the sorest-looking bottom cheeks I could recall seeing for a long time. Though lacking the vivid welts a sound caning would have inscribed, their condition was nonetheless a testament to the punitive power of the rod in the right hands. That day's determined application left flesh raw from a myriad tiny cuts over bruised mounds that seemed to glow with an inner angry throb. It rather put into the shade the results of my own twiggy encounter at the beginning of the week; while Cook had the muscle to do real damage she lacked the vindictiveness that plainly powered the Housekeeper's arm.

Molly's own healing lotion had done wonders for my admittedly less drastic state, so I took up the jar that had been set out ready. I sniffed witch-hazel with a hint of wintergreen, fondly imagining a folk remedy from times when a chastised bottom was a not uncommon affliction, at least among children and servants. Then a good dollop scooped onto the centre of each buttock was quickly spread to cover the whole.

'There, sweetie, just let that soak in for a few minutes.' I stroked the girl's neck till the shoulders began to relax, while allowing the other hand to stray to the crotch of the boy close beside me. Except for the fact that it kicked at my touch, the thing in his trousers was as rigid as an iron pipe. If the patently female spread of cunt and arse before us was jacking him that hard, once I'd soothed the ravaged mounds he should be ready for a spot of therapeutic penetration. Two-way, so to speak: it would do Molly a power of good and give me the satisfaction of having him up to his balls in a third party bum at my instigation. Which might help put some distance between me and the events of the night.

So I set to work without more delay. Faced with a bottom decidedly the worse for wear, I had found from experience that it was better to be brisk. To let oneself focus unduly on the extreme tenderness of the flesh was likely to induce a hesitant clumsiness that worked counter to the sympathetic intention. Firm without being rough was the rule and I stuck to it, shutting my ears to Molly's petulant complaints while the boy kept a grip on her legs. They soon died away, as I knew they would. For one thing the lotion was doing its work and for another the after-effects of whipping were visibly juicing the parted labia.

I tested the erotic temperature with a couple of fingers into the slippery interior, and was rewarded by a hoarse moan. It was, however, a different place I had in mind for the rampant lad at my side, and to ease his way I anointed the tight rim between the buttocks.

'Oh yes, yes,' breathed the maid, and pushed up her behind. I tapped the bulge in his trousers and the boy unzipped at once. What emerged wasn't the biggest specimen I'd met but it stood at a full ninety degrees to the slim body, and had a way of looking almost over-engorged, as if fit to burst from the pressure within. Feeling like the ringmaster of a circus of performing organs, I eased Molly's body down toward the table's edge and guided the shaft forward until its head nuzzled up to the brown pucker.

'Go boy, go,' I whispered in his ear, while slipping a hand inside his trousers to fondle the taut bum. With one push the glans was out of sight and a very few more had his thighs pressing against the birched cheeks. That was when my little scheme went wrong. One moment I was directing operations with a relative, if horny, detachment, the next a molten stab of lust hit my clitoris, shot up the spinal cord and exploded in the brain. It wasn't pleasure, it was pure demand, and brooked no refusal. That's my excuse for what happened next, though I am aware it has the ring of a piece of special pleading.

Grabbing the boy's thighs, I yanked him out of the speared arse, swung him round and hauled down my trousers. Hips thrust forward, I thumbed open my cunt and shoved myself onto the end of his cock. I don't flatter myself I was the efficient cause of it rather than the last and least link in a chain, but as the purple-headed beast nosed me it spat a jet of white, and another that welled up to dribble down my vulva. I remember to this day the lights that fizzed in my head like fireworks, and I remember the orgasmic jerking of my lower half. For a second or two, for a minute, I can't say. All that remains beyond, fragmentally, is a careering passage, clothing clutched, that made the stairs and up them to the safety of a locked door at the back.

I must have been spared a prolonged bout of self-examination, for the next thing I recall was an insistent rapping that broke into my heavy doze. The words 'phone call' were decipherable through the muffling of the heavy door, and with a splash of cold water to the face I was fit enough to follow Laura down the stairs and into the library. There she left me to make my own way into the study, where I lifted the antiquated receiver and announced my presence.

'Okay, I got the message. Behind those thick rims she's quite the chat-up merchant. I think I'm gonna be back if I can find an excuse. But you are not going to like it. Talk about a merry dance.'

'Tamsin, I shan't know whether I like it or not until I become aware of its contents. And that won't happen until you read the thing out to me.' The morning's excesses had put the scheduled call quite out of my mind; suddenly, though, I was consumed with impatience to know what the American academic had seen fit to tell us.

'Easy, boss, I'm coming to it. The first thing is that Belle Torman is in Brittany and the second that she's got the Notebooks with her. For safekeeping, she says. Some nerve that, from the lady who nicked them in the first place. I mean to say—'

'Yes, Tams, and the third thing, if you could bring yourself to get to the point?'

'Sorry, boss. She won't say where she is exactly, only that if it's imperative - that's the word, *imperative* - to see the things straightaway then there's a phone number. I didn't try it, thought I'd better leave that to you. Dr T certainly doesn't make life easy.'

'Okay, give it me in case, but I've had another idea. Can I call you back? Soon, half an hour tops.'

Before the promised thirty minutes was over I was making my way back upstairs, elation vying with apprehension that I'd gone a step too far. Then in my room, there he was, rising from the bed and holding out the paddle. I must have looked a complete fool grinning from ear to ear, but he was grinning too as I sat for him to drop over my lap. I attacked the cotton seat for a while and when I stood him up and pulled down the trousers he was in fine erect form. I took hold of the pulsing shaft and looked up at his face.

'Well, boy, I just stuck my neck right out and booked a trip abroad. For the two of us. Not exactly a holiday, but among the people we're going to visit a thing like this is just for starters.' I waggled the leather oval and he nodded knowingly. 'So what do you reckon? Are you up for it?'

'Yes, Miss. Please, Miss.' There was no hesitation and relief washed over me. I squeezed the cock in my hand and a drop oozed from its end. I hadn't blown it after all.

'Terrific. Now back over and let me give those chubbies the roasting we know they deserve...'

Chapter 14
En Train

The rest of the afternoon dragged by, though heavy rain cleared for a spell to permit the distraction of a waterproofed expedition into the dripping woods. Having chanced my arm, with initial success, I was eager to bring the business through to a conclusion. I had ignored the contact route we'd been offered and on a hunch phoned Judith at the Archive. It was becoming rather a habit to intrude on the seclusion of her eyrie at the top of the old library stacks, but when I confided my idea she was only too willing to help. I can no longer remember who told me of the one-time convent in the old town of Vannes that had brought her perverse love-affair with the rattan cane to its first flowering, but the information lodged in my mind and it was a fair inference that a devotee of s/m manuscripts who'd gone to Brittany would be found in that very place.

Judith told me of her own arrival some five years before in Rue des Vierges, unannounced and thence rather more into the thick of things than she was quite ready for. However, were I able to find the occupant in, then I might get a more official introduction to the Order to which it was a gateway. I turned down her offer to drop a line to the Thérèse in residence for my mind was already made up: I wanted us there pronto, before any mere note would have had the time to drop through the letterbox of the number ten in question. So I called Tamsin and paced back and fore while she established that if we left from Waterloo early in the morning we could be whisked to our destination from Paris before the end of the afternoon. That was what one called a high-speed railway. All that remained was for the exemplary PA to book the tickets and come to Ardingley End in time to run us to an evening train to town. That was before settling in herself for a country weekend devoted to supervising the packing and loading of the late Monty's collection of pornography. It was a good thing she was devoted to her work.

After what seemed an age the boy was folded into the back seat of the Porsche on top of our bags, and we were delivered to the station in time to find facing seats at one end of a carriage otherwise quite full. We were thus comfortably installed but I found myself at rather a loss. It was as though, having taken the plunge into an expedition *à deux*, there wasn't anything left to say. We both stared out of the window and I was thankful when the train began almost at once to move. And after a while even more thankful, if surprised, when the boy delved into his bag and came up with a volume that he began to read, seemingly with close attention. It was encased in a worn leather binding and I could gain no hint of what its contents might be without staring more pointedly than I cared to. Instead I followed his example and pulled out from my briefcase some papers that would at least give the appearance of providing some diversion.

At St Pancras a cab swallowed our luggage for the short journey, at the end of which I pressed a key into the hand of the new bookworm and pointed out the back stair to the flat. Without a word he took charge of the things while the driver took me off to collect the reserved tickets. As often his expression had given little away, but when I came back he was stretched out on the sofa with his shoes off, as if well at ease in the new surroundings. More so than I, in fact, who had recourse to a fresh bottle of Glen Grant for a nightcap somewhat stiffer than was customary. I'm afraid to say that I then left him sucking at the neck of the preferred bottle of beer on what was to be his makeshift bed, my will to face down the awkwardness I was feeling having failed me. Sexual frolics seemed completely out of the question. The difficulties I could - would - face the following day, when I had the sustaining framework of the mission to retrieve the works of the self-styled *uxor studiosa. We,* of course, not I, was how I should have been thinking. But then that was rather peculiarly *my* problem.

However the early morning brought a new perspective to things. A matching pair in black, rather as for the excursion to Miss Faversham's, we forwent breakfast in order to indulge ourselves on the Parisian leg of the journey. I had plumped for first-class tickets, a move that would require some creative accounting in the quarterly expenses, but one that was a big hit with my travelling companion. In the sparsely peopled carriage we had free run of two pairs of facing seats, but the boy slid in beside me after tossing our bags over onto the others. Thus we tucked in companionably into the 'full English' that seemed to set a fitting seal on our venture into foreign parts, and while we sped through the flat lands of northern France he began to make brief references to the former life of which I knew next to nothing.

It was not for me to comment, I felt, nor even react except to make the noises that signalled he had my attention. Our positions allowed me to keep my eyes on the passing fields as he spoke, and indeed allowed his not to meet mine. There was mention of a week below deck on an ancient coaster as stowaway-cum-assistant to a boozy AB, and of two months crossing parts of Central Europe with a thumb and a bedroll. There was more in similar vein on the theme of accommodation, prompted by our comfortable surroundings and the earlier contrasts with it.

'Ace,' he said, downing the remains of his coffee and leaning back. 'I could get used to this.' Something in the voice made me turn my head and when I caught his eye he grinned and let out a half-stifled giggle. I remember looking sternly at him but he simply said, 'I mean it, Miss.' At once the half-formed thought that I was being spun a set of travellers' tales felt unworthy of the occasion. For the remaining hour to Paris we settled into a silence that seemed mutually comfortable. The boy opened his book with no attempt at apology or excuse, and after glimpsing the words *Governess and Memoirs* in the running title I was quite happy to let the mind drift as the countryside sped by the window. Now there was a topic that could be picked up later.

We braved another taxi to cross the city, and by noon were in place on the TGV that would take us directly to Vannes and the purloined Notebooks. It occurred to me that their author would have found it scarcely credible that almost three centuries hence devotees with a mere taste of her writings would cross the Channel in pursuit of them. But it was no more than her due, and I was confident she would not let us down. Lifted by a wave of optimism I looked at the boy, and when he lifted his head, raised an eyebrow at his reading material. Tamsin had taken the trouble to put us facing across a table once more, and since there were a mere handful of occupants in the whole compartment, we were spread over the four seats on the left side with the opposite singles empty.

'Strict, she was. Very.' He pursed his lips. 'The cane, never thought twice. On the slightest excuse.' I took the proffered volume and opened it. The subtitle promised the detailed reminiscences of a disciplinarian who, for reasons of propriety, must conceal her identity. Apparently a first edition from 1893, it was not a work I was familiar with. 'She had a horse made specially. Thick straps all over. But after a bit they weren't needed.'

'So you think it's the genuine article? And really a woman?'

'Oh yes. I mean...' he went a touch pink and hesitated '...I mean, you can tell. The way she goes on about the marks you know she's touching them. During, like. Again and again.' I took in the earnest face, nostrils a little flared, startled at the vivid picture he evoked. He was quite right, too. Without wanting to endorse crude gender stereotyping, it would not commonly be a man's way to engage directly with the effects of what he was doing. Revel instead in the visuals: the gaudy stripes springing up on beaten flesh and the jerks and twitches of the outraged body. These were correlates of pain to delight the eye at a distance, safe from the intimacy attending the handling of the afflicted parts. With a pang of pure lust I thought of the paddle I'd used, and the delicious feel of the sore buttocks, and looked at him again.

'All that severity, though. I seem to remember even Miss Faversham's six was a bit much.' He gave a sharp laugh and nodded.

'Give us a chance. This boy was trained up over the years.'

'And the idea of it, being at her mercy - utterly—'

'Here. Gets me here.' He pressed a hand to his stomach. 'Like looking over the edge when there's just down. No end to it. And you can't stop thinking you want to jump.'

Never before had we discussed so much as the weather, and suddenly we were in deep. So it came as something of a relief, on my part at least, to be interrupted by the appearance of the stewardess come to take our order for food. The boy glanced doubtfully at the menu and seemed happy with my suggestion of fresh bread and cheese. We washed it down with some chilled Cava Rosado, and some while afterwards he took out another book and displayed it with a smile. I recognised it at once as the notorious *Guide to the Correction of Young Gentlemen* which had been seized immediately upon publication and most copies burned, although plainly one had found its way into Monty's collection.

A work in rather lighter vein than his earlier choice seemed to be, it allowed me to explain there was reason to think that the 'Lady' it was credited to was one Alice Kerr-Sutherland, distinguished by a flagellant career not so much as an actual governess, as with adult male clients. I pointed out the section titled *The Eternal Boy* as indicating the tongue-in-cheek nature of the writing which at first sight, and in the magistrate's view in the 1920s, could seem to advocate violence against children.

'So it was a kind of game?'

'In the book, yes, I think so. However there is no doubt she enjoyed chastising young men's bottoms as much as her contemporary Edith Cadivec did young women's.' He digested this thought for a moment, then flashed a cheeky grin.

'While some get off on both. Like you, Miss.'

'Oh, so you think you've got me all sewn up. Cheeky monkey! Now when I get you on your own, my boy, you'll find out just how...' I'd half risen to my feet, wagging a reproving finger when I became aware we had acquired an audience. By the single seats across the aisle was a woman turned towards us.

'May I?' She indicated the attaché case she was in the act of placing on the small table. 'I'm sorry, I did not mean to intrude...'

'Of course. Help yourself. Those are not our seats.' A further inspection showed me slim dark-suited elegance, auburn hair short at the sides sprouting longer mauve tints on top. From behind steel-rimmed narrow ovals of glass the eyes were amused.

'I fear I broke into a remonstration, if that is the word. And with such a book lying between you...' The carefully enunciated English bore what sounded like a German inflection, and the face had perhaps ten years on mine. I gave in to the impulse to pick up the hint that had been dropped and run with it.

'The boy has, I fear, not studied its contents as well as he might. Thus it occurred to me that a practical lesson might be required in more appropriate circumstances. By the way, I'm Jane Barrett-Greene of the British Library.' My hand was taken at once and the look was a warm one.

'*Offizier* Sibyl Metzger, of The Program. Unlike yours, it is an institution we prefer to keep out of the public eye. Now this is something of a coincidence. I had some dealings with your predecessor and I am pleased to meet the Dr Greene I was told had replaced him. But first things first, as I believe the expression goes. Circumstances may be more conducive to your lesson than you implied.' I followed her gaze round the carriage that contained half a dozen people, none less than middle-aged. Then she pressed the service button and before a minute had passed was engaged in an interchange in French with the young woman who'd waited on us earlier. It was *sotto voce* with a fluency that so far outstripped my limited grasp of the language, that I was little the wiser. In the course of it she was shown something that lay inside the case, after which she too cast an eye over the other passengers. Then she looked at us and gave a firm nod of the head.

'*Madame, ça sera fait. J'irais amener la fille.*' As the sliding doors closed behind her I was left with the feeling that I had consigned us to another's hands, though for exactly what was yet to be made clear. The boy was watching, a little wide-eyed, but I sensed he was ready for anything. There was not long to wait before the attendant returned in the company of a girl I guessed to be very much of his own age. She hung back, pouting furiously, and when forced forward with a twist of the arm, stamped her foot.

'*Ça suffit! Ou on rapport à ta mère. Tu comprends?*' The only answer was a scowl, but the fight seemed to have gone out of her. 'Bon. Restes ici.' She moved back the way she'd come, where two couples sat opposite each other, with two single businessmen in the seats beyond. All looked a little wary, but unabashed she leaned forward to draw in the attention of each one, and began to speak earnestly. This time I managed to hear the phrase *les jeunes*, and what seemed the key, repeated several times, la correction. It caught my ear at once, for unlike the slightly coy usage in English, the secondary sense of the French word is straightforward. It translates as 'thrashing', no ifs and no buts. As if in direct response to what we'd overheard Sibyl Metzger took from her bag an instrument and passed it over for my inspection.

'I brought this as a gift for my hosts. It is a martinet, though more compact and dense than I understand to be the norm.' She smiled as I weighed the object in my hands. 'One might say it was designed for the English short, sharp shock.' While less than a foot long, the thongs were a good quarter-inch of tough leather, bound into a thick bundle. I noticed the girl was staring at the thing open-mouthed.

'But you can't. Not - not *that*.'

'Ah, she has a voice and some words of our common language. *Oui, ma chère*, it is to be that. Come now, your aunt returns. Be brave; it is soon over and the pain will wipe out your misdeed.' She looked no more convinced by this than I would have been in her shoes, but things moved too quickly for her to duck out. In short order she was over the table with her shoulders in a firm grip while the German hauled up the hem of the mini-dress to reveal bare cheeks framed by the skimpiest of string briefs. There was not the space in our restricted situation for a full deployment of the arm, but the tall disciplinarian had the measure of the situation. Having raised her hand to the level of her head with the implement at the back of the shoulder, she brought it down with a flick of the wrist that splatted the tails into the meat of the buttocks. To her credit the girl stifled all but a gasp as we watched the fan of red lines form on the pale skin.

It took three more lashes, each harder than the one preceding it, to make her squawk, then another three to bring forth a real howl. The watchers were on the edge of their seats, goggle-eyed and with a discreet hand I found the boy's cock to be no less appreciative of the show. Sibyl Metzger announced that another six strokes would complete the matter, and proceeded to lay them on with force. When she was done and the victim's writhing had subsided, we were able to admire the tracery of blues and purples that decorated the swelling mounds. Let up, the girl clutched her behind, moaning.

'Oo-oo-ooh. Ça me fait mal!' But the worst already passed, her face lifted and she surprised us by giving her chastiser a quick smile. 'You were right, Madame. *C'est fini*. It is over.' With that she pulled down the clinging dress with some care, then wiggled her way past the audience and out through the connecting door at the end. The stewardess shook her head at the performance, but it was obvious she warmed to the girl's spirit.

'The young recover quickly, do they not? Now it is the other's turn to show us his mettle. It will be not so much a punishment, of course, as a demonstration to supplement his study. Ms Kerr-Sutherland, it must be said, is somewhat deficient in her treatment of the martinet in the *Guide*. However, to be fair, she did not possess an instrument of this quality.' She swished it twice through the air with a gleam in her eye. 'Now, Dr Greene, if you would oblige us by preparing our subject.'

'Jane, please; if I may call you Sibyl. *Et nôtre hôtesse s'appelle...?*'

'*Hélène. Enchantée.*' After my limited foray into the language we clasped hands: three women on first-name terms about to cement their intimacy over a lad's naked bottom. The baring was soon done by a pull at the waist string that dropped cotton trousers to the knees, after which I pulled up the T-shirt and held the torso down on the surface of the table.

'Excellent!' Sibyl bent over the target and I joined her in studying the expanse of uncovered flesh between the shoulder blades and the thighs. It was darker than the young woman's, but scarcely more masculine, having only a fine down by way of surface hair. There were a couple of smudges by the right dimple and just the suggestion of a darker tint to the main meat. Given the treatments of it I had witnessed or been party to in the few days of our acquaintance, the boy's arse was possessed of a resilience that begged to be tried to the full. From the way she straightened up and ran the thongs through caressing fingers, it seemed that the willowy German had reached a similar conclusion.

'Young man, prepare yourself. I begin.' The murmured exchange between the two men in suits died away to leave an expectant hush in the carriage. The first stroke was more vigorous than any before, and five more followed in similar vein. Our chastiser was developing the art of the swing in a confined environment with gratifying results. I tightened my grip on the protesting figure with a sharp admonishment to hold still, and in the ensuing pause we watched the weals spring up and deepen in colour.

Six further lashes, then another six were just as forceful, but the boy had found the stoicism to take them without further struggle, although they could scarcely have been less painful than the first. Six more and Sibyl was done, and I have to say I was glad of it, for by the end the tongues had bitten deep into places already raw and welted. In private I might well have inflicted worse on him without a qualm, so I suppose I was concerned less with his suffering than with how he would acquit himself before spectators. However, that he did quite splendidly, and after the other occupants were re-settled into their appointed seats there was a bonus.

After I rewarded the stalwart performance with an application of soothing cream to the inflamed parts, the boy straightened up and reached back to feel the damage with his own hands. At once three pairs of eyes found a new focus of interest in the erection that sprang jauntily into view.

'Bravo!' cried Hélène. '*Le garçon est fier* - he is proud, how you say...?'

'Proud to take the punishment of a Mistress?'

'*Oui, c'est ça. Mais la douleur...*'

'It is not uncommon for a sore behind to prompt a degree of arousal.' Sibyl's mime was quite explicit and the French woman nodded her comprehension.

'Not uncommon,' she repeated slowly. *'Alors, la fille aussi*, she too will be...' She straightened up, colour a little high and pulled at the hem of her uniform. *'Merci bien, mes amies. C'est très interessant, mais je m'en vais*. To my station.' We watched her head quickly off in the direction taken a few minutes earlier by *la fille* referred to, and recalling that one's reaction I thought it more than likely that the tawse had warmed her rather as it had the boy. And our stewardess seemed rather keen to investigate the matter.

'Does the aunt's concern for her niece stray toward the intimate side, perhaps?' Sibyl echoed my thought, one eyebrow raised, then turned back to the lad still holding his bum. 'It is in any case not our business, as I believe you say. However, this one most definitely is.' She brought a hand up under the organ that jutted between us until it was lying stiff in her palm. 'May I?'

'Be my guest.' For reasons of protocol I was gratified that the question had been directed to me, though it would have been little use to ask its owner. As I had come to know, the chastised boy withdrew behind his scrunched-up eyes when his climax was under the control of another, and so it was that afternoon on the speeding train. I assisted with a handkerchief spread on the table, then contented myself with fondling the hot swellings on the backside while keeping half a nervous eye out for the possibility of interruption. Closed fingers worked the shaft so that the foreskin rode up and back over the oozing head, and the crisis was upon us in streak after streak that pumped from the urethra. In what was little more than twenty-four hours of abstinence the semen factory had achieved a production level whose amount and reach had quite outstretched the capacity of my cotton square.

After I dispatched the post-orgasmic and awkward boy to clean up, I fumbled amongst my things for a bunch of paper tissues. Sibyl looked at me. 'Such a large quantity of desire, released by a little whipping and fondling. The simple pleasures of the young male, Jane, are they not a marvel?' I looked at her, we both looked at the tabletop thickly spattered with gobbets of sperm, and then, all at once, we were gripped by a manic fit of laughter. Neither before nor since can I remember such a side-splitting convulsion that forced helpless tears from the eyes, and I would guess that my companion was not one that laughed easily or hard. It passed, and before a solemn-faced lad returned from the lavatory to resume his seat, but in its wake I received some information that would give both of us a boost. Sibyl cleared her throat and spoke carefully.

'I had better, as you say, come clean before our journey ends. For I realised a while ago that we are headed to the same destination.' I remember blinking stupidly with the unnerving sensation of ground moving unexpectedly under one's feet.

'But how, I mean, why...?'

'I spoke this very morning with Samantha James, an acquaintance of longstanding. And she talked of eagerly awaiting new material from a collection in the country, and of some notebooks. Old ones from the seventeenth century that were missing. Of course, in the process your name was mentioned and when I saw the Englishwoman on the train with a boy and *that* book...'

'And you know why we are headed to Brittany?' I must have sounded a little sharp, but the eyes behind the steel rims remained amused.

'My dear Jane, our quarry is one and the same person. For I go there by invitation to take part in the disciplinary education of the fledgling American academic Dr Belle Torman.'

Chapter 15
Installed

Under the wing of our guide we were spared the task of talking our way into the unofficial access on Rue des Vierges. Though the entrance for visitors formally sanctioned was no grand affair: at the end of a cobbled street to the side of the cathedral stood a plain stone arch with a short flight of steps directly inside to the left. At the top of them, the sound of the iron bell-pull echoed and died to silence within, before the weathered wood of the door swung open. A young woman in a grey dress with pulled-back hair stood aside to let us pass through the modest opening, and bobbed her head to the one bringing up the rear.

'*Hauptoffizier.*' Even my scant German was enough to recognise the seniority of the title that was being acknowledged beyond its probable jurisdiction.

'*Annabelle. Conduis nos amis à la chambre à deux, s'il te plaît. C'est libre, n'est-ce pas?*'

'*Oui, mais...*'

'*Sois tranquille. Ça plaira Madame, j'en suis sûr.* I shall go to her now.'

'*Elle vous attend, Hauptoffizier.*' The girl bobbed again and turned, indicating that we should follow. While the tall German strode off down the passage that stretched ahead, we were led through a side portal that brought us to the foot of a spiral stair. Before I realised quite what she was doing, Annabelle hoisted my bag onto a shoulder, took the boy's out of his hand and twirled up the first half-dozen of the worn stone steps. 'Allow me,' she said over her shoulder, shaming us both by her agility and her grasp of our language, 'the space is narrow and I am accustomed to it.'

At the top she marched along a short corridor and opened the door at the end of it. Inside was a narrow room lit by a small window high on the far wall. Our luggage deposited on the nearer of two divan beds, she was gone without an opportunity for questions. However, the charge of us had been assumed by our 'officer', as if she spoke for the institution's real head, and I had no doubt we should hear sooner rather than later what was in store. An inspection of our quarters showed that we had a compact bathroom of our own, two chairs, two divan beds and not much else; appropriate enough to the bare boards and plain white walls of what was still a retreat. There was a single cupboard built into a corner of the wall, and I was in the act of peering inside when there came a sharp knock at the door. Sibyl Metzger swept in and steered a lad to the fore by his shoulders.

'This is *le garçon*. It is how he is known in this almost entirely female establishment. I thought he could take your boy down to the kitchen to eat then show him around. Meanwhile, we could share a light supper and a *tête-à-tête*, if you were so minded.' She smiled and I tried to look enthusiastic. The woman was the kind of organiser that left barely time to catch one's breath.

'Of course.' The boy was looking a little warily at the newcomer, who was kitted in a pair of cut-off trousers and a worn sweatshirt not unlike his own dress at home. Then he raised an eyebrow and his counterpart gave a little jerk of the head, after which enigmatic interchange they were gone out of the door. Sibyl walked to it and turned back on the threshold.

'My room is directly underneath. So if in a short while you feel ready it will not be hard to find.'

I made a pretence of unpacking the few garments brought with me, but once the bag was emptied I washed quickly and prepared to go down. The invitation had something of the tone of an order, and set off twinges of apprehension that took me back to my later schooldays. It was disconcerting though not perhaps inappropriate since I was, as then, in the course of engaging one-to-one with a woman older and more powerful than I. There was, too, a subtle change in manner since the encounter on the train: while it was difficult to be sure I sensed her watching me, as if in the interval she'd learned something that gave her an advantage. Backing out was, of course, not an option, though I had for the first time the feeling that I had rather lightly plunged myself - and the boy, for that matter - into an affair that might prove far from simple to negotiate.

At the foot of the stair I turned right to find the first door ajar. As I hesitated, uncertain whether to knock or announce my presence through the opening, there came an interchange from within.

'*Maîtresse, ce n'est pas juste. Je vous en prie...*' It was Annabel, pleading, and she was cut short by the icy voice of command.

'Go to Madame at once! Or shall I send word for you to be whipped twice?' There was a short silence. 'I thought not. *Va-t-en!*' The door was flung wide and I shrank back from any involvement, but the young woman stomped off in the other direction, shoulders hunched. Then Sibyl Metzger appeared, and seeing me, shook her head resignedly.

'You heard? It is for her own good. She knows this and I know this. I grow too lenient with age, so I send her to one who will do what is required. It is completely logical, yet we are treated to a tantrum. But I forget myself, dear Jane. Please, come in.' I was led through into a room whose old stone walls were hung with tapestries, where a dining table was set for two. My German host poured two tall glasses of a sparkling rosé from an ice bucket on the sideboard, and handed one to me. After we drunk each other's health she waved me to an easy chair and took up a position opposite.

'Perhaps you do not know that there have been changes in recent times within *l'Ordre Rigoureux*, as they name themselves. Since its originator withdrew, no permanent replacement has been found and I myself have been drawn in to assist on an ad hoc basis. Hence my presence here and our felicitous encounter on the train.' I explained that while I had been aware of the existence of the Rigorists for some time, the fact that they were a group of women devoted to a philosophy of corporal punishment was the extent of my information. 'So you are not acquainted with members of the Order, or, to your knowledge, with its acting head?'

'No. Indeed, no to both.' It was a curiously phrased question that revived my feeling that the *Hauptoffizier* knew something I didn't. Though what exactly I would have to wait to find out, for no sooner had I mentioned my connection with Judith Wilson at the Nemesis Archive, than I was treated to an account of those early years and the ethos achieved therein. Not that I was bored, far from it. Indeed, mere moments seemed to have passed when the flow was broken by a knock, followed by the re-entry of the maid.

'*Fais voir.*' A twirled hand accompanied the command, and it was a moment before I understood what was meant. Though the eyes were wet the petulance was undiminished, and the girl turned with a flounce and slowly dragged up her dress. Chastised she may have been, of which the cherry-red buttocks laced with purple left no doubt, but the little minx was not what one could call chastened. Good on her, I remember thinking, warming to the show of resistance in decidedly unfavourable conditions. However, it soon appeared that I had slightly misjudged the relationship between mistress and maid. After a brief inspection of the punished parts, Sibyl let the hem drop.

'*Ça suffit, ma chère. Bon.* You have received your due on my return: it is our ritual. Now there is another custom that you know as well as I, one that relates to the arrival of unscheduled visitors. *Tu comprends?*' The scowl cleared as if wiped from her face; it took me a little longer to move from a vague sense of foreboding to a full grasp of what was coming.

'*Maîtresse. Le docteur Greene, elle serat...*' Both looked at me, and I knew the worst.

'*Parle Anglais, mon choux.* Yes, I believe our guest will accept the usual means of demonstrating a commitment to the ideals of this house. Jane, I believe you understand what we speak of. It will be a token only, of course...' I bowed my head; at that moment I didn't trust myself to speak. 'Very good. Annabelle, you will go to the cabinet in the next room and select a rod from the middle of the rack.'

By the time she returned, Officer Metzger had placed a dining chair with its back towards me, and I bent over it with the best grace I could muster. While it was given to a teenaged Annabelle to sulk sexily, that was scarcely becoming in one of my years. As I found a grip on the crosspiece below the seat, sentence was pronounced at my back.

'Six cuts, twice. I like to exercise each arm equally. To one as versed in these matters as yourself, Jane, it will be a mere *aperitif.* Annabelle, uncover the behind, if you please.' I lifted my hips enough for the girl to open the trouser fastening in front, and when she pulled the garment down I heard a slight intake of breath that I assumed to be caused by the absence of underclothing. I managed a surreptitious wink, and was pleased to have it rewarded with a small but lascivious grin. Then I felt the cane pressed to my bare flesh and rubbed up and down over the curve of my arse. With the answering stab in my loins I was catapulted back across the years to a book-lined study, in which I more than once occupied a rather similar position under the eye of a senior schoolmistress. At that time I was modestly knickered in navy blue serge, but the use of the instrument in a preliminary caressing of the target area was identical. So was the beating when it actually began. In each case there was a positively cheerful air to the business: while nothing was audible, I had a strong sense of the chastiser humming under her breath while she worked. Vigorous canings both, short only of that last ounce of effort required to cause the toe curling hurt of which a length of rattan is capable. Instead there was the fierce stinging that for me remains the very essence of erotic pain. I can remember to this day how a brief touch of the sore parts in the corridor took me running behind a locked door to a climax that left me slumped and gasping on the lavatory seat.

When Sibyl finished I was able to exert a little more control than on that earlier occasion, but the cumulative smart of a dozen weals excited me to the point that I was afraid to move in case I should make my state even more apparent that it might have been already. Perhaps my host was aware of that, perhaps not. What she did was to announce her intention to spend a few minutes updating her records, thus leaving me in the hands of the maid, who made it clear at once that she knew exactly how I was placed.

I rose to explore the exquisite tenderness of the caned cheeks to find Annabelle at my feet. One foot lifted, then the other had my trousers off and her head was at my crotch. Such was my arousal that with spread legs I thrust into her face and bit my tongue to stop from crying out, while hers twirled around my throbbing clitoris. It was one of those rockets that was gone in a short cascade of brilliance, and in the anteroom I kissed her mouth thoroughly before she helped me to wash and dress.

'*Le garçon* - he is, er...'

'Not the jealous type, if that's what you're thinking. Might like to join in, though. But aren't you and, er, *ta maîtresse*...' Faltering speech seemed to be catching.

'*Oui*. I give her the service. *Mais pas tous les nuits*.' There was the sound of a door opening through the dining room, so the question of when Annabelle was next due a night off would have to wait. However, she'd asked first so I decided to remain optimistic of making a more prolonged connection with the delectable creature.

After such sexual shenanigans the supper went down a treat. I squatted on my satisfyingly tender backside and tucked into a cold table that featured, among other delights, salpicon-filled brioches and confit of duck, to be washed down with a fine Muscadet. While the full-time residents were said to partake of a spare diet consistent with their dedication to bodily discipline, it was plain that visitors, at least of my host's rank, were indulged with the best produce of the area. Fed and watered, I was only too happy to be quizzed by Sibyl about the volumes that had brought me to the home of the Rigorist Order.

'I believe they will prove to be doubly important. There are a few treatises on the benefits of whipping that begin to appear at the end of the seventeenth century, but they are typically unreadable, filled with pompous generalities. *Uxor juvenis*, as I think of her—'

'The young wife.'

'Yes, though in the odd pieces published she styles herself *studiosa*, which I gather means eager rather than studious. And that she certainly was. In what I've read there is an enthusiasm in her embracing of the perverse that is uncommon in any author of the time, but in a woman... When this is employed to log the activities of a household given over to the newfound passion for flagellation the result must be a treasure. Or so I expect to find, when I have the chance to examine it in full.'

'Ah yes.' The *Hauptoffizier* leaned back in her seat and swirled the wine round in her glass, studying it. 'The errant Dr Torman. She too, I understand, is an enthusiast, one who has let her ardour run away with her on this occasion. It is, however, inexcusable that she should have kept you from the study of your prize. I told you that I am to oversee our young lady's schooling in the rigours for which these walls are noted: her misdemeanour will be punished in the morning and I should like you and the boy to witness that justice will be done. But come, Jane, let us move to more comfortable seats. While you assist me in sampling this bottle of the local apple brandy - a prize in its own way - I should be grateful for some advice on historical writing about the institutional correction of women.'

When my eyes opened in the morning I closed them and groaned. But they'd seen enough to rule out lying in bed until the hangover eased its grip on my temples. It was already after nine, and while the later stages of our discussion were not easy to recapture, I did retain the clear memory of Sibyl Metzger's resolve to stage an early correction. So I forced myself out of bed, struggled with the shower controls and doused my head in water that was even colder than I intended. It was only when I emerged spluttering under a brisk towel that I saw the hump in the far bed, unoccupied at the time of my own collapse the night before. And nor was it just a hump, for it moved and snuffled before fingers lowered the quilt enough for eyes to blink up at mine.

I squatted and continued the process to uncover a rumpled T-shirt. 'You won't have a sore head like mine, boy,' I growled at the fresh-looking face, 'but I could work on the other end. Always assuming it didn't get too hard a night.' He turned coyly pink, but let me stand him up and examine the bum that poked out bare under the white cotton. Besides the traces of *un martinet fort*, as our steward on the train had admiringly called it, I could see no signs of a nocturnal instrument having been used. One of chastisement, that is. I wasn't going to address the question of what else might have been at work, probing between those inviting cheeks. Instead I pulled the boy down and he settled across my lap without a murmur. Several sharp slaps soon had him yelping and I was absorbed in studying the pinkening curves when there came a sharp tap followed by a head round the door.

'Oh, *pardonnez-moi, Docteur Greene.*' The maid put a hand to her mouth to stifle a giggle. '*Le garçon méchant...* I am sorry to interrupt.'

'Not at all, he rather likes an audience, don't you boy? But not so formal, please Annabelle. It's Jane.'

'*Bien.* I come to say there is the hurry. The Officer sends me to say she will be ready in ten minutes. *Ainsi la fessée*, er, the smacking...'

'Will have to wait. No problem.'

'*Le café* before, yes? I will come back at once.' Our visitor left with a smile and I hauled the boy to his feet. I fished a clean T-shirt out of his open bag and was amused to find a pair of white briefs that were little more than a genital pouch attached to waist and leg bands.

'Quick shower,' I ordered, thrusting the articles into his hands, 'and tuck the beastie away as discretely as you can in these. He'll get his exercise later, never fear, but it's going to be a stimulating morning and I wouldn't want you alarming the ladies. Right?'

'Right, Miss.' The cheeky grin as he disappeared made me itch to spank him until he came between my thighs, or better, until he was moved to bugger me as he had on that wild night. But with the arrival of our coffee I was able to rein in my lust enough to snap on a solid pair of navy-blue knickers, and in five minutes we made a sober couple in dark shades of grey. Very suitable, I remember thinking, for the promised severity of the event to which we'd been invited. And severity was indeed on the agenda, though at that stage I didn't know the half of what was coming. The half that was going to put me right in the firing line.

Chapter 16
Pain Old and New

Annabelle was waiting on the corridor below to take us to what she referred to as the place of grief: *La Douleur Ancienne*. The first letters were audibly upper case in a way that had me prickling. We were led down another of the spiral stairs with which the mediaeval core of the building was riddled; worn step followed worn step before at last we came out through a steel door that swung open noiselessly on greased hinges. It thudded shut behind us, and the drop in pressure made me catch my breath. For a long second there was only darkness, and then the click of a switch sent a dim glow flickering into the black ahead.

It was a low-roofed passage, and what had bound the stonework of its sides was long gone. Even below ground we were high above the shore and there was no dampness in the air. As we turned a bend the boy swayed into me and I slipped a hand round his arm, glad of the contact in the confined tunnel. Then there was another door, another disconcerting change of pressure, and we stood in what felt by contrast open space, flanked on two sides by rows of arches set on top of short stout columns. As we glanced up and down, a voice from behind us made me start.

'Welcome. I am glad you are here. It is good for one guest of the Order to invite others to see a little of its work. This is a place with atmosphere, I always find.' The speaker was Sibyl Metzger, who came out into the light in a white shirt, ruffed at the neck, tucked into what looked like breeches and riding boots. Her hands toyed with a short whip as she spoke. 'An ancient chapel, set apart from the cathedral itself and hidden. Although not well enough, for the authorities in Rome learned of irregularities and sent its officers to root them out. It was here, where we stand, that they made into the centre of their interrogations.' She paused, leaving us to contemplate the idea of walls that had resonated to the sounds of plainchant echoing to screams of torment. 'Naturally, when the inquisitors were done and the existing cathedral was sacked after their visit, this place could not be returned to its former use. The entrance to it was closed. The instruments are stored here still.'

To the left the long rectangle of the floor broadened into semicircles with the central area curtained off. Our guide walked towards it, and we followed until she indicated with the leather stock in her hand that we should position ourselves. Then she tugged on a cord that hung down from the dark above and the draperies swished apart. Now it was plain that where the altar must once have been located was a freestanding structure of pillars supporting a canopy that made, in effect, the proscenium arch of a stage. There was a flare of light and I saw a frame of rough wood that narrowed in to a high crosspiece, rather in the manner of the easel of an old blackboard. At its centre was indeed something black, but shiny and rounded... In a fraction of a second the image had resolved itself: what I was looking at was a pair of buttocks surmounting legs bound together by a single sheath of tightly-stretched rubber.

As we moved forward and to the side the full picture became clear. The arms, too, were encased in a single tube, wrists roped up to the top bar. Thus the torso was thrust forward with shoulders drawn back, and bare breasts swelled large and proud as if from a figure adorning the prow of a ship. The waist was held by a shaped piece of wood, and the knees pinned by another. Hair tumbled down in chestnut curls past a jaw clamped on the ball of a gag; then the head strained round and eyes caught mine. A touch wild - and whose would not be in such a situation? - but I could see nothing of desperation in them. It was my first sight of Dr Belle Torman, promising young historian of sexual mores, and one I would recall fondly on later, more conventional meetings. For that one she was simply The Penitent whose disciplinary education was in the hands of her strict Superior.

Without a word the older woman moved us back with the sweep of an arm, and raised the black quirt high in the air. *Crack! Crack! Crack! Crack!* The air sizzled with the rapid strokes that left the latex marked with four pale lines across the whole breadth of the splendidly full arse. Four and four again in short order, and I stood with a dry mouth waiting for the jerking of the hips to subside. So far there had not been a hint of protest, but the next batch was delivered at full stretch and the fourth of them was rewarded with a *nnngggg!* that sounded as though forced up from the pit of the stomach. Sibyl looked round with a smile of satisfaction.

'That is better. I was thinking our miscreant had been struck dumb. I chose the covering to save the skin, at least for a while, but it conceals the degree of our progress. Jane, since you are the ones sinned against in the matter, I wonder if *der Junge* would like to decide for me how far the punishment is to go. By how the bottom feels, I mean.' The last was added in response to my blank look, but the boy understood. I watched as he went straight to the frame and laid his hands on the rubber-coated mounds that were still rippling from the recent assault. With surprising self-possession he squeezed a little here and pinched a little there, all over the main area before cupping a palm to lift and let fall each buttock in turn.

'She'll take another dose, *Hauptoffizier*. But after that...'

'They will be good ones.' And indeed they were. When she drew back from the jerking and quivering hindquarters we stood silently in that kind of awe reserved for the soundest of thrashings thoroughly executed. It was maintained until the figure on the frame was finally still, then Sibyl Metzger placed her whip on a side table and took up a paddle in its place.

'I began with this before you arrived, and I shall finish with it. The thighs, you understand. Annabelle, take our visitors back please. Lunch will be in an hour.'

We followed her without a word up to our room, where I expected her to leave us to make her preparations downstairs. However, it seemed the maid had other plans. After closing the door she turned the boy to face her. Despite the restraining pouch there was an unmistakable bulge below the waist and she reached for it.

'*Le fouet a fait ça, yes?* Er, may I, if you do not mind...' She looked from one to the other, as if uncertain whether to ask him or me, so I came to the rescue.

'Feel free. Let's see him in all his glory.' From its performance on the train the day before, I felt safe in assuming the organ was not one to shrink under a novel female gaze. And I was right. Annabelle delved, rather expertly for one who claimed a dedication to women, and in a trice there was the thing exposed. A fine specimen, I thought fondly, and true to form it stiffened even more under our eyes.

'*Bravo!*' cried the maid, squeezing her find, 'there is no other like this here. *Le garçon*, he allows only the one the same as himself to touch. But I do not forget *le docteur. Jane, montre-moi ta chatte.*' The gesture made her meaning clear and I needed no urging to kick off my shoes and divest myself of trousers and pants. By the time I was ready the boy's cock was in Annabelle's mouth and he had his eyes closed. On her knees she pulled us together and boldly inserted the wet head between my equally wet labia just below the clitoris. Never had he been so near to the norm of hetero-penetration, but she wasn't to know that and he was in no condition to be complaining. Then with her mouth pressed to him and me, she worked the shaft with thumb and forefinger until I felt the hot goo flood the opening of my cunt while she sucked and slurped.

I didn't come at that point, but I knew my Annabelle wouldn't let me down. Rather breathless at the stage management of it all I watched her lick him clean and restore the wilting object to its place. Then with a wink she pushed him gently in the direction of the door, saying, 'Kitchen, *oui? Ils t'attendent.*' Once he was gone she turned back to me. 'On the bed, Jane. And very wide, please. *Il me faut travailler.*'

The promised lunch was a solitary one, for while two places were laid as on the earlier occasion, Sibyl Metzger did not appear. In her absence I was able to indulge without hindrance the appetite generated by the recent events, and I had no sooner swallowed the last mouthful of deliciously creamy quiche than there was a tap on the door.

'Entrez,' I called, pushing my plate aside and leaning back, glass in hand. The suspicion - hope, rather - that instantly formed in my mind was confirmed when the repentant one from the morning came in. I can't say she was none the worse for her starring rôle on the frame: the face surrounded by those stunning locks was very pale, and under cover of loose, high-waisted pantaloons the movements of the hips were perceptibly cautious. But there seemed no hard feelings after the harsh treatment: she declined the offer of a seat with a gratifyingly wry smile, and the eyes were untroubled.

'Dr Greene,' she began, but I cut her short.

'Jane, please, and I'll call you Belle. With some significant corporal punishment between us the need for formality has passed.'

'Well then, Jane, I have come to apologise for the game I played with your books.' When I raised an eyebrow at the word 'game' she went on quickly. 'Don't think badly of me. I was unsure how much you knew and curious to see how long it would take you to track them down.'

'Oh, I daresay all is forgiven.' I made it sound airy, though I couldn't help wondering how far I would have got without the boy's help. It was fitting that he'd been closely involved in inflicting the penalty. 'However...' I let a pause lengthen until I had the eyes watching me closely '...however, I reserve the right for a further comeback. When you are back in London quite healed, I intend to put you across my knee and spank that delicious bottom red raw.'

'Yes, ma'am.' It was delivered with a girlish pout that made me ache to carry out my threat at once. Then it occurred to me that there was something else necessary to complete our transaction.

'Excellent. Now if you would be so good as to bring me the missing materials...'

'I'm afraid I can't do that.' There was an odd look on the American's face, and I was once more uneasily aware of the ground shifting under me. 'You see, Madame has taken charge of them. Not ten minutes ago she told me that she wishes to have you collect the books in person this afternoon.'

No time was specified, so having learned where 'Madame' was to be found, I returned to the upstairs room we'd been given. It seemed only right that the boy should be in on the step that would conclude our mission, but there was no sign of him. Patience was never one of my virtues so I was already heading back down the passage when I was lucky enough to meet him at the top of the stone stair.

'The Notebooks,' I said, 'must be collected. From and by order of the lady in charge. Coming?'

'Yeah, course.' Despite the words he didn't look entirely happy, though kept mum until we entered the corridor with the director's rooms at the end. Then he turned to me as we walked. 'This boss, you didn't meet her?' I shook my head but he persisted. 'Before, I mean.' It was more or less what Sibyl Metzger had asked, and again I felt I was missing part of the picture.

'Well no one's told me her name. I had the idea they all went under pseudonyms anyway. Do you think she's somebody I know?'

'Bloody right. Heard them talking. Long time since.'

'You mean someone from my past?' But the question was to remain unanswered, for we'd reached the director's door and at that very moment it sprang open. A girl pushed between us, head down, and lurched off the way we'd come, hands kneading buttocks beneath a grey skirt. A middle-aged woman in a white tunic came out, shaking her head.

'*Oh, les jeunes! J'ai offris de calmer la douleur, mais...*' She stopped waving the tube of ointment and looked us up and down. '*Ah, pardon.* You are the English visitors. *Entrez, Madame vous attend.*' Inside there was a long bench seat opposite a padded table and a unit holding a variety of tubes and bottles. It was like the waiting room of a surgery and an examination area combined, except that all the treatments on offer from the 'doctor' were of a single, painful kind. All of a sudden I was beset by the conviction that our encounter was to be more than a simple returning of purloined documents, and the thought sent a shiver of apprehension through me. Then we were shown into the inner room where a figure stood outlined in a barred window that looked out to a distant rocky coast. But once she moved away into the light I had no longer any eye for the view. The hair was white, that was new, though the tight bun was unchanged, as were the strong lines of the face. Twenty years fell away in an instant and my stomach churned: the acting head of the Rigorists was Madame Mariselle, once installed briefly and traumatically as my resident stepmother.

'Madame,' I managed to croak, while attempting to get a grip on my whirling emotions.

'Jane. You are looking well, and little changed by the passage of time. And this is your young friend - they tell me he is popular in the kitchen.' She moved closer and studied him with seeming approval, then pointed the length of rattan she was holding at his trousers. 'I should like these down in order to make an inspection.'

She'd lost none of the dominating presence that had inscribed itself on my mind in those teenage years, and the lad complied without my offering even the feeblest of objections. While red-faced, he was not too discomfited to be sporting a semi-erection that soon filled out when Madame Mariselle stroked its underside with the tip of her cane. With the smallest of smiles at the effect of her action she ordered him to bend. Still he showed no reluctance, grabbing his ankles and holding the position while she tested the resilience of the hindquarters with her instrument.

'You may stand up and dress yourself. A sound beating would do you a power of good, boy, and you have the behind to take it. I hope you will give me that pleasure before you leave us. But now to the matter of the writings of the young eighteenth-century wife. Her *Commentaria* are a treasure indeed, one which prompts me to ask if I shall be handing them to a worthy recipient.'

Again I was reduced to silence, and she lost no time in developing her point.

'What impresses about the writer of these is that she is ever in the middle of things. She must experience it all for herself, at once, *tu comprends?* Only then will she inflict anything on another. Whereas, what I remember of your case, Jane, is rather different. You were quite ready then to impose your will without much consideration for its effects. I am asking you now, is that yet so?'

'Well, I...' The sentence ground to a halt as I struggled in my mind to rebut the accusation. *Uxor* was, from what little I knew that far, disposed to offer herself up to heightened experience, in a very active way of course, but nonetheless as a form of submission. Whereas I had from the start found the greatest pleasure in being the one in control. But in this there was nothing discreditable: it was the age-old couple of sadism-masochism, essential in practice if not in a neat jigsaw of theory. However, the idea that I was simply insensitive to the needs of others was a conclusion that had me beginning to seethe inside. Madame Mariselle was watching with, I suddenly saw, a degree of amusement.

'Aha,' she cried, 'it is good to see you rise to the bait. The half-truth that cuts to the quick. But it must be remembered there is truth in it. Come, Jane, let me ask you a specific question. You will have carried out a punishment not very long ago, a severe one. *C'est vrai?*' For a moment I could think only of the boy and spankings, then it came to me. Ama.

'Yes, I did, but she was willing. More than willing, in fact: she required it of me.'

'I am sure it was just as you report. That is not my point. Now you will tell me the details, please: the implement, the number of strokes, and the use of any special conditions.' I hesitated, and then realised I had lost my chance to dissemble. Only the truth would carry conviction and I gave her what she wanted with a horrid suspicion of where it was all leading.

'Very well, I shall give you the opportunity to show your good faith in this matter. The correct sadist has a duty to know at first hand what she does, is it not so? *Bon.* I possess the instrument of which you speak and the strength of arm to use it; we need only an item of clothing and we are there. So what do you say, Jane?'

What could I say? I'd been manoeuvred into a corner from which there was only one honourable exit, and it was going to be a painful one. There was nothing for it but to bite the bullet, and I bowed my head with what grace I could muster.

'Excellent. You may move the horse out from the wall.' While I did so she reached up to a high shelf and took down a long black rod that I recognised only too well from its rôle in my earlier life. Then she took from a drawer in the desk a pair of bottle-green knickers of a distinctly old-fashioned type. 'For our business you will wear these only, though you may keep the shirt. Use the dressing room. When you are ready the boy will be so good as to remain there until we are finished.'

It took only moments to strip off my trousers, shoes and socks and pull the knickers up into place. They were of a thick serge cotton that clung snugly to my buttocks, but would hardly serve as protection against the thrashing to come. I looked at the boy and he looked glumly at me, but I guessed the thought of it would be arousing him just as it would me had the positions been reversed. So I smiled a smile I was far from feeling and squeezed his shoulder, before returning to what felt like an execution chamber. Madame Mariselle looked me up and down, flexing the cane with a half-smile that chilled my stomach. She was going to enjoy herself.

'So twenty-four it shall be: *deux douzaines de coups. You will be afterwards a little warm, je crois*. There will be no need for the holding straps since you will show us a model of comportment, *n'est-ce pas?*'

I lowered myself onto the disciplinary apparatus with a sinking heart: an already bad situation had just taken a turn for the worse. At least a fastened body could distract from intolerable pain in a fight against its bonds; unrestrained it could only endure and suffer. I must endure and suffer: it was unthinkable to make an exhibition of oneself in front of Madame. I found a strut to hold between the front legs while I gripped the back end between my knees, and tried to mould myself into the padded surface. Twice behind me the instrument sliced the air as the wielder tested its feel, and the evil whirr made my insides contract. On the wall ahead hung a clock with its hands at almost twenty minutes past four; unless Madame were to draw the thing out, which had not been her way in the past, by the time they reached the half hour my ordeal would be over.

My shirt was lifted and folded up well into the small of my back, then fingers adjusted the underwear, smoothing out any wrinkles in the seat. I thought of the beautiful black mechanic whose stripes were to serve as the model for mine, and the wry amusement she would undoubtedly display at my situation made me resolve to acquit myself as well as I could. Then the space for such considerations was abruptly closed off. There was a swift movement at my back and a swishing impact that jerked my hips into the upholstered fabric under them. Two more in quick succession connected in like manner, and I was lifted by a glimmer of hope. While the mounting sting was bad, it wasn't possessed of the atrociousness I'd been dreading.

But I was clutching at straws, as I should have known. Madame was just getting her eye in for the real beating that began with a grunt of effort, a thump of her tread on the floor and a jolt that knocked the breath out of me. And then the pain came: an impossible, unendurable burning that sent the muscles into shocked spasm. Had I air left in my lungs I should have shrieked. It is possible -

nay, probable - that later I did and in full measure, though on that point, mercifully, memory fails me.

The next clear recollection is of coming out of a red haze to find the boy aiding my rise on trembling knees. As I wobbled, clutching his shoulder, there came the curt command: 'Show.' It was too cruel to have to offer for inspection buttocks that felt like so much molten lead, but I struggled dutifully to pull down the pants and step out of them.

'It is enough,' was the laconic response of dismissal, then the boy had a gown round me and was steering us out through the door. I don't like to dwell on the image of the winsome lad with the woman who winced clumsily along at his side. Thankfully there was no one to witness the odd couple's halting progress until eventually we were sequestered behind the locked door of our room.

Then it all happened very fast. The robe was whisked from me, pillows heaped on the bed and I was face down across them. I felt lips brush the traumatised flesh and a tongue that fleetingly licked before my legs were thrust apart and a hard shaft pushed impatiently at my vulva. In the wake of the rod I was wet and he sank to the hilt, thighs mashing into the throb of cauterised arse-cheeks. Our first fuck - brief, violent and unforgettable - ended as fast as it began in an explosion so fierce as to draw down over my consciousness a safety curtain of blackness and peace.

In the night I stirred to find the boy behind me again, and half-awake I moved with him to allow a second penetration. Thrusting slowly, a finger on my clitoris, he brought me to a climax that bore me up to a great height and rolled me out once more into the dark.

I surfaced as if from a deep well to the sound of a door closing. In the light from the high window I saw orange juice had been put for me on the small bedside table. Along with it lay the two rescued volumes and the aptness of the price I'd paid made them seem even more of a prize. Forgoing for the time being an inspection of the well thrashed behind in question, I rolled carefully onto my stomach and pulled the books over. Inside the cover of the first were a few folded sheets of A4, and on the last one of them I found what I hoped to see: *Uxor studiosa scripsit.* This was another instalment of the transcriptions Miss Faversham had produced. I swallowed a mouthful from the glass and with a keen sense of anticipation began to read.

Chapter 17
Switch'd

Today what I write begins its Life as a Cautionary Tale, in which our Progress in Matters Venereal is halted by an Episode of Castigation. However, my Abigail and I turn the Occasion to our own Purpose despite the Will of those who are set up as our Elders & Betters. To be plain, it is the Master I allude to, in full Knowledge that the critical Implication may be judg'd to come ill from a Dutiful Wife. Yet, I beg the Indulgence of my Readers until the Event is lay'd out in which he redeems himself, is granted Pardon and becomes the Means of furthering our Duty.

We were, I admit, a little childish early in the Morning, though not without Reason, and saving the Bad Temper of his Lordship I should not have been provoked into the Act. Once embark'd on a Game of Ball with the Gardener's Children we become, it is true, a little boisterous, failing to appreciate that the Lord Of All He Surveys is after sitting up late with Comrades in Drink and we are disporting ourselves directly below the Bedchamber where he lies groaning in Remorse. However, my State of Ignorance is soon to be dispell'd as a Window flies up on its Sash and we are treated all to a red-fac'd Bellowing.

The Youngsters scamper away in Dismay at the Racket, while I stand my Ground, irk'd by such rude Remonstrance. To put out my Tongue would demonstrate the Tenour of my Feelings but the Gesture seems insufficient. Thus I pull at the Tye of the Pantaloons donn'd for our Romp, and before Nabby can stop me I have them down to the Knee. It is some hours since the Darkness has pass'd and with it the time to admire the Splendours of the Moon; so in its stead I bend full over to show him another that has never belong'd with her pale Sister in the Heavens. Forthwith the Features at the open Window take on a Hue so crimson that for a Moment I fear that Apoplexy might strike the affronted Party down in his Prime.

'Do not move,' he roars, and vanishes from view. I turn to joke with my Maid that the Orbs I have uncover'd would become chill'd were I to obey the Order to the Letter, but she offers the Opinion that they will be suffering shortly from the converse Complaint. Given the Master's Tastes I have to own the Truth of this and begin to lament my hasty Response. However, I am spared the Indulgence of Regret by the Arrival of two Footmen carrying between them a Bench and a Coil of Rope. At the Sight of them I reach to resume my lower Garment but my Husband, hard on their Heels, forbids me with an unmistakable Signal. It is to be as Nabby has divin'd, and before the empurpled glare of the Lordly Visage I lie meekly along the wooden Seat, my face to it as directed. I am to get a Whipping and to protest is like to double its Severity rather than avert the Operation.

Yet, to be plain, I do not place myself in Readiness with any great Anxiety. Knowing Sir Montague's Predilections, I petitioned to sample the Birch Rod before consenting to a Marriage Contract that was sure to bring me into many close Encounters with its Twigs. At my Insistence he did not stint his Efforts, striking until the white Skin was bath'd in a ruby Dew and the Walls rang with my Squealing. It was a Shock indeed, especially to one whose Childhood lacked even one Occasion of a parental Hand raised in Anger, though to my Surprise, the Sum Total of its Effect was to induce in me an immoderate Degree of Warmth. I refer not only to the Rise in Temperature of the whipt Parts, but of the Heat induced in Parts adjacent. (With such Coyness the Reader must for now rest content: the Nature of such Fires and how a Maiden may slake them - with or without the Blessing of Society - is a Subject to which my Pen will return).

Thus it is that when my Wrists are pulled forward to be bound with a Cord and another used to encircle my Legs, I yield without Demur to what seems a superfluous Element of Staging. How mistaken is that Judgment becomes apparent when the second Man returns from the Trees with a Pair of stout Hazel Wands, by which Time I am bound fast to the Plank. It is with a Degree of helpless Horrour that I see the burly Fellows, duly weapon'd, take up their positions to left and right of my tether'd Nakedness. Scant Minutes past flaunted with Impudence, I now sense the bare Cheeks to quiver in Anticipation of the Lashing they are about to receive. At this point Nabby returns bearing a wicker Chair in which my Master installs himself at a prime viewing Place. His Colour has abated and he rubs his Hands in the undisguis'd Expectation of a Show.

'Strike in Alternation, good Fellows,' he enjoins them heartily, 'for with diligent Work we shall soon witness Contrition.' Sir Montague's Words turn me once more into the Rebel whose Fear is ousted by Indignation: a State that enjoys, I am ashamed to report, but a short Life once the Strokes begin to fall.

Dear Reader, if it has never been your Lot to suffer a Switching of the uncloath'd Buttocks, how am I to explain the Wickedness of the Smart that is so caus'd? In Truth I cannot, therefore I must run the Risk you will think me a Creature of no Mettle when I tell that before a dozen Cuts are landed I have cried Mercy. His Lordship, though, is minded to teach a Lesson and his Audience literally Captive, so her Pleas are no more than wasted Breath. In the end there is a lamentable and copious Flow of Tears at which the hard Heart is soften'd and the Footmen bidden to abandon their Whipping.

When the Knots are released, I struggle up off the Bench. The Sight of the discarded Rods, quite shredded by their Work, makes me fear to inspect the state of my poor Flay'd Bum that burns as though punctur'd by a Host of red-hot Needles. Now the Master is all Sympathy, as if my State is the Result of an Accident rather than his Orders, but my Resentment melts away at his Approaches. He draws me to him with soothing Noises and Nabby joins him in the Assessment of my Wounds. I am content to allow the Examination, aware that I am myself becoming a shade 'hot' (the Reader will be prim'd to take my Meaning) while my Maid is busy opening the Lordly Breeches at my back.

Then she lets out an 'Oh', I turn to see what has occasion'd it and gasp myself. Not at the Member that rears up at me - that is no unwelcome Sight - but at the Blemish that bulges from its Side. We have before us plain the Origin of the Day's Ill-Temper: no Act of Insertion will be endurable until the Wen has given up its festering Contents. Nabby and I exchange a Look that says it will be a good Thing to release the Pressure of the other accumulation in the Area, so I bend to allow the Organ to rub its end into the Crack of my Arse. Sir Montague is much taken with my Move and in mere Seconds I am sensible of his Spending, which stings the raw Cheeks as he crows in Delight.

Then he calls to the Footmen who look up as if startled from a complete

Immersion in collecting their Tools. They chastised with admirable Devotion, he declares, and now the Mistress's Bottom requires Attention that he himself cannot supply. No Rods need be cut, he adds, for the Servants should find each a Prime Specimen about their own Persons. I grasp his Meaning and plant a Kiss on the sticky End that begins to droop, then he directs that while the Men are to Avail themselves in Turn of the rear Entrance, and given the Circumstance of his Incapacity, my Abigail is charg'd to take Care of the front Lips with her own. It is most welcome News and I decide that my Master is wholly forgiven for his Mood.

The first of the Men deploys his Rod with a Vigour that takes away my Breath, and I am so fettled by his Ramming that I put the Head of the Master's afflicted Part into my Mouth where it is at once hard again. Now there is a veritable Truncheon that lunges deep in the Arse, while Nabby nuzzles the Cunt as might a hungry Horse its Bag; between the pair of them I am in Transports and a wild Idea takes Charge of me. To weigh such a Notion is by that very Act to cast it from the Mind, therefore I leave no Space in which Reason can do its Work. Two quick Movements suffice: one to bring the Shaft side-on to my open Teeth and the other to close them with Force upon the Root of the Pustule.

My Pen, I fear, is less than equal to the Description of the Events that follow. With a Sound betwixt a Screech and a Roar paining my Ears, I spew the foul Matter to the floor before the Stomach's Contents will be expelled in like Manner, a Tactic that has the Merit of a bare Success. At the nether Openings the Ending is near while the Shock and sudden Relief has made Sir Montague stand like a Pole. I close over the Gush of his renew'd Spending, greedy for the Mask of its Taste, as the Cock ramm'd into the Passage behind sluices out the very Bowel with its pumping Flow.

Thus it is finish'd and with a bare fourteen Nights to pass before the Spectacle we have achieved, more by Accident than Design, an excellent Rehearsal of some of its Features. So pleased are we with Ourselves that my Abigail and I retire to Savour the intimate Pleasures of a bath between Mistress and Maid. No sooner, however, than it is done, I am summoned by my Husband who is renew'd in his Manhood and impatient to reacquaint it with my delicious Hinder Parts. I give the exact Phrase inscrib'd in his Note, that further requires Nabby to assist in the Matter, and it causes us not a little Merriment as we make our Way refresh'd to the Master Bedroom.

Uxor studiosa scripsit on this 1st Day of August 1728

Chapter 18
Stuff'd!

The next several days, in fact the better part of a week, passed in a whirl of sex. Fucking, I should say. Neither buggery nor masturbation, nor yet the games mouths can play but plain and unadorned penetration of the vagina by the erect penis. In the first twenty-four hours of meeting him I had seen for myself the boy's powers of recovery to be beyond those often ascribed to late-teenaged males by their lust-stricken elders. In the first instance, to have his bottom warmed or see another's suitably chastised brought him to a condition where ejaculation required only a few deft movements of an obliging hand. What singled him out from the imagined pack was that if the conditions pertained, the result followed without apparent need for recuperation. Every hour on the hour, if one had a mind for it.

I exaggerate a touch, and I was not on his case with a stopwatch while engaged with the relevant body parts. It must also be admitted that since the organ in question was inside me at the crucial moments I was not in a position to assess if its customary spurtings became, over time, reduced to mere drops. No matter: what I did know and shall not easily forget was the frequency with which I found myself bent forward and spread to allow entry to the stiff meat.

We were delivered a few miles out of the town to a cottage on the coast belonging to the Order, nominally to give a space for me to mend and for quiet perusal of the prize of the Notebooks. The garden was large and enclosed, sloping right to the sea, and over the four days I must have sampled the greater part of it on hands and knees, bum in the air, though I did put uxor juvenis aside while the actual deed was done. In retrospect, I can hardly have been as grudging as this makes it sound for I had been, unusually, ready to abandon trousers for a borrowed skirt. Lacking knickers beneath, it could be flipped up on demand to permit me the untrammelled impression of a bitch in heat. I blush to think of it.

However, I was in good literary company. Between times, I was able to feast on the lubricious prose of the young wife as day followed feverish day in the run up to the spectacle. Her Master, it seemed, had been quite rejuvenated by the lancing of the boil, and was demanding frequent servicing by both Mistress and Maid as his imagination worked on the details of the tableau soon to be staged. Thus their nightly antics took on the aspect of rehearsals as the active men of the household were called upon, singly and severally, to test the feasibility of entering the chosen orifice from positions that had popped into Sir Montague's overheated mind. More often than not, while penetration could be achieved once ejaculation began the strained cock would spring from its hole and spew its load messily onto the floor. Quite the thing for a porn shoot maybe, but less so for a display being planned with military precision. Back to the drawing board.

Then with the event just three days off, a working centrepiece was achieved. *Uxor* tells it as only she can.

I have expended Words before to describe the Bench, but shall endeavour to do so again. It is a curious Thing, near square in its Proportions and low slung. The narrow Slats that make its top, of the same Oak as its stout Frame, follow a shallow Curve that might invite the uninform'd Observer to rest his Person thereon. But Readers of my foregoing Scripts would not be so deceiv'd: far from making available a Seat, it provides for a person's Seat to be presented for Castigation. Once it is buckl'd down, no Efforts by the protesting Body will discharge the arrayed Cheeks of the Posterior from their painful Encounter with the chosen Instrument of Correction.

This night I am the one with her Belly press'd into the wooden Ridges by the thick Belt that has been made tight across the Back. It is scarcely a Position of Comfort, though my Attention has been diverted by the sheath'd Member that has found its Way between the nether Lips from behind. Not a difficult Entrance, I must own, since the Portal is quite slick with my Anticipation, and once it is accomplish'd the Master leans over me with his own Beast proud before my Face.

Its Moment, however, is not yet come, so I content myself with a Taste of the wet End. Then he delivers a Volley of Smacks to my Rump that has me squealing. There is, I will confide, a Degree of Duty to these Cries, for the stinging Spanks cause me to bounce agreeably on the Shaft that spears my Vitals. On the Day itself I shall, of course, be most soundly whipp'd, a Fate spared me this Day for fear of the Marks that might remain. The Thought of such Treatment gives me no little Anxiety, though I dare to suppose I shall rise to the Occasion, in the Company of the Men's Members before the Sight of my Squirmings.

Meanwhile, my Husband has at last desisted from his Exercise and declared the burning Bum it has produc'd to be ready for Invasion. It is where we have before come unstuck, in a Sense all too literal, so I hold my Breath as the Man behind me leans back while another straddles his Thighs. This time we are bless'd with the Choice of a long-shanked Fellow, for his Organ slides into the greas'd Arse-Hole to its very Hilt without Mishap. I have learn'd how to facilitate Access to that Place polite Society does not speak of, but this Entrant must vie with the Occupant of the neighbouring Opening for the inner Space. Reader, these are well-endow'd Men whose splendid Erections are planted side-by-side in the trim Form of a young Woman. Thus it is that I am stuff'd as full as any festive Goose readied for the Spit, with a Bottom as hot as if the Roasting was already started. My Abigail, who has been watching with Interest, now intervenes by taking hold of my Hips and moving them up and down.

'Take Charge, Mistress,' she counsels, 'and you shall have these Boys properly seated.' I follow her Advice, lifting to pull the Organs out a Touch and lowering to push them back. The Sensation causes me to laugh, for all at once I am pleasuring myself with the formidable Insertions. Sir Montague is beaming at the evident Success of his Arrangement, and his Smile grows wider yet when Nabby kneels to take his Organ into her Mouth. At the Performance the task will, in the Nature of the Occasion, fall to me but it is consider'd Ill-Luck thus to complete the Tableau in Advance. So it is that I am allow'd but to press my Lips to the Shaft while the Maid's are at work on the bulbous Head. It swells and leaks in Response to her Efforts and my own tell me that the Fellows are in a similar State.

Three Cocks are to be cajol'd into firing as one (the Master has laid Stress on this Stipulation) and under the Burden of it I am as preoccupied as the Director of Animals that performs in a travelling Circus. However, the Moment arrives of a Pulsing before my Eyes, and a double Kick inside overtaken by a Clutching of the Vitals that stops my Breath. Dear Reader, I am stunn'd as by a Poleaxe and drench'd in a Delirium as rapturous as though the Celestial Gates themselves had open'd to admit me.

Reading this writing left me with mixed feelings: my Joanna, aka *uxor studiosa*, lodged as she was in the early eighteenth century, was more adventurous than I who should have had the advantage of all the later twentieth-century years of sexual liberation. Fortunately, these maudlin reflections were cut short by the arrival of the car that brought us to the cottage, and within the hour we were jolting along the rough track towards the old city. Madame Mariselle was waiting to explain that a message had come from a Miss Bingley at Ardingley End: without specifying why, it indicated that our early return would be appreciated. Something was clearly up if the unflappable Tamsin had been moved to get in touch.

'So I have taken the liberty of booking seats on the morning train. You will be fit to travel?' The grey eyes were looking at the snug-hipped trousers I'd risked for the first time since our encounter and I nodded, trying not to flush. Then they swivelled to the boy but he was staring down, pointedly failing to meet the enquiring gaze. I knew the Director of the Rigorists was itching to have him bent over as I had been, but I knew also that I must not push him into such a thing.

It was already mid-afternoon, and for the rest of the day the boy and I went our separate ways. I rather luxuriated in the personal space after our close-closeted spell by the sea, and following a pleasantly solitary supper decided to wander. The guest quarters were set apart from the main body of the one-time monastery where the residents went about their daily business, and beside the grim underground chapel I'd seen little of any of it. So I pulled on a pair of trainers that would allow quiet movement over stone floors, and a black zip-up jacket. I had no torch so would have to depend on there being lighting, at least in the areas I was likely to reach.

Two flights down I headed off in a new direction, passing a series of doors to reach a T-junction with blank stone walls heading to left and right. Then there was a noise, and something about it made me duck into the last recess. Footsteps drew closer and amongst the rustling of clothing there was a snuffling that made me prick up my ears. Surely it was - and yes - there came a distinct sob to confirm the suspicion that I'd heard the sound of suppressed weeping. I pulled back, holding my breath, as the cloaked procession swayed by, the unhappy member, female I was sure, tightly flanked by the remainder. In itself it was a sight more curious than alarming, but that was not all. Bringing up the rear was a taller figure in a black gown that distinguished itself from the grey of the rest, and over its shoulder dangled the long tails of a cat. And as he passed under the light I saw that the knotted leather strips of it were stained dark with something still wet.

Heart beating, I waited for what seemed an age, though no doubt it was mere moments that passed before a door closed and there was silence. There could, of course, be other explanations than the one that leaped out at me, but when I heard indications of the party's return I was off. My alcove would hide nothing from a group passing the opposite way so my best chance was to get ahead and find, if I could, some means of avoiding them altogether. In retrospect, it was hardly likely that one whose presence had become sanctioned by Madame herself would be seen as an interloper ripe for summary justice. At the time, however, the thought of that evil-looking whip striking my bare body was quite enough to drown out whatever small voice of reason might have been trying to speak.

Round the next corner was a straight corridor, brightly lit: could I reach the end of it before the approaching inmates came into view? About halfway along was an opening, and hearing a voice suddenly clear behind me I panicked and lunged at the catch of the inset door. It opened and I pushed it quickly closed, my back pressed to the cold stone to the side. The sounds were of an altercation that grew heated as the parties approached; for a horrid moment they seemed to stop right outside while the pulse thudded in my temples. It was only when the voices moved on and died away in the distance that I realised what I'd done. The door had latched shut and I was on the wrong side of a lock without a key. And apart from a barely discernable strip of light between the wood and the floor, I was standing in darkness.

By the time it took to call myself ten kinds of bloody fool my eyes should have started to become accustomed to the dark. But there was little to show for it. It was true that the glow under the door was slightly less faint, but it cast no illumination on the space around me. If I was going to find a way out I would have to do it blind, and the wall behind me was the obvious place to start. With one arm outstretched I inched away from the door, moving my hand forward by degrees until I reckoned I'd moved about a yard's distance. The stone surface was still there, unbroken, but the next tentative step found only empty space. Instant vertigo made my head reel and I leaned heavily on my support until it passed. I tried again, poking a leg out and down, and found a solid footing a few inches below. Exploring with the other foot established that there was a straight edge from left to right. Very good. If my luck was in I had just descended the first step of a flight of stairs and it should be a relatively straightforward matter to take the next and the one after that. Then, at the bottom of the whole thing there ought to be another door. Whether it would be one I could actually open, well, that was another matter. But first things first...

It went according to plan, except for one bad moment when the fourth step failed to appear and my nose came up against a wall right in front of me. While not a spiral stair, the thing was turning down to the left, and once the penny dropped I was able to take the next bend in my stride. After a straight run there was an end, but instead of the wall that was my guide my hand found a length of banister rail that terminated in a wooden knob. And then nothing. Afraid to let go I searched the surrounding area at arm's length with the same result: nothing. The floor was a little rough but basically flat, and it seemed I'd been delivered into the middle of an empty space.

Then I noticed the air. On the way down it was slightly musty, as if the way I'd come was little used; but as I stood uncertainly at the bottom it was tinged with something else. Suddenly I had it: cheese. That utterly French smell of ripe brie or camembert with just a touch of rottenness. It was faint but distinct, and had me hoping against hope. Cheese would be in a kitchen or at least in a larder near to a kitchen; the question was how to find my way to it through the impenetrable dark. Or was it? At first I thought my eyes were playing tricks, nerve endings firing off small volleys in the absence of the usual stimulation. But no, there was something. Right in front of me there was a line, a fine line that seemed to dance in front of my eyes. I reached out, emboldened and took a step, then another and realised what I was looking at. It was a crack of light under a door, much like the one I'd left behind, but it was a long way off.

I edged forward carefully, scuffing the stone flags uneven under my feet. As long as I had a line of sight to the target I should be all right. Before very long there was a change of atmosphere and I brushed against something to the side. And then I realised I could see. Very dimly, almost more by intuition than vision, there were walls to the left and right. I was back in a passage and it was leading directly to where I wanted to go. The door opened with the turn of a knob and at the end of a short corridor was another with a high glass panel. I caught the sound of voices beyond it: a quick interchange I couldn't make out, and a giggle. There was nothing threatening, in fact it sounded more like play, and it was followed by a sharp noise and a laughing yelp. A repeat left me pretty sure of what was going on so I moved up to the small window and cautiously raised my head to it.

I was looking down from the head of a short set of steps into a kitchen area with a large stove to the left and sinks to the right. In front of me was a counter, and splayed across it was the *garçon* I had briefly met, trousers down round his thighs. On the bare bum the red splodges amply confirmed what I'd guessed and I watched, a little dazed, as the boy - *my* boy - lifted a wooden spatula and cracked it down again. The spanks soon fell into a rhythm with the shrill little gasps belied by the way the lad pushed out his backside for the next. As if to remove all doubt of the nature of the game between the two, the 'punisher' crooked an arm round the throat of the 'victim', pulled him upright and put a hand to the erection that sprang into view. Then it was back over the top, and when the boy's trousers came down too it was plain what was coming. I almost gasped out loud with the stab of arousal that hit me as he parted the red cheeks and pushed his hard cock at the hole between them. That cock - the one that had subjected me to a sweet orgy of penetration - was in the process of spearing what I assumed to be its default target.

I felt no jealousy, rather a strange kind of relief. But most of all I shook with an intense voyeuristic lust that had the fingers stuffed into my cunt awash. On our first meeting the boy jerked off unashamedly beside me while we watched a behind being made tender; now I was wanking at the sight of his cock spearing one. While a detached corner of my mind registered the thought that there was something poetic about it all, the climax broke over me in concert with the raised voices crying out below.

Chapter 19
All Change

That night I was out for the count. The boy must have come back at some point for his bed had been slept in, but when I woke in the morning he was nowhere to be seen. I'd just decided to begin collecting things together for our journey when Annabelle came in carrying a breakfast tray. She put it down and glanced over at the rumpled sheets, then turned to me a little anxiously.

'He has *le rendez-vous, tu sais? Avec Madame. She comes to me in the evening with le rotin.* Er...' She looked to me for help and I began to see where this was heading.

'Rattan is what we call it, if you mean a cane.'

'*Oui.* It is special to her, like the black one. I must make it *en trempe, toute la nuit. Comme une marinade, mais dans le vinaigre.*'

'She wanted it soaked in vinegar?'

'*C'est ça.* She says it will be *un chauffe-derrière pour le garçon.* The boy's request. Your boy.' If my French was not leading me astray, the key phrase translated as 'bottom-warmer'. It was no doubt Madame Mariselle's idea of a little joke, for a supple length of wet rattan was likely to be up in the same league as the vicious black rod. And yet it seemed the boy had, quite literally, asked for it.

I was still digesting the implications of this when the door opened. We gawped as the subject of our conversation entered, closed it carefully behind him and came forward. His movements were visibly stiff and he was very pale, but appeared quite in control of himself.

'Knew she wanted to. So I thought why not. Kind of parting gift.' At this we rather fell on him, I'm afraid, one each side to lower the trousers as gently as we could manage. Not only was there no objection to our blatant curiosity, the boy's face was acquiring a distinct smirk. As the beaten buttocks came into view, Annabelle sucked in her breath.

'*Dieu qu'il était sévère* - Madame was not easy with him.' I wasn't going to disagree. By repute, hard judicial canings produce the effects before us, as indeed did my own, though I was not then in the position or condition to give the damage detached scrutiny. There were only six marks that had been executed in unrelenting parallels, but what marks they were! Coloured somewhere between purple and black and the thickness of a forefinger, they stood out in hoops that ran from flank to flank: vivid testimony to the rule of aiming each stroke six inches below the target. But more shocking still - to one who was acquainted with the body in question - was the crimsoned swelling of the whole hindquarters from waist to the upper half of the thighs.

The pain at infliction had been certainly formidable, and when we straightened up I looked at the boy with a new respect. While I too had suffered Madame's rigours, I'd been trained up for the part; he was just a lad, an *ingénue* in these matters. Now, however, in the space of our rapt study, there appeared a sizeable erection and Annabelle grinned at it.

'Jane, I would love to assist you. *Mais après l'épreuve should come the time for two, n'est-ce pas?*'

When she'd gone I bent him over and worked a small bead of lubricating jelly into the tight hole. Then I found a slim dildo in the goody-bag that always travels with me, and eased it in to the hilt. He grunted and stood up. I wagged a firm finger under his nose.

'Boy, when those bruises have quite gone, I am going to give you the spanking of your life, for being so foolhardy as to offer yourself to that woman. Right?'

'Yes, Miss.' The colour returned to the face under the shock of hair, but I thought I saw something deeper in the eyes than before. I took hold of the stiff penis and drew him on top of me on the bed, sliding down until I could reach the hot welts with my fingers and close my mouth on the erection. Rash though he may have been, he had earned his pleasure and I was going to devote myself to it.

Our trip back was essentially uneventful. Thanks to the smoothness of the TGV the boy was able not only to sit, if gingerly at first, but to fall asleep in the corner seat. Changing stations in Paris went without a hitch, though it was not made easier by the awkwardly long package we had acquired. Not content with the leaving present of a beating, Madame decided at the last minute that the boy should take with him as a memento the instrument itself.

Back across the Channel, the rail travel was rather more of a trial to one with a tender behind, and by the time the train pulled into the stop for Ardingley End it was late. Although I'd left a message on her mobile, there was no sign of Tamsin's Porsche at the station, so I was reduced to pleading with a part-time cab driver to take us the last few miles. As the vehicle at last drew up at the imposing entrance, Mrs Jencks came running out.

'Dr Greene, quickly please! She's in the library...' She waved an agitated arm at the lit mullioned windows to the right and I shoved my wallet in the boy's hand for the fare and took off. The outer reading space was empty, but a cry came from the interior room where the collection had been housed. I hurried through the half-open door and stopped in my tracks. My PA was on her feet with miniskirt up round her waist, clutching her bum. Between her fingers I could see the flesh glowing red, and standing over her, holding the polished dark wood of a hefty paddle in both hands, was a tall man with a thatch of white hair. He had to be the new Master of the House and it looked as though he'd started as he meant to go on.

'Jesus fuck.'

'Language, young lady. And I am not finished with you yet.' The Texan vowels, gently chiding, carried the weight of authority. I took a breath and stuck my oar in. For all it achieved I needn't have bothered.

'Excuse me, I am Tamsin's employer. If you have a quarrel with her perhaps you should take it up with me.'

'Jane, it's all right. Really. Let's just get this over with. Two more, sir, I believe you were saying.' He nodded without so much as a glance in my direction and Tamsin went back across the desk with an odd little sigh. Wielded with energy, each impact of the weapon spread and lifted the buttock cheeks most impressively. When he was done she hauled the skirt down and rubbed through it, breathing hard. Then the patriarch turned to me for the first time.

'And now, ma'am, you are...?'

'Jane Barrett-Greene, of the British Library.'

'The Librarian. Am I to understand that you are the one responsible for this?' He indicated the shelves around us that stood mostly empty.

'Er, I arranged for the removal of the collection, yes.'

'Very well.' He looked down at the paddle and slapped it on his palm, then fixed me with clear blue eyes. 'You will join me for breakfast at eight-thirty sharp. I will hear then your proposal for rectifying the situation.'

'I'll consider the invitation, if you'd be good enough to tell me whom I'm addressing.' I was fuming but no doubt managed to sound merely petulant. He simply drew himself up and turned to go.

'"Sir" will suffice for the present.' And that was it, unless I was going to lose it badly enough to shout at the departing back. I'm glad to say I didn't, and then Mrs Jencks hurried in.

'You will go, won't you Dr Greene? I couldn't help overhearing. It's been a nerve-wracking time since he came but he is set on the place and would keep on all the staff. There is only the one difficulty of the books. It seems Sir Montague's reputation was such that the new Master - well, so he'll be if only he stays - anticipated a collection to match his own, er, special tastes. We're depending on you to explain and talk him round.'

'Hmm. Is that what Tamsin was trying to do?'

'He was very angry...' the PA was still holding her bottom, though without the earlier distress, '...and it did calm him down quite a bit.'

'Tell you what,' I waited until they both had expectant eyes on me, 'there's one thing I don't fancy and that's that plank of wood for my breakfast.'

'Oh no,' said Mrs Jencks quickly, 'he wouldn't. Not to you. And I heard him discussing hash browns, I believe they're called, with Mrs Beaton. Very amicable they were. It's only his manner sometimes, really.'

'Right, I'll do it.' I decided it was time to bite the bullet. What the story was going to be I had no idea, but there were several hours before the morning.

'I don't know about just his manner being the issue.' Tamsin pouted at the Housekeeper, who took her arm.

'Yes, dear, you're sore. We'll have to see what we can do about that.' She led the girl away and I'd cooled down enough to flash her a wink. The odd couple were seemingly still on. As for me, I needed to do some thinking.

Back in my room I found the bottle of Bowmore, liberated for me by Mrs Beaton from the stock downstairs, as a remedy should insomnia strike. Unused for that purpose, it could perhaps be deployed to stimulate thought. I poured a solid dram with just a spot of water, took a good slow swig and lounged on the bed. It seemed our 'astute' lawyer had overlooked the possibility of the buyer being a man with s/m leanings who was aware of the Everett line's long history of such predilections. Any one who did would be expecting there to be such books; this one was demanding them. Well, he couldn't have them: not the ones the Library had acquired, nor those that had gone to the Nemesis Archive, given the financial arrangement reached with Samantha James.

My musing had reached the third glass when I heard the latch of the door. The boy's head appeared, then the rest of him with Molly close behind.

'Jane, I know it's late and I don't want to disturb you, but I saw those bruises and they could really do with some of my oil. So I thought - we thought - er...' it started with a rush and then dried up. The idea of a threesome made me prickle for a moment, then it occurred to me perhaps I wasn't actually being invited. Maybe my blessing was being sought for them to go off *à deux*, and Molly was having trouble spitting out the request.

'Hi guys,' I remember saying, 'good of you to call. But I'm a tad tied up, y'see. Important meeting in the morning and all. So if you could manage without me, I'd appreciate it.' Looking back, the atypical and whisky-induced warmth must have been blatant. I only hope the words weren't slurred. Whatever they thought, the pair disappeared with a haste that confirmed my suspicion. I chuckled to myself: Molly would soon discover the boy had developed some new inclinations, if indeed she was to be favoured with them. What the hell. I drained my glass, taken with an idea that might grow into a plan. The bottle had hardly been touched really, and another good splash of malt might just bring it all into focus.

When my travelling alarm went off at eight it felt like being pulled out of another world that was deeper and more true than the one I was being forced to reoccupy. The feeling stayed with me as I showered lazily, though my head was quite clear. Annabelle had seen to our laundry before we left the Order, so I was able to put on a crisp white shirt and a pair of pressed black trousers. Freshly washed, the hair was brushed easily back into unobtrusive neatness and then the merest dab of an astringent perfume behind the ears finished the preparations. The creation of an impression entirely out of superficial items is not my favoured style, but I wasn't normally called upon to sweet-talk an unbending paterfamilias whose world view was likely to be found at the opposite end of the universe from mine. And there was a lot at stake.

I arrived on the dot of the appointed time to be met by a frillier-than-usual version of Laura complete with black stockings. 'Go for it,' she said into my ear, ushering me into the small dining room that looked out on the rise at the back of the house. He was already there, standing framed in the morning light of the window.

'Good morning. I understand it is *Doctor Greene* I am speaking to.' It seemed I wasn't to be offered a hand or even a name in return.

'Yes sir, it is.'

'Please take a seat.' He pulled out a chair for me then took his place opposite. As we drank the freshly squeezed juice in front of us he said, 'A PhD, I take it; and the subject of the thesis?'

'DPhil. Oxford, you know. Banned books.' It was a while since anyone had asked. He was looking at me curiously, so I elaborated. 'After the printing press was invented, all books had to be licensed until the Act expired in 1695. So I was looking at how prosecutors and publishers went about doing their respective business in the following century.'

'I see. I own a number of volumes from that era myself.' He paused for a moment. 'Venus in the Cloister is one and, if my memory can be relied upon, one called Discipline in The Ladies Academy.'

'Well, both of those titles were the subject of legal action, though not necessarily the editions you possess.'

'Very interesting. Perhaps you would be able to cast an eye over the rest some day.' It was a promising remark that I could let lie while Laura took away our glasses and served us from the hot trays on the side counter with a mound of soft scrambled eggs, home-cured bacon and the hash browns Mrs Beaton had been asked to cook. I was glad to see the southern gentleman had an appetite as healthy as mine, so we ate in a surprisingly companionable silence. When the plates were nearly empty I broke it, feeling the moment had come to make my pitch.

'I know you're upset, sir, about the empty shelves in the den. But from what you say, they will be easily filled by the contents of your own library.'

'And more.' He was staring at me with no expression I could read. Maybe I'd gone too far, but I was in a mood to go further yet.

'To be blunt, sir, the books were never part of the sale. You may have hoped to find a collection, but such a thing was not promised. Sir Montague always wanted them to go to our national collection.' That was stretching matters to the point of untruth, but there were occasions when I felt the facts should not be allowed to get in the way of arguing a case.

'Can you tell me to whom exactly these books are available where they are held now?'

'"Bona fide scholars" is the phrase used, and those who qualify are allowed only to request specific titles to be consulted in the reading room on the premises. However, if you became Master of Ardingley End and were to give your, shall we say, retrospective approval to the donation, then I could arrange that you be granted direct and unlimited access to our material. There are precedents in the treatment of past donors of important collections. In addition, while I can't at present guarantee it, I am confident I can arrange visiting rights to an unparalleled archive of women's writings that is stored not far from here across country. Again these would be granted in view of the late Master's generosity in the past.' My breakfast companion had been listening intently and took a swallow from his coffee. When he put the cup down he wasn't actually smiling, but the craggy face had softened enough to make that look like a possibility.

'My father used to say it was a foolish man who, in his private life, refused an inducement to do something he was already inclined towards. So, Dr Greene, there is a good chance I shall be taking you up on these offers.' It sounded as though I was home and dry, even without resorting to what I expected to be my ace card. It was time to play it and clinch the deal. I'd brought with me one of the two volumes of the Notebooks, and when our dishes were cleared I placed it on the table and pushed it towards him.

'This is something that has a direct connection with the house; in fact it belongs here in a way the other items under discussion don't. It's a journal that was kept by the new bride brought to Ardingley End the best part of three centuries ago.' The prospective Master took the old leather binding and opened it carefully. His eyes skimmed over the faded writing on the pages in front of him. 'It's not that easy to make out at first. The writing can be a bit of a scribble and she has a kind of shorthand all her own. But if you look inside the front cover you'll find a few sheets printed out.' He did as indicated and I waited a little nervously while he finished reading.

'*Uxor studiosa* - now is that the studious wife?'

'Not exactly. More like eager. Keen to be initiated into the sexual games of the age.'

'You are the expert, Dr Greene, though I would guess this volume is quite a prize.'

'It is one of two, so there's quite a lot of material. I was hoping to arrange for an edited version to be produced.' The patriarch made a gesture of acquiescence.

'I'm sure the task is in good hands.'

'Thank you, sir.' I didn't want to put at risk the progress we were making by any lapse into informality. 'There is one more thing. The Notebooks contain a number of passages about a grand tableau that was mounted on August 15th in 1728. It seems to have been a kind of stylised orgy of flagellation and copulation whose elements were rehearsed weeks in advance and recorded in some detail. Now, I wondered if, as an inauguration ceremony for the new Master...' I stopped, suddenly apprehensive. We knew the man had an interest in erotic literature, but my thought of a full-blown staging might be an idea too far. However, I needn't have worried. The piercing blue eyes had come alive with interest.

'The fifteenth of August, you say. That is barely four weeks hence. Planning ought really to start without delay. My daughters will arrive tomorrow and they are sure to want to be involved.' I didn't bother trying to suppress the silly smile that had taken over my face.

'We shall need transcripts of the relevant passages, sir. Leave it to me and I'll get on to it straightaway.'

Chapter 20
Instruments

'You mean you did it and he's not pissed off about the books any more? Ace. So now I can keep my bum well away from that board.'

'Don't bank on it. You might well be called upon next month to present the cheeks publicly. To say nothing of the rehearsals that'll be needed.' Tamsin was perched on a kitchen counter, having begged an extra pot of coffee from Cook after sleeping in. The news had gone down well but the last bit left her staring at me nonplussed. I tried to explain. 'In the summer of 1728 the then Sir Monty put on a show starring the young wife he had recently acquired. She kept quite detailed records of the whole thing and the new man would like to honour the anniversary of the occasion.'

'A show? Would I be right we're not talking about a wholesome evening of family entertainment?'

'Well, Tams, saving that you're a couple of centuries early with the concept, I'd have to say yes. It seems to have been a rather, er, heated affair, as the young lady herself might have put it.'

'Let me guess. Given the period, and in this house we'd be talking about very hot bottoms and even hotter sex.'

'Flagellation and fornication.'

'Or flogging and fucking.' The PA giggled. 'All the fs. And you've signed us up for parts in a replay?'

'Well, you decide for yourself, of course. But given what we've got from the place, it seemed a little churlish to refuse.'

'Right, you've twisted my arm. As long as I get a rôle that's not too heavy on the pain bit. So, guv, what do we do next?'

'You can drive me out into the country, to the lady who worked on the Notebooks before. We're going to need some transcripts PDQ.'

On our way out to the car the boy came round the corner and I waved my document case at him.

'The Notebooks are going to Miss Faversham, for more copies. Fancy a spin?'

'Well, er...' The response was not enthusiastic and I guessed he was remembering what happened the last time.

'Don't worry. She won't lay a finger on you in that state.' It seemed to reassure him into joining the expedition, though he made a great fuss squeezing into the space behind the front seats as if to rub in how sore he still was.

We bowled, or rather boomed, our way along the country lanes with Tamsin's stereo sparing us the need to make conversation. In the light of a cloudless morning the village green shaded by its ancient oak looked impossibly idyllic, as did the cottage nestling under a thatched roof. Its owner was expecting us and appeared as soon as we drew up. The jacket had been discarded in acknowledgement of the weather, though the tweed skirt was still in place. She beamed at us.

'I'm pleased to see you again, though I don't believe I've had the pleasure...'

'Tamsin Bingley. Without her, Rare Books would certainly come apart at the seams. Tamsin, this is Miss Faversham.'

'Edith, please. Well, do come in.' Once we were installed in the small living room I handed over the Notebooks and gave an abbreviated account of their retrieval.

'It's good to see them safely back. Now, I'm familiar with many of the passages you are interested in so I should be able to have a printed version for you within the week. And, of course, I'd be very happy to take part in a longer-term editorial project. At least I shall no longer be accused of making away with the materials.' She turned to the boy who looked down, embarrassed. I came to his rescue.

'He is sorry for that, Edith. And at present he's in no condition to risk chastisement, given his recent experience.' It took little coaxing for the ill-treated posterior to be offered for inspection, and our host was suitably impressed. I had to agree that the technicolour hues surrounding the central six-barred grid were rather startling.

'My, my. The work of a formidable rod, I would say, with a technique to match. As it happens I might be of service here, having been blessed with an older brother who was always getting it in the neck... so to speak. Not quite to this extent, but enough for me to have developed some methods for dealing with the aftermath of a good beating. The marks are, I believe, quite recent.'

'Yesterday morning. Early.'

'Very good, boy. Then I take it you'd be willing for me to have a go. It is a while since I was last so employed, but I don't expect the hands will have lost their touch. So let's make a start, shall we?'

'Yes, Miss F. Thank you.' Deferent and polite. She seemed to have a way with him, whether dishing out discipline or dealing with its after-effects. The two of them disappeared through to the back and I dragged Tamsin out the other way. There was no garden at the front for the house gave directly on to the quiet cul-de-sac that separated us from the grass. But there was a long bench, and on it we basked in the sunshine while she filled me in on the politicking at the Library during my week's absence. It seemed no time at all before the boy came out followed by his new carer. He was giving off the slight but unmistakable glow of the young adult male who has had a basic need catered for.

'There,' she said with a little sigh. 'That should improve matters no end. Now, Jane, I wonder if there's any chance I might borrow the lad for a day or two. There's a new computer system on the way - the one I've been using is so behind the times, you know - and I remember from my work at the End that he is quite the expert. It would save me a lot of trouble.' I looked again: there was more to the boy than the sexual proclivities for which there seemed to be a growing demand.

'No problem, Edith. Help yourself. Unless there are things he should be doing at the House.' Not knowing exactly what his duties were, I thought it only right to ask.

'Nothing special.' He shook his head. 'Anyway, this is work. We get the transcripts quicker.' I bowed my head before the blunt logic and then remembered what else I wanted from our visit.

'So that's settled. There is one more thing, though. As far as I can see, Ardingley End lacks any standard canes, being equipped only with fearsome things from the most damaging end of the scale. I am going to be called upon to do a little instruction soon, and I wondered if you could help out, Edith. I'm after the kind of thing once to be found in a Headmaster's - or Headmistress's - study, for use on misbehaving senior pupils.' Edith Faversham was nodding vigorously.

'I know exactly what you mean, Jane. The idea was to cause short-term distress without putting the offender out of action altogether. An excellent tool, and indeed I possess a number that fit the bill.'

'Well, if I could have the loan of - actually I'll be needing two...'

'Oh, please, you'll accept them as a gift. No, no, I won't hear of any other terms. Now if you'll just be patient for a few moments, I'll go and fetch what you require.'

We dawdled back and succumbed to the temptation to make a detour to *The Greene Man*, whose landlord's embarrassed fascination with disciplinary matters had entertained us on the first visit.

'Afternoon, ladies,' he called out, and when we approached the counter lowered his voice for it not to carry to any of the occupied tables. 'So how did you get on at the House, if I might ask?' I shifted my hand to let him see the handle of the cane I'd been hiding behind my back, and his eyes bulged.

'Oh, don't bring up the subject,' said Tamsin plaintively, putting a hand to her backside. 'I wish we'd never gone near the place.' For good measure I leaned forward conspiratorially and added my two pence worth.

'I can tell you, in confidence, that I've learned a thing or two about keeping an uppity young miss under control.' Again I touched the instrument with a meaningful look, and his complexion darkened almost to the colour of a beetroot.

I picked up two menus from the bar, and as we looked around for a table, Tamsin said to no one in particular, 'I only hope the cushions are good and thick.' Taking our seats, it was all we could do to keep the giggles at bay, but the promise of another excellent lunch kept us in check until we had given the landlady our order.

Afterwards, Tamsin stopped at the car and took the cane from me. She bent it into a curve, swished it through the air and tapped it smartly on her palm a few times. 'So did the boy really ask for a beating? I mean, those marks...'

'Indeed he did, and without any prompting from me. Though he may have got a little more than he was bargaining for. He brought the weapon back with him: it's a good foot longer than that, a deal thicker and very pliant.' Tamsin shuddered but continued to size up the one she was holding.

'If we find somewhere quiet, do you reckon I could get an idea - that's just an idea, mind - of what this thing actually feels like?'

Just three hundred yards beyond the pub was an open gate which a quick recce showed led into a smallish area of pasture, unoccupied and shielded by overgrown hedges. Tamsin nosed the vehicle in until we were out of view of the road, and turned off the engine. We sat in silence for a few moments then she opened her door.

'We'd better get on with it.' Outside she lay across the bonnet from the side, then frowned. 'I don't think I know what I'm doing, guv.'

'Okay. Think Bingley of the lower sixth: a wayward girl caught smoking behind the bike sheds yet again. The headmistress has decided a short sharp shock is the only answer.'

'Right. That sounds good. Well, not good really 'cos I'm terrified. Is the skirt all right on?' The short grey garment reached just to the tops of the thighs, and its stretch material was moulded perfectly to the shape of the buttocks. Suddenly I felt distinctly warm.

'The thong won't get in the way, so a layer on top of that will be quite acceptable. To begin with.' Standing slightly ahead of target at the front bumper I measured up the instrument. It was a bit of a stretch, which was all to the good since it removed the danger of the tip biting into the far flank. 'Three first. Let's try to take them in one go.' The cane was well balanced and I brought it down dead centre with a good whack.

'Shit. Oh shit.' The bottom quivered but the body stayed put, and the next two were received in silence. Then a small voice said, 'Can I have a minute, please?'

'Of course.' She shot up and kneaded with both hands, legs doing an impression of walking on the spot. Then she went back down without a word. 'You're doing well. How about three more bare? Then that'll be a decent six of the best.'

'You're the boss.' With the skirt rolled up the double-edged tracks were surprisingly vivid, and I painted another three on the compliant flesh without more ado. I busied myself returning the implement to the back seat beside its twin, during the brief burst of blowing and jumping. Then we got back into the Porsche and after another short silence drove off.

At the End, Tamsin pulled up round the back with rather a flourish and made a beeline for Mrs Jencks, who appeared in response to the noise. She said something into her ear and the pair vanished into the house without a backward glance. No doubt Mathilde's special lotion was going to be put to good use again. As for me, I'd been feeling decidedly lickerish ever since the triumphant breakfast and the caning of those peachy cheeks had brought me to a pitch that was crying out for attention. And who better to give it, I suddenly thought, than a certain black mechanic, if only she was in the mood...

In the yard there stood a gleaming Cadillac, all pastel blue and fifties chrome that resembled the fins of a spaceship, but there was no sign of life. At the top of the outside stair to the flat the door stood open, so I called a hello and there was an answer from within.

'Jane, is that you? Come on up.' Ama was standing with her back to me at the sink, cleaning her hands. 'I heard you got the books.' She turned to grab a towel, sleeves of the boiler suit pushed up to the elbows. The zip was open to the waist and it looked very much as though there was nothing underneath. In two paces I was behind her, hands through the side openings onto bare hips.

'Sure did. Though that wasn't all.' I pulled her close, feeling the warmth of the body against mine. 'I got my comeuppance for lamming into you. Do-as-you-would-be-done-by sort of principle, the other way round.' Ama twisted out of my grip with a laugh.

'Oh, did you now? Show. Pronto.' I dropped the trousers at once and she had a good look. 'Mmm. These must have been sore. Bit difficult to say at this late stage, Dr Librarian, but I'd guess the swishy stick was quite like the one in the other room.'

'Almost identical.'

'Oh Jane, what have you been up to?' She found my wet crotch and I came clean about my recent exercise. 'Here, I have just the thing for one in your state. Get over and don't argue.'

'Yes, Ms Mechanic, anything you say.' She stacked two pillows on the edge of the bed and I did as told. An oval-shaped object was dangled in front of me that gave off the smell of new leather. She pressed it to my bare behind and I pushed back in a kind of reflex.

'Ooh, the lady's begging for it. So here we go.' There was a whoosh and a smack, then another and another. The slaps were soon falling thick and fast and my arse was burning with a fire that connected straight to the groin. Afterwards, Ama opened me wide where I lay and brought me slowly to another peak that left me gasping. By the time I spread her out to inspect the faded marks I'd made, with all that followed, it was just half an hour short of dinnertime. Since the Master-elect, as it were, was away to meet his daughters, it would be the sparky kind of gathering of staff round the kitchen table that I did not want to miss.

We showered together under the device fitted to a large, old-fashioned bath, and Ama asked me what I thought of the prospective incumbent.

'You mean, ahem, "Sir"?'

'Yes, he's not exactly given to informality. He came and found me yesterday when the Caddy downstairs arrived. That's not my type of thing really, but he's got some top flight Euro stuff on the way. Like a 1934 Bugatti.'

'Sounds like you're going to have a whale of a time under the new management.' While I soaped her back she went on in a low voice that had me straining not to miss the words, with their edge of agitation. 'I don't know if I should tell you this, but he cornered me in the workshop with a bag and took out this whip. His great-grandfather's slave whip, believe it or not, and he's showing it to me. Can you imagine? And it's obvious, just obvious, that it's no ornament or souvenir. The evil bastard of a thing is for use. What's worse is - and this is fucking shameful - I got so juiced it was like a tap. To see my pants after you'd think I'd peed myself.' She turned to me and I held her tight.

Then after a minute I said gently, 'Look, lover, if there's even a hint of blackmail in this, we'll give him a bloody good talking to. But if it really does turn you on...' I reached over, pulled down a big towel from the rack and wrapped it round her. 'Come on, let's move. You'd better find a drier, otherwise we're going to arrive late together with wet hair and set the tongues wagging.'

Chapter 21
Lessons

Mary Lou and Maybelle were not happy about the situation I found them in at our first meeting.

'Daddy, we so don't deserve for this to happen.'

'Bel's right. Please, Daddy. It was a teensy little thing, not at all bad really. Okay, stern talking to bad, maybe, pants down bad no way.' But the pants were down and were plainly going to stay down until patriarchal justice had been done. They were of a cream stretch material neatly folded around the thighs, and joined by a narrow band of lemon-yellow underwear that matched the crop tops of the upper halves. The young ladies were arrayed side by side over the rounded top of a trunk with their hands gripping a floor-level rail on the far side. Thus the bodies were pulled well forward making the buttocks, bared for six inches above and below, into the outstanding features of the display. The piece of furniture occupied the centre of the room that was to become the new study: a choice recommended by the first-floor prospect across sculpted garden hedges to the tree-lined drive and the ornamental gates in the distance. However, at that point the more arresting view was undoubtedly to be found on the inside of the windows.

'That is enough. Rules are rules and you will do well to accept your chastisement with good grace.' The voice was not raised; it did not need to be. The gravelly tones forbade disagreement and the sighing and lowering of heads indicated the girls had been there before. I was at one time acquainted with such a place myself, and I knew that when resistance only made things worse it was better to bow to one's fate and get it over with. That morning I was to be one of its agents, called upon to give instruction in 'the English instrument', and I had arrived suitably equipped with Edith's gifts. The Master took one from me and flicked it a couple of times. I guessed it was being compared unfavourably with his solid paddle so I demonstrated that, properly wielded, a humble school cane could slice through the air in a way that meant business. Since his preferred hand was the left, we were able to stand one at each end of the trunk with easy access to a bottom of our own, as it were. I laid the rod across the cheeks of mine to begin the demonstration, and he copied my movement.

'One of the cardinal points, sir, concerns range. Since rattan is very flexible, if one reaches too far across the target the tip of the rod will whip into the opposite flank with an excruciating bite. In severe punishments one may intend to do just that, in which case the body would need to be restrained. For ordinary purposes, though, one should aim for the end of the rod to land here...' I indicated a point perhaps an inch beyond the summit of the right-hand mound '...bearing in mind that exerting force is very likely to extend the arm further than anticipated. Then one is free to strike unstintingly without fear of overdoing it.'

'I see, Dr Greene.' While I still had his full attention I thought it better to round off the brief introduction before it became too much of a lecture.

'The rest is more obvious, and then it's simply a matter of practice. The fleshiest parts, say between the top of the cleft and the undercurve of the cheeks, are ideal for vigorous work and well-spread strokes may be multiplied at will with no lasting damage. While the backs of the thighs are not ruled out, a sustained attack on their sensitive surface would properly belong in a thrashing of the severest kind. And I understand, sir, that that is not our present task.'

'Indeed not.' The odd sound he made was indeed a chuckle, as the hint of a smile confirmed. 'No, my beauties have earned such a thing before and doubtless will again. This time, however, I had in mind a more moderate lesson, yet sharp enough for its effects to be felt well beyond a single day.' A man after my own heart! Whatever his failings, he had hold of a basic principle of corporal punishment, one that I felt the cane was uniquely placed to fulfil. There was the chance win of a fresh convert to my belief, and I remember a distinct sense of anticipation as I raised the implement to inflict the first cut.

When I brought it down there was a gasp at impact, then an 'Ow-ow-ow' as the pain hit home. But despite the shocked squeal the body stayed in place for the next. Good girl, I thought. Two more, progressively harder, had the bottom cheeks a-quiver yet still there was total compliance. Then it was the Master's turn. He spent a long time measuring the cane against the unmarked surface and adjusting his stance. With a jerk he delivered a stroke from on high that I sensed was wrong from the start. It grazed the underside of one buttock and slashed across the backs of the legs. The hands shot back and with a howl the young woman writhed on her belly like a stranded fish. The patriarch tapped his instrument impatiently on the wood.

'Back in position, now! Or when we're done it will be the paddle.' Not one to admit a mistake, it seemed, and I waited for signs of rebellion against the injustice of it all. However, there was only a heavy sigh as the girl resumed her grip on the bar and showed us the angry weal already purple on the fair skin.

'You'd do better to get your eye in.' It came out snappishly so I went quickly on in a more conciliatory fashion. 'Once you're sure of the aim, sir, then you can up the force.'

'Right.' He appeared less than happy, but proceeded to lay on two nicely controlled cuts that the girl was able to take with no more fuss than her sister. Three more apiece and it began to look as though we had a canesmith in the making. He traced with a finger one of the raised tracks he'd made, and nodded approvingly.

'Dr Greene, what would you say to another six before we call time?'

'It should be enough to make an impression, sir. May I suggest a change of places first?'

It was done and the caning resumed. We were both hitting harder than before and the bodily responses showed it. However, the recipients proved themselves to be stalwarts who held fast and remained in their places until told they could rise. We turned our backs to admire the outside view, allowing a discreet minute or two for mutual commiseration and restorative rubbing, before the rather well marked bottoms were given a final inspection.

Lou and Bel restored their clothing to its proper place and embellished the thanks required for the punishment with an exaggerated formality. With each bare midriff adorned by a thong emerging from hipster jeans they made a fetching sight, and were plainly not the airheads I had first supposed. The father drew his offspring to him, and they seemed happy enough to accept an arm on the shoulder as he explained to me that a birthday was approaching.

'They have been raised under a curfew for as long as I can recall, and it was for a breach of that in my absence that they've now paid. However, less than a month hence these young ladies reach the age of majority and will be free to come and go as they choose. In addition, I have undertaken from that date to forgo the right to impose discipline as I see fit. As it happens, Dr Greene, the date coincides with that of the tableau we are to commemorate, so there will be cause for celebration indeed.'

First one twin and then the other had dropped into a squatting position beside the paterfamilias during his little speech. When he finished, Lou pouted up at him.

'Now, Daddy, do we get a promise you won't go for overkill in the final weeks?'

'Too right, sister,' Bel chipped in quickly. 'We could be facing a new policy to max the whacks before it's too late.' As the father looked down at them, shaking his head indulgently, my suspicion was growing that there was more to the trio than a Victorian father ruling with a rod of iron, and it came back to me that the estimable Mrs Beaton had said as much.

'And that's not all, Bel. Can we be sure that the heavy hand really does a vanishing trick on the 15th? Ka-boom, puff of smoke, never to be seen again.'

'Good question, Lou, and I got another. If - and we are totally in the if-ness here - the paddles disappear—'

'And the canes, Bel.'

'And the canes, then I don't know about you, but I might, just might, even just a tiny bit, start to miss them.' By now the mock seriousness of the discussion had given way to giggles and I had the uncomfortable feeling of eavesdropping on the reputed family business that was none of mine. So I mumbled a quick excuse and made for the door, though I couldn't help hearing the Master declare that what he would give up was a right, so he would still, of course, be open to invitation. Then, as I closed it, I couldn't help seeing that the paternal trousers were flaunting a quite substantial bulge only inches from the faces of the daughters that seemed, to my - by that stage - rather fevered eye, to be turning purposefully in that very direction.

Monday morning, early, we returned to London. There was little that could be done while the transcripts were being prepared and the boy was reportedly content to sit in on the process until the following weekend.

'Ambient okay with you, guv?' said Tamsin, and I grunted vague approval to avoid showing my ignorance. The car's speakers began to pour out a slow, cocooning pulse and I was happy to sink into a reverie while she negotiated the motorway traffic with an easy flair.

Back at the BL the first few days passed in a whirl. While Dominic had held the fort admirably as usual, there was still a mound of paperwork and a string of rescheduled meetings, at which I was obliged to disguise myself in a suit either to argue our corner for a slice of funding or defend it from unwelcome restrictions. Then on Wednesday night I returned from a well-earned glass or three of cold beer to find a message that had been switched through to the machine in my flat on the top floor.

Hi, Dr Greene, this is Lou. We thought you oughta know Daddy's headed your way to see the books. More to settle was the drift and I guess you already know his way of getting things settled. He's been practicing, too. So you better watch your - er - back. Sorry!

There was a burst of giggling cut off by the click of the receiver, and the home taped voice telling me that was the lot. I went to the cupboard and poured out a nightcap. Was the patriarch on the warpath? Or was there a joke I wasn't getting? Or both? I would find out soon enough and it was difficult to take the warning seriously with the amber liquid so agreeably tickling the throat.

As soon as the doors opened the next day I left instructions at the main desk that a tall Texan in his later years asking for Rare Books or me should be sent straight over. He would not give a name let alone offer credentials, but I was prepared to vouch for him. Then I briefed Dominic that he was to keep the man waiting while he buzzed me down below in the half-basement where our collections were stored. There I planned to lurk amongst the new acquisitions, whose loss to the house was apparently still rankling its master.

It was an hour before I made it downstairs, where Rachel was putting stuff into the computer database from a notepad filled with tiny neat writing. Her main work was across the road, but permitted secondments to us from time to time when a need arose. She had short dark hair with appealing hazel eyes kept hidden behind thick lenses and, I'd had occasion to notice, was quietly interested in some of our documented 'deviations'. Open on the desk beside her was a copy of *The Model Household*, of 1853, and I tapped on the illustration of a mistress birching her maid.

'The way it's been drawn, you'd think the thing was a broom she picked up from the corner.'

'Yes, it's a bit comical really. That doesn't look like it would do much.'

'No, the proper thing, I'm told, is made of a small number of slim switches. Very whippy.'

'Ouch.' She smiled shyly. 'Well, I'm only supposing. I never...'

'Oh yes, it's the very devil. Feels like the skin's being flayed right off. But actually it soon mends.' My authoritative pronouncement had rather given the game away, but Rachel looked suitably impressed and I decided it was as well she knew our department was no ivory tower.

'I'm afraid I've led a very sheltered life.'

'There are remedies, you know. Now I keep a list out here...' I'd gone through the connecting door still speaking, but what I found brought me up short. A figure huge in silhouette against the window moved forward without speaking and laid a cane on the desk between us. After the initial shock I saw it was no more - and no less - than the visitor I'd been expecting. He must have come down the back stair and that implement was very like one that lived in a stand in the office. And that meant that Dominic...

By that time Rachel appeared in the doorway, wide eyes moving from the Master to me to the crook-handled length of rattan. Still he was saying nothing so I broke the silence.

'Rachel, I'm going to need a few minutes here in private. If you've got plenty to carry on with for now...'

'Of course, yes. I'll do that.' After an anxious glance at the intruder she was gone and the closing door made a reassuringly solid sound.

'I took the liberty of asking for a loan of the rod from the young man. I have to admit that the qualities of these articles become more and more evident with use.' Wondering quite how all this 'use' was being achieved, I was briefly diverted by an image of the staff at Ardingley End being summoned to the study one by one, with Mrs Jencks herself perhaps being saved until last. However, he was now in my domain and I needed to take charge of the situation.

'Am I to assume, sir, that you plan to extend your experience with the borrowed instrument?'

'I do; that is, if you agree there is cause.'

'Cause?' If submitting to a demonstration of his new prowess would secure a blessing on the books residing where they were, then I was game. But first, he would have to spell it out.

'Do you not own to being unscrupulous in removing the collection?'

'It is my job to secure what items I can for the Library. In my position you would surely have acted in the same way. And it is done: you were too late for negotiation.' The silence that followed told of his reluctance to accept what I was saying, so I made a bid to cut the knot. 'I'll be blunt, sir. Nothing technically wrong was done in clearing the books from the house. However, you have hard feelings that you would like to take out on somebody. Well, here I am, at your disposal.'

There was a longer silence but at the end of it he said, 'Thank you, Dr Greene.' Then he cleared his throat and for the first time in our acquaintance I detected diffidence. 'There is one more thing you might clarify for me about these English practices.'

'Ask away, please.'

'I have found mention of the way in which a master in your old public schools might, ah, make free with a boy's rear end after he had striped it.'

'Not exactly a *practice*, I have to say, but it did happen. Prefects, even, were known so to indulge themselves.' If he wasn't going to name names nor was I, but my poker face was threatening to crack at his euphemistic turn of phrase. So I rummaged in a drawer for a packet, took from it a small capsule and passed it over, after which I felt able to continue in an appropriately serious tone. 'I am happy to oblige, though I would suggest you insert this right at the start to achieve adequate lubrication for the finale. Now, sir, when the business is finished, can I count on that also being the end of the matter of the books?'

'You have my word.' I took him at it, lowered my jeans and stretched out over the desk. He parted my buttocks with a grunt of approval and pushed the pessary home. Given my rather spare appearance, he was no doubt agreeably surprised by the meatiness of the area I'd uncovered. It was a pleasing thought but short-lived, as the situation I'd talked myself into so gaily began to hit home. There I was, face down and arse up for patriarchal displeasure to be vented thereon. It was now a matter of honour - as with Madame - to stay the course, only this time I didn't yet know what that course was. Nor did I know how proficient the southpaw had become, though what he was equipped with could impart a wicked lick and I feared the worst.

There wasn't long to wait. One touch of the cool wood was all the aim taken, and the first blow was delivered to the exact mark. There is a moment following an accurate and forceful cane stroke that is quite literally breathtaking: one stops breathing as the body struggles to assimilate the jolt of pain. Repeated assaults may lose the sheer shock of the first, but the space to recuperate between seems to shrink. Thus after six full-blooded cuts I found myself gasping between clenched teeth, 'You're hurting me, sir.'

'That is my intention. We've done six and I'm of a mind to do the same again. And then once more for good measure.' There was a quiet relish in the words that chilled me into silence. I could have walked out at any time, but it was out of the question to admit defeat on my own ground.

And take it I did - just. The final three were the hardest of all on flesh that was achingly tender. I writhed speechlessly until firm hands took charge of my hips and there was a hard nosing at the hole between my buttocks. He was wet and the jelly had done its work so there was no friction to impede his entry. But he was big, both thick and long, and I was distended beyond all prior experience.

To cap it all, he was given to an energetic thrusting that soon had me hanging on with the same grim determination necessary to survive the cane. It was a mercy that its use seemed to have so excited him that ejaculation took place almost at once, and I was allowed to slump on the unyielding surface while he disappeared to wash up. When he returned I struggled to my feet, clutching at my dropped jeans, and pushed him through the door. Rachel's capable hands could take charge while I took five minutes to restore myself in the bathroom. But I was rallying well and had to admit that now the thing was done it was certainly one for the book.

The two of them were huddled over a manuscript when I emerged, making an effort not to walk as if I'd spent an unaccustomed day in the saddle.

'The young lady has been showing me how it will all be set out,' he waved an arm at the half-filled shelves put by for the new collection, 'and it rather pleases me that other enthusiasts will have the opportunity to benefit from these fine books. I expect to return myself if the invitation still stands.' He was graciousness itself and I decided my throbbing bum had been a price well worth paying.

'Of course, though perhaps the next time you'll not feel the need to take such vigorous exercise on your arrival.' The Master laughed and wished us farewell before making his way back up the stairs. Rachel was looking at me curiously.

'Did you really let him cane you? I was trying not to listen, but...'

'Yes, my dear, and I am sore. But he's been made sweet, which is what matters. Now if you want to stick a very cautious toe in the water there's an Irish girl in Soho I know who will hold your hand. I'll email her right now, tell her to get back to you here and then you can take it from there. Right?'

'You are telling me you thought it was what I really wanted?'

'Well, I was reading between the lines.'

'You thought I wanted to be flung over a desk and assaulted with two vicious weapons? That's how you see me, is it? Just begging for it, can't get enough, so we'll set the big Texan on her?' I was working up a good head of steam that had Dominic looking a little surprised. But it was really no more than a variation on a scene we'd played before and he fell in with it without objection. In short order he was the one over the desk with trousers and underpants round his ankles.

'Right lad, in future, before you do any reading, make sure you've got the right glasses on, okay?'

'Yes, boss. Sorry, boss.' I was still holding the cane I'd brought back upstairs and proceeded to lay on six stingers that had the downy cheeks bouncing. When I lifted him up he was beautifully hard and I couldn't resist planting a kiss on the end of it. Then I made him sit on his stripes while I straddled him and lowered myself so his cock slid wetly into my sopping cunt. Oh what bliss! I drew it out for as long as I could, pulling back until I could just see the glans between my thighs, then sinking the whole length in again, exquisitely. But all too soon the rather cherubic face contorted and the climax was on us in a welter of juices.

Eventually I eased myself painfully off Dominic's lap and retrieved my discarded trousers. The episode played out, it was back to the routine business of the department.

Chapter 22
Uxor Nigra

Tamsin cried off the next weekend, so I set out for the country on a slow Saturday morning train. At the station I made a beeline for the taxi with a rather winsome young man behind the wheel. When he learned where I was bound he looked at me with new interest, and as we drove eventually managed to ask if Ardingley End lived up to the stories that circulated about it. Rather than get him to say exactly what he meant, I took the chance to drop enough dark hints of deviant doings to feed the gossipmongers for weeks. Not purely out of mischief, for it was obvious to anyone that a tableau in the manner of the Notebooks would require more able male bodies than could be provided in-house. So once I'd satisfied myself there was some substance to the claims of being 'well up for it' by my driver that included at least two of his mates, I took a contact number and promised to be in touch before long. A rehearsal would establish quickly enough their abilities to rise to the occasion on demand.

He sped away grinning immoderately, and shouldering my bag I headed up the stairs. In the study the daughters were sitting side by side with their noses stuck into the newly arrived transcripts.

'Awesome,' said Bel, after a glance to register my arrival.

'Totally,' agreed Lou. 'Way back when and she is core. Caps. But, Dr Greene, we are looking at a problem. Those guys—'

'Guys, wow.'

'Footmen, she calls them. More like *dickmen*. Ready with what takes a girl's fancy.'

'Even girl-lovin' girls can have fun playin' with one.'

'Sure can, Bel. But two birthday girls, now, what they need is two of them. One each. So they can fuck.'

'Yeah, Lou, fuck. Out in the open. Daddy can watch if he likes but he can't stop them. Not these two, because they'll not be minors any longer.'

'The magic age, Bel. But where are we gonna get our dick-bearers?'

Leaving aside the intriguing notion that one's twenty-first should be marked by having public sex under the eye of a parent, I reassured the double-act that the matter was in hand and would be dealt with promptly. It seemed the Master had seen his copy, but I'd have to wait until he got back from a tour of the woods to discuss it. My query, though, reminded Lou of his recent visit to me and I thought it as well to confess to the caning if not the rest of the 'English practice'.

'Show us,' she demanded. It was true I'd not only seen their marks but seen them being made, so I decided it would be churlish to refuse. They gathered round to inspect 'Daddy's stripes' and made commiserating noises about the number of them and how vivid they still were. Duty done, I zipped back up and left the girls to their eighteenth-century studies with the sudden thought of another problem that had not yet been broached. We could probably draft in local cocks to fill one gap, but there was the scribe herself: no bystander but a lynchpin of the show. The question was, where were we to find our *uxor studiosa*? Little did I realise then that an answer would be found very close to hand.

I was too late to have a sociable lunch, and Cook bade me help myself to some bread and cheese and glass of beer that was left in the big jug. She was stood over a mixing bowl, formidable arms floured to the elbows, and explained that the Master was getting a real English steak and kidney pudding for his dinner.

'Very particular, he is, to sample traditional recipes. Not that I know much about that; I just make what I always made, you understand. But it seems to suit.' She was plainly content with the early days of the new regime, and as I ate I wondered aloud about the man's reluctance to be identified.

'Well, I heard tell that the lawyer weren't happy about making do with "Mister X", though he granted there were nothing illegal about it. Anyways, the house has already got a lad without a name, so what's new? In fact we could follow their lead and all go by what we do, though it's true we'd have a bit of trouble telling apart the maids.'

Her comments reminded me that I'd not yet seen the boy anywhere, but I was rather hoping he'd come looking for me before the day was out. So instead, when I finished chatting with Mrs Beaton I set out to find Ama and see how she was faring under the changed circumstances. There was nothing doing in the yard, so I went straight up the stairs and peered into the hallway. When there was still no sign of life I carried on into the small kitchen to leave a note.

I was scratching my head about the message to leave in the space below a shopping list when I realised the outside door had clicked shut. About to call out, I was stopped by a low mutter of voices followed by the sound of steps into the living room. There was no line of sight to where I stood at the counter, and there was a kind of urgency to the interchange that made me disinclined to intrude. Leaning forward, I saw the door they'd gone through was almost shut. It was time to make a swift exit, but the hall was quite dim and I risked what was intended to be a quick peek into the room. But what I saw through the crack brought me up short.

They were facing each other, profiles sharp against the white wall behind: the black mechanic and the master of the house. Tall as she was, he was half a head taller and she looked up at him intently. Behind his back I could see he held a tight coil of black leather. Then Ama stripped off her T-shirt and in a single languid movement draped herself over the cushioned surface of the restraining machine beside them. He flicked his wrist and a yard and a half of dark snake slithered across the boards; when he flicked it again the thing rose up and fell, soft as a kiss, across the far shoulder. Above the heavy denim of the work jeans the naked back looked shockingly vulnerable and I waited, heart in mouth, for the weapon to strike. But it was not to be, not then. He began to speak quietly, and I watched mesmerised as he traced line by line with the forked leather tip where each lash was going to land. If...

Her response to the question in his voice was to push herself up and go over to the wall. There she thumbed down jeans and pants and offered the man a bare rump. This time he took the stock of the whip, parted the buttocks with it and thrust it between her legs. At once she arched her back and rode on it, back and forth, and the moaning that came from her throat made me suddenly flush in shame at what I was doing. Wrenching myself away I heard him pronounce, 'You must take all. The alternative is nothing. You understand?'

Ama's answer, 'All, oh *all*,' was a shuddering gasp that seemed to follow me

113

fleeing down the steps. All: the whip, the house, *him*.

Safely out of the yard I slowed down and took a detour along the edge of the pasture beyond the vegetable garden to gather my thoughts. Its form was unconventional, to say the least, but there seemed little doubt that what I'd spied was a proposal of marriage. And it had been accepted: in the heat of the moment, but if I knew my Ama, no less surely for that. The new Master of Ardingley End was to be joined by a new Mistress.

In the evening I tracked down the man himself to the den at the back of the library, where he was busy unpacking a special delivery of books. Able to begin filling the shelves our acquisition had emptied, he was amenable to sampling the bottle of Talisker I presented, even to forgoing ice in favour of a little cool water from the adjoining pantry. After I spent some time admiring a copy of *The Wandering Whore from 1660, and a Manon la Fouëtteuse* from two centuries later with finely rendered ink-drawings, I poured out a second generous tot. He sniffed it and rolled a good sip around on the tongue.

'Distinctive,' was all he offered, apparently without irony, though I wondered at one used to bourbon taking so quickly to the sharp smoky taste of the Skye malt. 'Now, Dr Greene,' he said, pulling the transcripts towards him, 'about this tableau. What would you say if I put the whole matter in your hands?' I must have looked startled, for he went on to explain. 'What I would like is to reproduce as closely as we can what the young lady sets out. I believe the description allows that, since she spares us none of the, ah, details.'

'She is nothing if not explicit.' I smiled, nodding.

'I have not yet compared our resources here with the cast used in the original, but it strikes me we are likely lacking suitable men.'

'Indeed sir, that's right, and I have already taken the liberty of finding a contact among the local lads. I'd be prepared to screen them personally to see if they, er, come up to scratch.' The euphemistic speech seemed to be catching. 'It occurs to me too that we are missing the young wife who not only recorded the event but played a major rôle in it.'

'Well, Dr Greene, that is one base I do have covered. Trust me, by the time we shall have a performer licensed for the very part.' He took a drink and so did I. It was all I was going to get out of him at that point. However, I hadn't quite done probing.

'Fine, sir, I'll pencil in a young woman, as yet unspecified. Though there is one more thing. She plays, as it were, second fiddle, second to the head of the house. The original event, as I understand it, was intended to be a setting for the patriarchal seed to find a symbolic receptacle; to be transferred before the eyes of the whole company, to—'

'I have read the material.' He cut in as I was warming to my theme of the spouting semen as an object of veneration, justified I felt by the use of the word 'sacrament' in the text.

'Excuse me, sir, I am merely trying to be clear about this. Am I right in assuming that you do intend to display the organ for all to see, and to, to...' I faltered and let the sentence peter out. His gaze was fixed on the top of the desk and the well-worn features turned a curious shade of puce. There was a silence, then he downed the contents of his glass.

'Dr Greene,' he said heavily, 'the apparatus will do what is required of it when the time comes. Now, if you would oblige me with another splash of your special whisky, I would like an opinion on a few more of these volumes.' It was good of him not to remind me that I knew at first hand how the 'apparatus' functioned - not that it was something I could quickly forget. Perhaps he was averse to sexual talk as opposed to writing, or perhaps it was talking in those terms to me that was the problem. In any case, I was happy to pour out more drink and look at more dirty books of a certain age. The forthcoming wedding had been confirmed in all but name, and I could also look forward - if with impatience - to feasting my eyes on the monster of an erection that had violated my innards.

In the meantime, though, there were other potential erections on my mind, and after a while I left the Master to the last dram, pleading the need to make a phone call. It was a mobile number the driver had given me, and he answered it almost at once. From the buzz in the background I deduced a pub and got straight to the point.

'It's Dr Greene here, at The End. Do you recall our conversation in the car earlier today?'

'Um yes, I do.' He sounded a little startled.

'Well, how would you feel about coming over tomorrow afternoon? For a kind of screen test, shall we say? And any other keen young men would be welcome.' I heard sounds of a hurried consultation, punctuated by some decidedly sceptical snorts.

'Sure. It could be just me or it could be three of us. Depending on whether I can get these dickbrains to believe me.' There was audience laughter at his remark, though it had a nervous edge to it. I thought it likely we should get our quota.

'Well, you can tell them they'd better keep the dicks tucked away in the interim. We want specimens in prime condition. See you at half-past two, okay?'

After lunch the following afternoon, a small reception committee gathered in the library. The young men Molly showed in to the panelled room looked somewhat abashed, I daresay with reason, for they faced us across a long table on which had been placed the instruments for the occasion. They consisted of only three items: Edith's cane, my paddle and a strap that belonged to Cook, none of them formidable in itself. But to novices in their use it must have been a daunting array, and not made less so by the maid's asking if they would each please remove their trousers. While that was done I explained that the show for which we were auditioning involved some preliminary corporal punishment followed by oodles of scrumptious sex. As a first step they were requested to stand where they were while the young ladies made an assessment of the relevant parts. I added that, of course, anyone who wanted out was free to go at any time.

Mary Lou and Maybelle homed in on the lad in the middle in cheerleader mode, all cleavage and tiny pink hotpants. They fussed over him, making sure their charms were amply displayed to his popping eyes, then Lou tweaked down the boxer shorts enough for Bel to rub the arse-cheeks that emerged with the oiled leather of the strap. While they were thus occupied I became aware that the ringleader seemed more interested in the cane than what was happening beside him, so I took it for him to have a closer view.

'Ever felt the benefit of one of these? Used on the place it was designed for, of course.' I turned him a little and stared down at the behind neatly sheathed in black cotton briefs.

'Er, no, but there was a teacher and she... she had one, in a glass case on the wall. And there were stories... boys said she threatened... but she never... though I know she saw me looking at it once... she never...' It came out in blurted phrases and he licked his lips nervously. I saw that the whole shaft of his cock was outlined long and stout under the tight cotton, and my own genitals gave an answering pulse. It looked as though we'd found a natural.

The daughters were busying themselves with the third boy, having left the second as stiff as mine had so quickly become. But they were making little headway with a penis that dangled limply in defiance of their best efforts, until the boy went round from behind the table and paddle in hand fondled the exposed bum. At once the organ gave a kick and the girls giggled. Another natural, maybe, with a preference for his own gender.

'Did you know?' I queried softly, and he shook his head, grinning at what we'd seen. 'Let's go next door, all right?' I didn't want to be sidetracked and nor, I guessed correctly, did he. Once the door to the den was shut behind us I stood in front of him holding the length of rattan in my two hands.

'Well, Colin,' I began, dredging up the name he'd offered when we first spoke, 'it may be a pity the mistress didn't take you in hand. But it's far from too late to start now.' I couldn't resist drawing the tip of my cane along the hard bulge that ran from the groin along the crease of the thigh, filling the skimpy material between waist and leg band. He let out a semi-stifled moan of pure lust that hit me straight in the vitals. It was time to cut the cackle and act. He bent over the chair I offered and gripped the seat as instructed, presenting me with a delicious sight. The thin cotton garment would do very well at the outset, especially when the recipient-to-be was new to the game.

'This instrument hurts a lot, properly applied, and that means, among other things, hard. But if you're the young man I take you for, you'll come through that. And then... well, you'll find out. Three before the pants come down, agreed?'

'Yes, Doctor.' I was happy to let the designation stand: after all, my intention in making the lad suffer was not vindictive but therapeutic. It would thrill me of course, but I was going to give him a life-changing experience, and that's what I call service.

I made the first stroke a moderate one that Colin took in silence. It left a mark in the cloth across the dead centre of the buttocks, and I let rip with the next two a half-inch above and below the target line. Each time he sucked in air and jerked up, but each time he went back down into position.

'Good lad,' I said in a reassuring tone, taking hold of the black waistband, 'but a proper caning is always on the bare bottom. Right?'

'Right.' It lacked the cheery ring of my question, having rather the quality of being issued through clenched teeth. Never mind, I had faith in my choice of subject and, as it turned out, one that was well placed. He endured three sizzlers with only the white knuckles clamped to the sides of the chair betraying the pain of them. I pressed a hand into the small of his back and ran consoling fingers along the tramlines flaming in earnest on the fair skin. Then I leaned forward and spoke quietly into his ear.

'There is space for two more, in between the rest. It would make a neat finish to the job, if you agree.'

He sighed, but I signalled an end and got the hoped-for consent in a resigned, 'Okay.'

At the last he made a choking noise and I held him tight round the waist until the thigh muscles stopped working. Then it all happened very quickly. Thumbing down my jeans with one hand I pulled him up so that his bum pressed into my groin. In front the cock was stiffening fast and in a trice it was standing proud, so I sat on the edge of the counter with legs spread and pulled him to me. In my hand the organ oozed a clear drop, then another and his face was a mask of slit-eyed lust.

'Told you,' I breathed, bringing the tip of the cock against my throbbing clit, and he gasped.

'It's coming... I can't... stop... uh...' I held him as the hot flow spurted over me, until milked of its yield the penis drooped. But when I gave the tender behind a loving squeeze it kicked, and in seconds the thing rose again to nose against my sperm-spattered belly. What followed was the messiest fuck I have the pleasure of recalling, before or since. Gloriously awash in his fluids and mine, my bum slithered and slipped on the wet wood as he pumped us both up to the grandmother of all shattering climaxes.

With the resources of only a dishcloth and the cold tap in the adjoining pantry, mopping up took a while. In the end, though, our bodies were restored with relative ease, although after such a vigorous coupling I was a little worried at the noise we might have made, but on the other side of the door no one was paying any attention to our entrance.

The closing stage of the afternoon's trials was underway with Bel kneeling, camera to her eye, behind the third of the volunteers. The bum in the frame was ruby-red, with the kind of inner glow that betokens a determined application of leather. The cock looked firm enough as it was, but the boy put down the paddle and rubbed it into full glistening rampancy for the close-up shot. The young Texan pressed a button and studied the small display screen.

'Awesome,' she announced to her twin. 'Daddy is so going to appreciate our hard work for his show.' Lou, however, was shaking her head.

'A dick in that condition is gonna make him think a dick poking where it

117

shouldn't. Daddy sees these and he's like, "pants down and over my knee now, girl".' Bel pouted.

'Ouchville. But it's all in a good cause, sis.' They succumbed to a small fit of the giggles, nursing imagined spanked bottoms. I guessed 'Daddy' would get shown the pics regardless and that the heavy hand would give way in the end to the patriarchal phallus. The centrepiece of the tableau would amply confirm Mrs Beaton's original suspicions of a somewhat eccentric family set-up, but that was still a fortnight away.

The photography complete, the lads were ushered out promising to return in a week for a run through of their parts in the event. For the present it was up to me, closeted with the uxorial original and a good dram, to sketch out a workable choreography.

Chapter 23
Bottoms Up!

A week later, as we bowled along the country lanes on the last leg of the journey back to Ardingley End, I mooted the part I'd pencilled in for Tamsin in the tableau's centrepiece.

'Sure, I know the kind of thing. Set it up just so and the top of your head blows right off, yeah? But what's the deal with these strap-ons?'

'The deal is no cocks, at least not till he gets there. Unlike Joanna, aka *uxor*, this is a brand new wife. But she has to be plugged, or it won't pass muster as a pukka rerun.'

'Gotcha.' There was a silence while the PA squeezed us past a tractor with a wave at the vest-clad driver showing off his pecs. 'Though I expect I can guess which of the openings I get.'

'Well, speaking as the one pinned down underneath it doesn't look too bad. You get the room to wiggle about and hit the spot. Plus it will be a bottom that's been, shall we say, well prepared.'

'Okay, okay, back door is no problem. So everyone's gonna be, er, prepared, right? And how exactly will I, if you've got that far with the plans, boss?' I let the sarcasm pass from one less than enamoured of corporal punishment.

'I thought maybe Mrs Beaton's strap. If you agree, of course.'

'Been there, done that, and it bloody stings.' She gave a sour little laugh.

'I could offer the cane, or there's always that fine hardwood paddle—'

'God, no way.' She sighed and squared her shoulders at the wheel. 'You win, guv. For the greater good, I suppose, or some such tosh.'

'If it helps, it is everyone we're talking about, saving his Mastership. So Cook will be joining Edith Faversham over the trunk, with of course, your pal Mathilda Jencks. Though afterwards I thought they could be excused the gymnastic fuckfest and left to their own devices with a jar of unguent.'

'No skin off my nose. I'm actually rather looking forward to my piece of tasty black arse. But if you haven't already picked a weapon for the matronly cheeks, can I suggest the board from hell? I wouldn't like to see it idle.'

'Wicked girl. Though how appropriate: it will be, as they say, a learning experience. And I hear the Master has been joined by a muscular secretary-cum-minder who'll be looking to help out and is bound to be a dab hand with the instrument.'

After lunch I met up with the Master. He was happy enough to endorse the disciplinary schedule I'd drawn up, which ended with its author, flanked by the daughters of the house, at the mercy of the patriarchal cane. Once more down with the breeches, though I wasn't planning to invoke England or St George. Next the new Mistress was to take centre stage, but on the subject of her treatment he was keeping mum. I gathered, too, that Lou and Bel were to play a critical part in the culmination, but given his reluctance to call a spade a spade in sexual matters I didn't even get to outline my scheme for deploying the organs at my disposal. I would just have to hope that faithfulness to the original would see us through.

Coming across Molly and Laura in the kitchen, I imparted the news that maids had been allocated to the order of the birch. With only a week to go, rods had better be set pickling, and sooner rather than later. However, I was able to sweeten the pill with an undertaking that the Housekeeper's hindquarters would, in their turn, be bared and expertly tanned with the slab of polished wood. The idea went down so well that the girls were still chuckling between themselves when they headed off armed with cutters.

At the garage buildings I spotted a pair of boiler-suited legs protruding from beneath the canary-yellow Bugatti, and decided to own up.

'Hi, Ama. Confession time. I'm afraid I was snooping on you and the big man. I was trying to creep out from the kitchen when I heard the answer. Sorry and all that.'

'Jane. So you know. I've been and gone and done it, haven't I? Good and proper.' The mechanic swung herself out from under the car and looked up at me from the low trolley. 'Tell me what a fool I am.' I shook my head. A part of me, admittedly small and kept well in check, craved the moment of utter submission, and was undeniably jealous.

'Each to her own,' I muttered. It wasn't the place to elaborate on my feelings.

'Let me show you something.' She scrambled to her feet and led the way inside. At the end of a long workbench stood an upright object, and coming in out of the bright afternoon my eyes took a few moments to adjust. There was a broad base on which was planted a trunk as tall as Ama herself, and on that was fixed a crosspiece hung with straps. Then the details coalesced into a perception that made me shiver. The thing was a whipping post and was being finished by the woman who was going to be fastened to it. She drew me in close through the shavings that littered the floor; in the enclosed space the air was heavy with resin and the sickly reek of new leather. I felt suddenly unsteady and clutched the wood for support.

'It's for the tableau; a departure from the bench but one we thought justified. He picked out the tree himself and had it cut to size, including a branch for the T-section. The platform came from a lectern out of the disused chapel.' The deadpan snippets of information added a weird chill to an already bizarre situation. 'Jane, you don't look well. Are you all right?'

'It's very close in here.' It was no more than a touch of dizziness, but I wanted away from the gruesome apparatus. I am not usually squeamish about severe treatments; indeed I'd given Ama a pretty good going-over myself a few weeks before. However I had set limits, but who could say what the man she proposed to consign herself to would consider enough? Then, of course, that was exactly the point. It was why she was doing it. Had to do it. But I spared the lady a repetition of what she knew well herself and went with her up the stairs. In the flat she handed me a bottle of oil.

'Do you feel up to giving me a rub? It makes the skin supple and resilient, more able to withstand, well, you know...' Again I cringed inwardly in contemplation of what might be in store for that beautiful body. Her fingers began to unbutton in order to strip when a voice called out from the door and Ama responded with a loud, 'Hi Jill!' The little kitchen maid came in, but when she saw me she coloured and took a step back.

'Sorry, I'll come another time.'

'No,' put in Ama, then explained to me that Jill had been 'doing' her all week. It gave me the chance I needed to escape from an uncomfortable situation.

'Don't go, please. I was just on a flying visit.' I moved myself nearer the exit as Ama emerged statuesque from her boiler suit in front of the pale girl with her elfin features. She was looking up in wide-eyed awe as if before a manifestation of the goddess. I thrust the bottle in her hand and made myself scarce.

By the end of the following Saturday all participants had been fully briefed and were content, if not always enthusiastic, to accept the impending discipline. Early Sunday was spent finalising the running order and checking and double-checking the times it would take to inflict the fourteen doses of, variously, strap, birch, paddle and cane. After all that I felt like a latter-day de Sade in the throes of composing *The 120 Days of Sodom*, and took myself off up to the wood in the clear morning air.

On the way back I found Jill sitting on the steps to the garage flat. With the Mistress-to-be away formalising the union she looked thoroughly out of sorts, and I thought I could see the traces of tears. It was too late for pussyfooting, so I plonked myself down beside her.

'Hey, girl, I heard you're going to be the personal maid. Is that right?' She nodded glumly so I pressed on. 'Cheer up then, that's good news, isn't it?' There was no reply and the eyes welled up. I put my arms round her shoulders and held her while the sobs came and eventually subsided.

'Sorry,' she snuffled, pulling a wet face away from my jacket. 'I'm being silly.'

'No, you're not,' I said sternly. 'But there is one thing you must realise. Ama's got to do what she's got to do. You can't change that. I know it's hard to accept but you can't protect her. What you can do, though, is look after her. Right?' Before she could disagree I got up and held out my hand. 'Come on. Instead of moping about you can give me a hand in the Hall. And then, there's something we really need to do before you come back here to meet the new Lady of the Manor. Something that's been unaccountably left out of my schedule...'

The birching block and the trunk with added rail from the study had been left ready in the passage. So we carried them in between us and moved the benches from the long dining table to provide seating for the small audience, each of whom would in turn participate. And that included the one temporarily forgotten. After making some small adjustments to the block I turned to Jill.

'Well now, sweetie, have you worked out what it was that slipped my mind? Until just now, that is.' The expression of wide-eyed innocence with which she shook her head was too much, and I burst out laughing as she gave me a cheeky grin as if to say it was worth a try. 'So let's get down to business. I take it that you didn't get a Welcome.'

'No. I was very young when I started doing bits of work here, and they sort of forgot after.'

'Okay. I think we can leave the twigs out of it for the present, so how about an old-fashioned over-the-knee spanking; nothing too alarming about that, hm?'

'Um...' She looked around at the double doors standing open and I guessed the problem, so once I had her in the small room beside the fireplace I turned the key in the lock and sat down on an upright chair, patting my lap.

'Over you come. No one's going to disturb us here.' When I lifted the dress the chubby little buttocks were quite knickerless, and I'm afraid to report that I chuckled rather lewdly. She turned to me, scarlet with embarrassment.

'I usually leave them off when I'm going to... to...'

'Of course you do, dear. And you couldn't have chosen better today. For this pretty bottom is soon going to be in need of all the cooling air it can get.'

Before I'd done there were tears again, but I judged them to be of the healthy kind that stem from a fiercely smarting rump. They were soon dried and then I pinned up her clothing at the back so that the results of my efforts were clearly visible. As Jill left she passed another figure coming in. The woman stopped and her head swivelled to watch the red arse jiggle out of the room. She put down her case of equipment by the benches and mouthed a whistle.

'You must be happy in your work, Dr G.'

'It has its rewards, Mo, I have to admit.' It had been Tamsin's idea to make a record of such a once-in-a-lifetime event, a brainwave I thought, although the trick would be to avoid the disruption of a film crew bent on documenting every detail. So I sought advice from Judith at the Archive, who said she knew exactly the person for the job. There was a camerawoman who would capture the whole thing from the broad sweep of the action to the most in-your-face close-up, and she had the latest digital stuff. Most importantly of all, we would hardly know she was there. Patriarchal approval was granted at once and that was that: Mo was booked.

The Sunday before she had installed a few supplementary lights amongst the chandeliers and was, it transpired, having last minute doubts about their adequacy. I was offering to fetch the tall stepladder used the last time when a voice chipped in.

'I'll go. It's in the store at the back of the kitchen, right?' It was Tamsin, and Mo turned to flash her a big smile.

'Hi there, T. How ya doing? No, don't go just yet, not before I check the meter again.' She took out a gizmo with a lens and a small screen from her pocket and looked over at the disciplinary apparatuses. 'It's a thing about skin, yeah? You gotta get the level on the nose or you're fucked.'

'Okay. Will I model for you, Mo? Like I was going to get whacked. Correction: like I am going to get whacked.' A tug on its zip turned the microskirt into a strip of cloth that she laid over the trunk before dropping down beside it. The bum-cheeks stuck out, split by a tiny thong, and the camerawoman began to swoop around them with ecstatic noises, zooming in and pulling back. The speed with which our PA got herself on the case suggested that more than technical assistance was on offer. It felt rather as if I were watching a new courtship ritual of young females, and my presence was at the very least surplus to requirements. So when Tamsin told Mo to feel free to raise a bit of colour if that would help, I quietly left them to it.

Three hours later I was able to kick off the proceedings in style. It wasn't something I'd given much thought to, let alone dreamed of doing, but when I saw the dark gleam of the bronze plate as wide as the span of my arms I was captured. It had lain neglected in an outhouse until seized upon by the new attendant and restored to prime position at the foot of the main staircase. He was a man of even fewer words than his Master, but I had up my sleeve the inducement of applying the 'Board of Education', for which he was indeed an enthusiast, to three very well fleshed behinds. In return he demonstrated to me the technique by which a first, barely audible tap with the soft mallet, primes the gong for a second strike to launch a mighty crescendo.

Thus prepared I delivered the hammer-blow that sent a wave of sound booming and crashing into the tunnels of space ahead and above. When the echoes died away a single file of figures came into view, descending the broad stairs in slow procession. Each was dressed in a plain, calf-length shift of unbleached linen, chosen with an intentional nod to the times of the young wife whose writings had formed the basis of our performance. As an undergarment it carried an aura of the bedroom, though with a distinct penitential tinge: stripped of all else the wearer was available, at the raising of a hem, for chastisement as much as for sex.

The players had been arranged in the order of their appointments with a disciplinary instrument, so Tamsin headed the line of ten bodies. She had a face that attracted attention however the rest of her was clothed, but its individual quality was on that occasion muted. Instead she was suffused, as were those that came after, with the kind of gravity bestowed by absorption into the larger whole. One by one the company passed into the hall and took their seats on the oak benches. When all were settled, I threw a switch on the panel by the fireplace and bathed the trunk in a warm glow of light. A clap of the hands and we were underway. The PA and the boy came forward, lifted their gowns waist-high and lay forward together over the rounded top.

Mrs Beaton was to do the honours with a replay of the strapping at which the lad first grabbed my attention. This time, however, his cock was tucked out of view in the interest of making available a second target alongside the original. They made a fine pair, his wickedly spankable bottom jutting quite as provocatively as Tamsin's lusher curves as the flat piece of leather thwacked repeatedly into reddening flesh. No one was counting strokes: the plan for the early stages was to continue until the recipients were judged to have undergone a suitably testing experience. As it was, Cook's brow was wreathed in perspiration before the muscular arm discarded the instrument with a sigh, and we watched the writhing victims nurse scarlet cheeks before resuming with some circumspection their places on the hard wood bench. Mrs Beaton and I grinned at each other: with the first two behinds so well roasted, the evening had really begun.

Chapter 24
Consummatum Est

Next on the programme was a birching in the manner that had become traditional to the house. Maids Laura and Molly dragged the heavy block into position and put down next to it the tub of brine and vinegar complete with its steeping contents. Then they hoisted their shifts and knelt side by side on the padded wooden step while the Housekeeper secured the leg straps.

'Over,' she commanded, and the girls went forward and stretched out their arms. My local lads had jumped at the chance to take part, and Colin took hold of Laura's wrists while his straight mate gripped Molly's. They may not have been in the best place to view the effects of the whipping, but they would feel the reaction to every cut of the pickled bundles. Already both boys were visibly erect under the linen as they leaned back to take the strain.

Soon the small audience was being treated to a fine spectacle. Mrs Jencks worked with an energy that belied her years, and the air was filled with the swish and snap of wet saplings on naked skin. Given their time at Ardingley End, the maids should have been well used to such treatment, but there was nothing about their responses to suggest the experience was stale. In fact, if the squealing and writhing and the clenching and unclenching of buttocks had become part of the show, their prior exercise had served to render them only more convincing as expressions of pain.

When two rods had been reduced to tatters the Housekeeper paused, allowing us to savour the sight of hindquarters scored with a tracery of angry lines amid welling spots of red. Then she took a new instrument dripping from the barrel, and brought it down in brisk alternation on the pairs of cheeks: back and fore, back and fore, back and fore. Behind her camera Mo had been as unobtrusive as promised, yet I became aware, even above the anguished shrieking, of the excited hiss of her breath as she homed in for the kill.

I'd allowed for a brief bathing of inflamed parts *in situ*, estimating that the girls would not want to miss the turn of the lads who'd been so keen to hold them down. So Tamsin set to work with a cloth and a bowl of cold water while the next victims were given the job of sweeping up. Then, the trunk restored to centre stage, it was three male bottoms that were presented for the company's delectation. Edith and I selected a fine springy implement each from the collection she'd brought with her, having agreed that while the outer two should receive a stiff six apiece, our budding submissive in the centre could be taken to the full dozen.

And so he was, with twelve swingeing beauties that had the flesh of the arse-cheeks all aquiver. At the finish a riot of weals was emblazoned thick on the flanks, Edith's to the right and my backhanders to the left. The lads were let up and given a minute for the fits of squirming and clutching to pass. I noticed my partner say a few words into Colin's ear, at which the pale face lit up and the head nodded keenly. A future date had been set at the country cottage, I guessed, for remedial work on the bruising and, given my boy's experience, what would surely follow.

The entry of the Master's man, tanned and fit in singlet and shorts, caused a distinct stir. He had with him a range of instruments to cater for targets of differing size and resilience, and decreed that he would take 'the older ladies' one by one. Each was to lift her own garment and bend over, placing the flat of the hands on the top of the trunk. Legs together and a straight back would ensure, he promised, that no untoward display was afforded to the watching juniors. Oldest first, we'd already decided, so Mathilde Jencks stepped out and with a visible effort at appearing composed, bared and bent as ordered. It was scarcely a lip-smacking sight, I have to report, and even the enthusiast for the board seemed a little taken aback by the scrawniness of the rear on offer. But he found a whitewood paddle drilled with holes and his duty was soon done.

Edith Faversham was a different proposition, presenting two hams that broadened steadily and seamlessly from knee to base of spine. Again our man did not appear best pleased by what he saw, but settled for the application of a medium weight board until the upper region of the display had turned a pretty salmon-pink.

Then came the unexpected treat of the evening. On a scale of age Mrs Beaton was the youngest by some degrees, but the contrast was absolute. When she took up the prescribed position there came into view two luscious hemispheres, white and silky. Large, certainly, but perfectly formed with a dark enticing smudge between the undercurves, they begged to be treated in exemplary fashion. The attendant reached for the heaviest slab of polished wood, then checked himself.

'Madam, if I may feel... that is, to be quite sure...' Cook made no reply except to push the buttocks out into even more prominence. The man's hands patted and prodded, lifted and palpated and an expression of wonder crept over his face. Then he took up the instrument and with a, 'Brace yourself, ma'am,' set about the appointed task.

With a smack that echoed round the room, the first swat lifted the body up onto its toes. The flesh bounced and rippled in aftershock around a band of colour that sprung up instantly.

'My, oh my,' breathed Mrs Beaton, sounding oddly more surprised than shocked, then settled her heavy form firmly back on its feet. Five more strokes were accepted in silence, after which the man adjusted his aim to land six across a line a few inches higher. Another half dozen to the ample undercurves were taken in like manner, with only a small rocking movement to absorb the impact.

'I don't mean to speak out of turn, sir, but had you in mind finishing off soon?' The tone was almost conservational, with only the slightest quiver in the voice to show that the worthy lady was feeling somewhat, shall we say, stretched. Once more the hands assessed the globes, whose milky complexion was transformed into a rich ruby.

'Six full-centre, with your permission, ma'am.' Cook bowed her head and took them without a word. Afterwards she stood flushed, kneading the beaten cheeks under her shift. The attendant collected up his paddles and offered her an arm.

'You were magnificent, if I may say so, ma'am. Now will you accept some cooling lotion?' An almost coquettish smile crossed her face as she murmured a thank you then made her exit, albeit a touch stiffly, at his side. I caught a glimpse of his shorts filled out at the crotch and suspected there would be little standing on ceremony in the anteroom. Indeed, no one who'd witnessed the encounter was surprised when the announcement came a week later of a second wedding.

There was one more disciplinary exhibition scheduled before the bride of that morning was due to appear before us. I was to take my place with the daughters for the Master's cane. In the scheme I'd drawn up, it was down as a reprise of the earlier caning to the detail that the central figure - me, of course - would endure a double dose. However, there was one critical difference: the instrument was of the synthetic variety already burned into my memory in Brittany. But while inclined to rue the insouciance with which I'd consigned myself to it, I had no real complaint. It was only right and proper that one so fond of chastising buttocks should now and then expose her own to a degree of severity.

Holding the thought close, I assumed my position and managed a wink and squeeze of the hand to Bel and Lou, who were looking no more eager than I. Then the Master was beside us silently, shrouded in a grey monk's cloak. The feel of the cold black rod against my naked flesh made my stomach tighten, then came the two words, 'I begin.' He might have wanted to minimise the impression his own figure made on the watchers until later, but there was nothing perfunctory about his performance. I will not dwell on those dreadful, measured strokes that wrenched cries from deep in all of us before he was done. Suffice to say I was glad of a short respite before having that part of my body pressed into any surface, however yielding, by the weight of Ama's on top.

And then, in short order, the beautiful lady herself was present and there was the final scene setting to distract me from the throbbing of my ill-used buttocks.

The new Mistress waited quietly at the periphery while we shunted the rough wooden post into prime position across from the trunk, which had been transformed by a flat cushioned top. Tamsin and I belted on our phallic appendages, as did Molly, who was to use Laura as the boy was to use the third lad in the culminating orgy. Thus equipped we joined the rest in a row, and watched while the now blindfolded Ama was led by her naked maid to stand before her designated place of pain.

The long gown parted to allow first one arm then the other to be cuffed to the crossbar. A tug at the neck cord released the garment to fall in two halves around her feet. Next the waist was cinched tight to the wood and I saw there had been an addition to the device. A padded wedge fixed in a groove was slid up to the level of the crotch, after which the knees were secured to the squared sides of the post. The effect was to thrust the arse-cheeks up and out, in a posture that seemed indecently to invite their impending violation. To complete the preparations, Jill took a pessary between finger and thumb and pressed it into the puckered hole that winked between the globes.

There was a sudden hush, a collective catching of breath, and the Texan strode down the line, looming over us in heeled boots. The whole outfit was of hide, from the black leather chaps with a bulging pouch between the legs to the sleeveless vest, and the reek of it was heavy in the air. We stood stiff, straight, as much by instinct as from rehearsal, and no one moved when he passed behind us raising hems to inspect the marks of corporal punishment that each bore. One by one the line of ten was approved, until he reached the boy at the end. Whereas the PA's fair skin had held a good colour, her partner under Cook's strap was not so lucky. Sent to fetch a school cane he was summarily bent and subjected to a juicy six that had him hopping.

It was a pleasing diversion, but I don't believe that any present had forgotten what was about to come. Indeed, once he returned to his place the room grew very still and I was aware of my own dry mouth and quickening pulse. In the silence the Master took up a stance to the side of the bound body and signalled the maid to attach the ball-gag to the victim's head. The job done, she was waved away so I pulled her in beside me and held her firmly by the arm. There was no announcement, just a rapid movement of the arm, a whooshing noise and a crack loud enough to make me start. For a frozen instant the breadth of the dark-skinned torso was encompassed by a darker line that curled up over the right shoulder. The head snapped back and the fists clenched as the whip sprang away, only to land again with that gut-wrenching sound. Again. And again. And again and again. The air was a dizzying blur of snaking thongs and the figure jerked in its bonds like some marionette come to brief demented life.

When he stopped I found myself gasping for air and holding on to Jill for dear life, although she had made no move to intervene. Across the whole of the back the marks stood out like purple cords, but there was not a single break in the flesh. As we stared in mute fascination the muscles began to unlock and the flogged girl shifted her weight with a sigh. The Master was motionless, expectant, and after a moment from Ama's turned head a barely perceptible nod passed between them. Then his man appeared from the shadows and the long coil was exchanged for a new one, not even a full yard in length. Except for a braided handle, the thing was of a uniform thickness from end to end, hanging from the chastiser's hand with its tip grazing the floor.

Once more the arm rose and fell in a whirl of action and the lash buried itself six times in the soft flesh of the buttocks. Six cuts had landed but there was only one line, dead centre, which ripened and darkened under our eyes as he fine-tuned his position on the opposite side. Aimed a tad lower, the whip struck six times more to leave a broader band of plum-coloured contusion. The accuracy was breathtaking, and the thought of the pain inflicted by such a concentrated attack made me feel weak. Yet it was not over. Twice again the body was required to submit to the changing of stance and the fierce volley of lashes that followed. At the end a hand's breadth of swollen flesh crossed from hip to hip, oozing a little where the last inch of leather had bitten deep into the flanks.

The Master drew back, gathering his offspring to him, and the three maids closed round the figure hanging from its restraints. Tamsin touched my arm and I came back to earth; it was time for the final stage. She started to fuss over laying me out on the padded slab, but I told her, a little snippily, to save her energies for the arse about to arrive in a much worse state than mine. And so they came, half-leading, half-carrying the wilting body until it could be lowered onto the six inches of black rubber that sprouted from my crotch. There was no need of lubrication: in the midst of all the scalding lashes the lady was blessed with the delicious ache of a sopping cunt. The hands withdrew and I was forcibly reminded of my own tender stripes. At the same time the spur on the device dug sharply into my clitoris, and I felt the PA's stubbier strap-on nose in until our bodies were plugged together in a pulsing mass of sensation. Above me, Ama's eyes were closed, though the way she rocked and moaned was making me shiver with lust.

To the left boy was slowly buggering boy, and to the right Molly pumped her dildo in and out of Laura's willing bum. From my supine position the scene in front was unfolding in bizarre inversion. With the codpiece gone, the patriarchal organ stood out, huge, from a forest of black hair, while the daughters' puckered mouths teased its shaft and tip in turn. As the ensemble moved toward us the girls peeled away to open their legs for the waiting, stiff-cocked lads. Fucking under Daddy's nose, as promised, but Daddy had other things on his mind. His erection loomed above me, positioned with a thumb and forefinger encircling its root. What a specimen it was! Every inch that had plumbed my rectum was before me in bulging splendour, foreskin half back to show a clear bead of pre-ejaculate hanging from the urethra. Ama's eyes flicked wide open and before the drop could fall her tongue had taken it.

I watched, mesmerised, as she nipped the glans between bared teeth then pulled back to lick the tip, over and over in a sequence that had the juice welling. The veins of the distended shaft pulsed and I could hear the rasp of his breathing above the thumping of my own heart. For a moment I took in the lens of the camera to the left, trained on the weirdly formal dance of body parts and wide eyes of the maid to the right. Then the lips closed and sucked and the loins pressed sharply into mine. All at once the crescendo of sensation was unstoppable and the room erupted with the sounds of bodies helpless in the throes of orgasm. And as I bucked and cried with the best of them the mouth above spilled over with thick white sperm. At another time and in a different place I might well have shied from such an effusion, but in climax I opened and swallowed the surplus of the gift from Master to his new Mistress with something approaching eagerness. It seemed only fitting.

In little more than an hour the company was reassembled and seated, with varying degrees of comfort, at the long dining table. Mrs Beaton's sister had been loaned from her employment for the occasion, and her small army of assistants set to assembling the components of our celebratory feast. We had not planned a formal affair of set courses, but to have an array of dishes from which each could pick and choose at will. Centre place was occupied by a boar's head skewered with truffles *à la bourgogne*, joined by plates of beef and pork and dishes of potatoes and vegetables. It was not an occasion of polite conversation or interchanges cultivated to match the quality of the food. Evidently I was not alone in feeling ravenous following our bouts of disciplinary sex, and eating took precedence over all else save the supping of chilled chablis or a ruby shiraz according to fancy. Only after plates had been loaded with second or third helpings, and glasses recharged many times over, did it seem any one had attention to spare. And when they did, it was perhaps predictable to what end it would be directed.

Giant plasma screens had been placed to the sides, elevated to a height that allowed an unobstructed view to all, though of what exactly was unclear since they'd been dark and silent throughout. Then I noticed a glow that grew brighter, and in half a minute had resolved itself into an image of arguably the finest pair of buttocks we'd seen all day. They loomed over us, at least twice life-sized, before flattening and bouncing back when the paddle cracked down. The maids whooped and clapped and despite her crimsoning features it was plain Mrs Beaton had no objection to an action replay. Mo left the controls she'd activated and moved in behind Tamsin, seated beside me. We had all exchanged the coarse penitential linen for a satin garment of similar type, and out of the corner of my eye I saw fingers creep under the hem while others fondled the outline of a breast.

Across from me lips met lips, and what could have been at first a sisterly kiss grew rapidly into an incestuous thing of deep tongues, while to right and left eye engaged with lascivious eye and hands began to wander. It was all too much, and easing myself out from between my neighbours, I moved round to the seated Molly and encircled her with my arms. As I hoped, the strap-on was still in place and I found myself in the grip of an alcohol-enhanced lust that would not be denied.

Brazenly I went forward on my elbows, Molly greased her weapon with a dollop of butter that lay to hand, and with one steady push she was in to the hilt. I need not have worried about the reactions of our fellow diners, for at that very moment the black bride took to the table herself on all fours, gown up round the neck. Behind her the Master rose to his feet and stood while Jill rubbed a final millilitre or two of distension into his already impressive erection. Then she spread the whip-seared cheeks of her mistress and guided the beast into the pink wetness of the gaping vulva. Whether she was consciously aping the handmaid of *uxor studiosa*, or making it up as she went along, the outcome was the same: Ama's deranged squawking set in train the orgasms that were to explode all around amidst the detritus of food and drink.

And that was that. It was not the end of the evening, of course, but it was the last part memory allows me to recount with any presumption of accuracy. However, I console myself with the thought that our model narrator of the Notebooks was similarly unforthcoming about the later stages of the original celebration. What I can say is that the lurid fragments of the commemoration that do stick in the mind leave me confident that we did her proud.

Chapter 25
New Blood

The weeks following our grand finale were, as could have been expected, a little flat. Occupied with mundane if essential business for the Library I was unable even to revisit the House, and the mood was not improved by the news that Tamsin intended to resign from her post. Having hit it off with Mo, the PA had decided to throw in her lot with the camerawoman's scheme of producing s/m erotica tailored for a female audience. *Folie à deux* or an idea whose time had come? I didn't know then, and the verdict is yet to be delivered as I write; either way Tamsin was not going to be easy to replace. So I was not in the best of humours on my return from viewing an exceedingly dull collection at Bodiham House, when Dominic greeted me with something of a smirk on his face.

'I made an appointment for you, boss. Saturday morning at eleven. I hope you don't mind.'

'Should I?' Something was afoot and I was quite happy to let him draw out his moment of disclosure.

'No, far from it. Do you remember that old battleaxe of a teacher, Miss, er...'

'Marston, if memory serves. Don't tell me she wants a heart-to-heart.' Dominic's grin broadened.

'Not her, but the peachy girl she had in tow.'

'Ah yes, rather dragging her feet.'

'Well, she seems to want back into the lion's den. Something about an offer to show her more of the instrument case.'

'Mm, Becca Miles. Very tasty, and by the end she did seem to be warming to the experience in more ways than one. Shame you won't be here, Dominic.'

'Actually, I could do with putting in some extra work on those new lists.' I chuckled at the slightly pink earnestness of the expression. The poor boy had missed out the last time with the old dragon in the outer office.

'By all means, feel free. Nothing wrong with a little discreet eavesdropping. But now I feel a plot hatching, and you can reward me by getting a line to Ardingley End. I'll take it inside.'

The boy was happy enough to fall in with my little plan. I knew he'd been occupied with his new friend, but I guessed, correctly, that he would not pass up the chance to take part in the training of a female novice. I plead not guilty to any charge of matchmaking: what I had in mind was more that he could use a bit of hetero input and she could benefit from an entry point to stimulating weekends in the country.

On the day the boy had been collected from his train and installed in good time for the arrival of our visitor. She was even prettier than I remembered, and the skirt was perceptibly shorter and tighter than before. For his part the boy was quite fetching with his mop of hair and black roll-neck giving him a Gallic air. The girl glanced at him curiously after we'd shaken hands, so I hastened to explain.

'Some young men, Becca, seem to require correction on a regular basis, my boy here being one of them. So I have taken the liberty of inviting him to take part today. It will, I hope, make for a stimulating demonstration, if of course you have no objection.'

'No, er, none at all.' She looked a little nervous, but not unduly discomfited by his presence.

'Good.' I had already selected what I intended to use on them both, and passed it over for her inspection. 'I believe I showed you the Lochgelly before. It is a serious instrument, but I believe that a girl with a real interest in the world of corporal discipline deserves no less. Do I have your approval?' I was putting her on the spot but I wanted to leave no room for misunderstanding. She licked her lips, staring at the three-tongued piece of leather in her hands, then held it out to me.

'Yes. Though may I ask how many strokes? I mean, I think I'm up for it anyway, but...'

I smiled in what I hoped was a reassuring manner. 'Of course, dear. The boy needs a sound dozen, but I wouldn't think of giving a first-timer more than six. Naturally, they will be good ones.' When she nodded in acceptance I turned to the boy. 'Right, lad, let's have those trousers off and you over the desk.' He obeyed without a word, and I spent some time lifting and tucking in his top to make sure the hardness of his penis was not lost on young Becca. 'Okay, boy, get a good grip. This is going to hurt.'

There is something supremely satisfying about the way heavy supple leather strikes the naked buttocks, at the same time lifting and embedding itself in the yielding meat. That day I excelled myself with the force and accuracy of my strokes, so that when the last had fallen a dark crimson rectangle, sharply defined, clung like a wet cloth to the swelling mounds. The boy, too, rose to the occasion. Though his pain was clear to me from the intensity of his gasps and grunts, he remained exactly where I'd put him. Becca looked a little pale, but I pressed a jar of herbal cream into her hand with a brisk air.

'Come, girl, he deserves a little reward for taking his punishment like a trooper. Rub it in well now.' After a diffident start she was soon massaging the abused flesh with dedication, and when she was done her own complexion had turned quite pink. When the boy straightened up I took hold of his stiff cock and stroked it, catching the clear drop that oozed from the tip. 'It seems the aftercare went down a treat.' As was his way, he was looking down saying nothing while her flush turned as red as his behind. But she managed a laugh and I felt confident her embarrassment would soon pass once I was out of the room. But first, there was her delectable behind to deal with.

'Now, Becca, I think the skirt should come right off. And if you can take up the same position...' I waited while she unzipped the garment and stepped out of it, then took it from her. She bent over and I folded up her blouse while admiring the way the bottom filled out the lace-trimmed silk of the knickers. When they came down I was pleased to see the crotch visibly damp, and allowed myself to run a hand over the exposed cheeks. 'Go with it as best you can and keep these relaxed, dear. Now, are you ready?'

'Yes, I suppose. I mean... yes.' She took the first two with only a little squeak, but I laid on the third as hard as I could and she shot up with a yell, clutching at the injured parts. But almost at once she dragged her hands away and went back down. 'Oh sorry, sorry. Please, give me that one again and I'll try harder.'

'Certainly, sweetie, if you say so. So that's four to go.' I made each one count, but she found her resolve and stayed put to the end. I let her rub for a minute, then pushed her gently over once more and handed the cream to the boy. 'Right, I'm going to leave you to it. Take your time, you won't be disturbed.' Nature could take its course for I had needs of my own that were becoming rather insistent.

Dominic was waiting just outside the door, which was standing ajar, and I wasted no time. Inside his pants I found the rampant organ I was looking for, hauled my jeans down and went over, bum in the air. We were in no need of lubrication: with practiced movements he worked my cunt until I oozed and dripped with lust, then pressed himself against the tighter hole above. There are few sensations in my experience to match that moment when the muscle opens, half-willing, half-protesting, to allow access to the head of an invading cock.

So my story ends in as regrettably lewd a fashion as it began, though this time there were no interruptions from unexpected callers. Only the Keeper of the National Rare Books, bare-arsed across her own desk, enjoying a wonderful protracted buggering by her handsome secretary...

www.ingramcontent.com/pod-product-compliance
Lightning Source LLC
Chambersburg PA
CBHW060938120626
46557CB00003B/1052